Anguish & Anarchy

Broken Realms Book 2
Jane Rose

Jane Rose Publishing, LLC

To the ones who have lost...
May you hold onto the broken pieces of your heart
knowing one day, you will be whole again.

To my sister:
No matter where
No matter what

THE RUINS
THE BANISHED
TWILIGHT KINGDOM
N
W
E
S
OLYRIUM
KRYSTAL MOUNTAIN PASS
CITRINE CITY
KORIN
ALICANTO STABLES
SUNSPARK KINGDOM
SPHINX FIELDS
MAREEN
LUAR
REFLECTING POOL

CONTENTS

BOOK ONE RECAP

If you're anything like me, you read a book and instantly mind dump to make room for the next story. In case you may have forgotten what happened in book one, here is a brief recap of events!

The scene opens with Aliyah and Saraphena being totally awesome and stealing cake together. This crap sack Cyrus whipped Aliyah on the post for being late on their rent and when that wasn't enough, he forcefully took her virginity from her. Aliyah got her back stitched up by Saraphena before passing out and waking up to her entire village being burned down by skeleton creatures called The Kalari, who wear human skin for fun.

Let's jump over to Olyrium where Enzo and his band of witty sidekicks are living it up in Korin, totally unaware their life is about to be changed forever. Fast forward to Enzo deciding they need to go to Luar to save the villages from being burned, the group fails to understand if they bridge "on three" or "after three" and ultimately end up separated from each other during the fight. It's probably for the best though because Enzo gets saucy during a fight with a strong- willed Aliyah in an alleyway. Deciding he wants to keep her forever, Enzo kidnaps her intent on bringing her back to Olyrium. Unfortunately, Aliyah gets an ax to the chest which later becomes a hilarious talking point when Enzo gifts her a necklace with a battle ax on it to remind her of the day they met.

Aliyah finds out she has actually always been fae when Saraphena drops the bomb on her that she is actually Aliyah's Soul Guardian since birth when an old hag came to her and bound their lives together. Aliyah was marked with a moon scar and Saraphena with a sun scar to signify this bond. Saraphena can't be mated while their souls are bonded, so that's a real bummer for her and Gunnar, who is her lost love from before she escaped with Aliyah to the human realm.

Let's fast forward again to the tavern where Enzo killed a man for touching Aliyah without her consent by making him drink shards of glass. Aliyah then matches with a beautiful alicanto she names Mirage due to her color changing feathers from maroon to indigo. Then a bunch of other crazy stuff happens with her and Jade connecting, the enchanted book of names goes up in flames when Aliyah touches it, and she finds this sword that belonged to the queen that she can touch, but not pull from its protective bubble.

After Aliyah destroys the ancient relic which has survived hundreds of thousands of years before she came along and touched it, they decide to go to SunSpark to have her float in the Reflecting Pool. Hopefully doing so would show her an image of her past or her future, but when has anything ever worked out for the hero in books?

Aliyah discovers the others have powers when they fight in training. Saraphena can disappear, Duncan can teleport, Gunnar has fire magic, Enzo can manipulate objects/people with his mind, and Jade can predict her opponent's next move before they even know they're going to make it. Technically this isn't a real power since she was low borne, but it may as well be for how good she is at it! Oh yeah, and Jade's parents were traitors from SunSpark selling secrets to the Banished King so they were hung and Jade was sent to the military academy where she met Gunnar and Enzo.

Enter Liliana. Gunnar's younger sister and a ball of sunshine. She has the ability to read and change another's emotions. She has an instant connection with Duncan. Much to his dismay, he can't seem to pull himself away from her either. After his first love died, he never expected to fall in love again, but his grumpy personality is no match for Liliana's sparkle.

They decide to have a huge ball in honor of Gunnar coming home. Kaleron, Gunnar's older brother, makes a deal with Aliyah to come with him to the ball and makes her swear to not tell anyone about the threat he made against her in order to get her to comply with his demands. But Saraphena overheard and told Enzo. Naturally, Saraphena had to go. Kaleron tries to poison her, but Marigold rushes in at the last moment and attempts to save her.

A fight breaks out and the whole ballroom goes up in flames...literally. Marigold tells Aliyah she needs to get out of there and will send the rest of them to find her. That was right before she got beheaded for helping them. Oh, I almost forgot, the Queen of SunSpark gave Aliyah a ring she brought with her from Twilight when she was a girl. The queen saw herself giving Aliyah the ring in her vision from the Reflecting Pool, so she knew Aliyah was meant to have it.

Where was I? Oh yeah. Aliyah flees to Krystal on the back of a sphinx. Saraphena is likely dead because Aliyah had to leave before she knew if Marigold saved her. She hikes through Krystal forever and has a dream where Enzo tells her to keep walking north and he will find her. Well, ten days pass and he still hasn't found her. She is out of water and food and is basically on the brink of death. She has a super heartfelt goodbye, but then right at the last moment, Enzo finds her. Also, SURPRISE, Saraphena lives!

They decide to go to Twilight since Kaleron marked them all as traitors, so they can't go back to Korin. Duncan brings them to his home, which he hasn't been to in ages since his father killed the love of his life. They find charred and skinless bodies littering the villages and discover the Twilight palace has been completely overtaken by The Kalari.

Plot twist! Duncan's older brother, Aramot, aligned himself with the Banished King and killed their parents before letting The Kalari wear their skin like a warm, bloody blanket. The group meets Aramot on the battle field and surprisingly, due to Jade's amazing battle strategy, win! The mate bond awakens between Aliyah and Enzo and it is this super cute moment where Aliyah tells Enzo she loves him! Everything is happy, Aramot is dead, and The Kalari are retreating. And that's it! That is the end of book one!

Wait....I feel like I'm forgetting something really important. Let me think. Let me think. OH! That's right.

Right before Aramot died, he stabbed Aliyah through the heart...killing her.

Okay, now you should be all caught up!

Content Warning

In book one, I promised to wreck you emotionally and physically. Nothing has changed. The title of this book is "Anguish & Anarchy" and I can once again promise you these pages are filled with unexpected events, likely to elicit copious amounts of anguish and anarchy.

I took special care while writing this book to bring you through each step of the grief process alongside the characters. You will join them in their denial over the events of book one. Wrestle with anger that comes out twisted and sideways and most likely directed at me for the things I am going to put you through in this book. You'll be willing to strike bargains you never dared to consider before. You will feel the darkness of depression cloud your mind as you process the carnage I delivered in the first three parts, but in the end, you will learn to accept that fate is not always what it seems and just when you think you have the ending figured out, I'll gut you once again.

"Anguish & Anarchy" is darker than ever before and filled with events you likely won't survive. I ask that you take care of your mental health throughout this journey and seek professional help if you feel nothing at all while reading this book. If you prefer to go in blind and accept whatever fate I have planned for you, please skip to Part I: Denial. (For those of you that are about to skip ahead, I think it is interesting that you are already in a state of denial thinking you can handle what is to come without checking the trigger warnings.)

For you normal people, please see the list below for potential triggers. While this list is not exhaustive, I have tried my best to pick out any potential triggers that may arise in this book. I wish you luck on this journey, and I'll see you at the end...if you survive.

And for the record, some of the characters in this book do unspeakable things. In no way, shape, or form, do I condone these actions in real life. This is *fiction,* so if you are at all uncomfortable with, or sensitive to, morally gray or unhinged actions, **PLEASE DO NOT CONTINUE READING THIS BOOK!**

!!! SPOILERS AHEAD !!!!
This is your last chance to turn back!

<u>Trigger Warnings may include, but are not limited to:</u>

Alcoholism

Closed Door/Fade to Black Sexual Scenes

Death of a minor

Explosive Characters

Grief/loss

Hallucinations

Illness

Mass Murder

Murder

Self- harm

Suicidal thoughts

Chapter 1

ENZO

"There has to be a way! There has to be! I won't accept anything else," I yell.

"Enzo, we need to be realistic here. We may not find a way," Saraphena says.

"So what then? You don't want her back? Is that what you are saying?"

"No. That's not what I am saying at all, Enzo. Of course I want her back, but I don't know how it would even be possible," she snaps.

"Let's look at our options." Gunnar cuts in. "We could always go back to the Reflecting Pool and see if it will show us anything helpful. Saraphena has never been in the pool. Maybe since they were Soul Bonded, it would show us something about her future and Aliyah will be in it."

"I'm not sure we are going to be allowed back in SunSpark right now. We didn't exactly leave on the best of terms and Kaleron has yet to lift the bounty on our heads," Jade says.

We sit around the kitchen table back in Korin. I buried Aliyah not a fortnight ago and yet my heart is already pulling me back to her. I thought I could learn to live without her in time, but my mind refuses to accept she might be gone forever. There has to be something we can do to bring her back. Someone, somewhere, somehow, has to know a way.

"What about the Twilight Kingdom's fallen star? It's said to grant any wish, right? Maybe we can wish Aliyah back," Liliana perks up.

Since the incident in SunSpark, Liliana decided to stay with the group. After she fought against her brother, Kaleron, the future king of SunSpark, she is now tied to our band of traitors.

"The relic hasn't been seen in ages. I wouldn't even know where to start looking for it," Duncan adds.

"Someone must know something!" I yell. My teeth grind together and I feel a headache creeping up behind my eyes.

"Enzo. I think...I think it might be time to consider—" Gunnar starts.

"No! Do not say it. She can be brought back! We will find a way! We have to find a way— I need—" My voice breaks as a lump in my throat forms. "I need her."

"We will find a way." Jade walks over and puts her arms around me. "Let's go to Twilight. Maybe we can find something in the library about the fallen star. We won't give up yet. Right, everyone?"

"Right," they say in unison. I see the hesitation in their eyes, but I can't let their reservations about bringing her back stop me. I need my dove. My fingers trace the small battle ax hanging around my neck. I wrap my palm around it and let the edges dig into my palm.

A knock comes at the door. I stare at the group for a moment before walking over. Opening the front door, there stands Kaleron.

"Enzo—"

I don't give him the chance to finish before I punch him straight in the face. "What are you doing here?" I yell.

"Enzo, please. Give me a chance to explain!" Blood starts dripping from his nose as he rights himself.

"Explain what?!" I yell, cocking my arm back to hit him again.

"I'm here to apologize!"

"Enzo, stop!" Saraphena's voice clears the red haze from my mind.

"How can you not want him dead?! He killed you Saraphena."

"I remember, but he also wouldn't show up here without a reason. I want to hear what it is."

"Thank you—" Kaleron starts.

"Do not thank me yet. Now say what you came here to say," Saraphena says. Gunnar approaches from behind her and wraps his hands around her waist. The death glare he gives his brother matches the umbrage I feel in my heart. My pulse races and I grip Aliyah's necklace to center myself.

"I heard what happened to Aliyah. I am so sorry Enzo. I never meant for any of this to happen," Kaleron says.

"You're sorry?! *Sorry?!*" I can't help the exasperation seeping through my tone. "She is *dead* Kaleron! DEAD! Do you hear me? DEAD!" I go to reach for his throat, but Duncan's arms are around me faster than I can move. He pulls me back into the room and away from Kaleron.

"You never meant for Aliyah to die, but you meant for me to?" Saraphena asks.

"An unfortunate circumstance of being the future king. Well, I suppose now, *the* King of SunSpark," he says.

"What?" Gunnar snaps.

"King Aramos is dead. He passed in the scuffle the night you all left. Terribly unfortunate, but this now makes me king. Given the circumstances, I am formally rescinding my decree that you all are traitors. Clearly, you have suffered enough."

"Don't do us any favors, Kaleron. We have bigger things to worry about right now," Saraphena says.

"Are you trying to bring her back?" he questions. For a moment, I see a flicker of hope in his eyes. *He doesn't get to feel hope at the prospect of her living and breathing again.*

"That's none of your business! I wish she had never met you! I wish we had never taken her to your court! If it wasn't for your actions, we would have never been pushed to go to Twilight in the first place!" I scream.

"Enzo, enough. He isn't worth it. Let him leave so we may as well," Duncan says to me.

"I think you should go. Thank you for rescinding the bounty. Consider this forgiveness for trying to kill me. Now leave," Saraphena says with a sharp edge to her voice.

"If you find a way to bring her back and you are in need of any assistance from SunSpark to do so, please let me know. I will do whatever I can to help bring her back." He turns on his heel and walks back towards the street. Saraphena closes the door behind him.

"The good news is the bounty is lifted. We can now search every realm for anything to help bring her back without fear of death. Gunnar," Saraphena looks to him then over to his sister. "Lil, are you both alright? I am sure hearing of your father's death and your brother taking over as king must be difficult."

"Our father wasn't much of a father to us. He had Kaleron to focus on. While it is sad, I am not surprised he's dead. It was only a matter of time." Gunnar places a kiss to Saraphena's lips. I turn away, not wanting to subject myself to such emotions.

"I am sure we will find a way to move on. Aliyah was a far better person than my father ever was. If we could only bring one of them back, I would choose Aliyah every time," Liliana says.

My heart rate has calmed since Kaleron left. I palm Aliyah's necklace once more before tucking it beneath the collar of my shirt.

"Let's get some rest. I think we could all use some. We leave at first light," Jade says.

We each depart to our bedrooms. As I walk up the steps, dread accompanies each footfall. Going back to my bedroom knowing Aliyah will not be there tastes sour on my tongue. I close my eyes and try to block out the thoughts knowing she is not there. I clench my jaw so hard I swear my tendons pop.

Enzo. I hear her soft voice creep into my mind. It's faint, like a soft whisper I can barely hear.

"I'm sorry, little dove." I open the door to my room and push her voice from my mind, knowing it will only hurt me more. I'm going to bring her back. I refuse to believe otherwise. I promised to protect her and yet I failed time and time again. I will not fail her this time. No, this time I *will* bring her back or die trying.

She can't be gone forever. Without her I am nothing but flesh and bones. This hallow feeling inside my chest grows with each passing day and I fear if any more time passes without her, I will never be able to recover.

Enzo, please. Her voice filters into my head, still faint, like the soft caress of a light breeze. I close my eyes and pull the necklace from under my tunic. I squeeze it so hard the edges of the battle ax break my skin. I pull my hand away and watch it heal only to grip the ax again, and again. The pain in my palm distracts me from my memories.

Little dove, why do you taunt me in death?

I need you, Enzo. I don't want to die again. Please save me. Please come for me—

Her voice cuts off as the sound of choking fills my mind. My nerves fray and burning spreads through my chest. I grip the skin where my heart would lay and push my fingers into my flesh as if to rip out the beating muscle and rid myself of this anguish. Here she is in my mind begging me to save her.

I couldn't save you. I scream at the top of my lungs as my chest burns. It's as if a hot blade is piercing straight through the beating organ. This must be what she felt in those last moments. This reminder of how she died is like a poison to my soul. I cannot continue this way. I need her back. She cannot be gone forever.

The pain in my heart subsides and the voice in my head dissipates with it. These last few days my heart was filled with hope. Hearing her voice in my head just now felt like a blessing, but I fear she will drive me mad even in the afterlife. I'm bringing her back. I can feel it.

I lie awake several hours after tossing and turning and stare up at the ceiling. Memories of Aliyah float through my mind. Some bring a smile to my face, while others cause tears to slip from the corners of my eyes. I used to be ashamed to cry. I was told crying makes us weak, but when it comes to Aliyah, I can't help the sting of fresh tears at the thought of what life is without her. I have lived over 700 years without loving anyone this way, and one blonde, sassy, beautifully stubborn girl walks into my life and I am ruined forever.

I remember the day I first brought her here. She laid in this bed with an ax in her chest. Then she laid in this bed after I locked her in here the night she went to Adryanna's for the first time. Now, she may never lay in this bed again. I grip my sheets so hard I tear holes in the fabric. I hear the blood rush through my ears and the steady beat of my heart.

I sit up and stalk to the washroom needing to splash some water on my face. I stare at the broken reflecting glass laying in shards around the basin and floor. Aliyah had shattered it the first day she was awake and I never bothered to clean it up. Everything happened so fast after that day. I thought I would be bringing her back here safe and sound and we would pick out another glass...together. One she couldn't break so easily with her little fists. I smile at the thought.

As I stare at the shards on the counter, tears brim in my eyes once more. There, reflecting back at me, is not only the image of myself, but a depiction of what my soul looks like. Broken and in pieces. Tears drip onto the glass, blurring the image. I grip the ax on my chest if only to feel something from the pain the little edges cause.

It isn't enough. The pain is still too much. I pick up a shard of glass and bring it to my wrist. I promised I would find her in the afterlife. Maybe I can't bring her back, but I can go to her. I push the tip of the glass into my arm—

A soft knock comes at the door. I let out a breath, drop the glass, and shake my head. *What am I doing? How would this help me? How could ending it all be fair to the others?* They want her back almost as much as I do. Aliyah laid in that mountain pass praying to the Maker I would find her. She tried to live for me. I must try to live for her now.

I think of the first night on the road to SunSpark as I walk to the door. I had overheard Aliyah talking to Duncan. He told her to fight for me, even when I couldn't fight for myself. That is what I must do for Aliyah now. *Fight.*

I open the door to see Saraphena standing in the doorway. "Come in."

"Hey, Enzo." A soft smile pulls at her lips, but I can tell it isn't genuine. She is trying to be strong, but I can see it in her eyes how much she's hurting. It was the same look staring back at me in the reflecting glass not moments ago.

"What can I do for you Saraphena?"

"It seems silly to ask how you are, so I figured I'd just assume you weren't good and come check on you anyways."

"Thank you. But I'd rather be alone right now."

"If it's alright with you, I'd like to be alone together."

"If that is what you wish."

I stalk back to my bed and lay on top of the covers. Resting one hand behind my head, I try to find some peace. Saraphena makes her way around to the side of the bed and lays down next to me. She stares at the ceiling and we let a few beats of silence pass between us.

"It's quiet," Saraphena starts.

"Too quiet," I add.

"I miss her in my head. I miss the sound of her voice. I miss her laugh and the way she always made me smile. What are we going to do without her if we can't find a way to bring her back, Enzo?"

"I'm not sure. Before her, I thought I had everything I could have ever wanted. But I realize so much of who I am now is because of her. How can I just let her go?"

"I don't think we do. I think we need to hold onto the best parts of her and make them a part of who we wish to become. I know she wouldn't want you to be sad. I think it would hurt her more knowing you are struggling."

"Then how do I make it stop?"

"I'll let you know when I figure it out." She huffs out a laugh.

"I feel as though you are the only other person who knows what this emptiness feels like. You knew what it was like to have her truly be a part of you. What if I lose the parts of myself that made me the person she loved?"

"All we can do is try and be the people she wanted us to be. I know she wanted me to be happy with Gunnar. She wanted me to build a life with him. While I never imagined building a life without her, I know even if she isn't here, she is always with me in my heart. 'Til the end." Saraphena smiles at the memory of what Aliyah and her used to say to each other.

"I want to kill him. The Banished King deserves to pay for what he caused. If Aramot hadn't been working with him— if he hadn't been working *for* him, Aliyah would still be alive. I want to rip every bone from his body until he knows half of what this pain feels like."

"You'll have to get in line." She smiles at me.

I reach over and grab her hand. "She loved you more than anything, Saraphena."

"We won't let him get away with this, Enzo. We will avenge her, but first, we need to bring her back."

A knock comes at the door. "Can we come in?" Gunnar, Duncan, Liliana, and Jade all stand in the doorway.

"Of course," Saraphena says. I give her a side glare as she smiles back at me. They come in and find a space on the bed with us. My whole family is piled together, yet somehow, it still feels empty without her. *Almost* my whole family.

I miss you, little dove. I'm going to bring you back. I promise.

Chapter 2

ENZO

I wake to the feeling of pins and needles pricking down my arm. Jade's body is half laying on my arm, disrupting the circulation of blood flow. The others are all sleeping on the bed around me. I wipe a tear from my cheek and crawl out of bed.

Walking down to the kitchen, I begin packing food for the journey. It seems not so long ago we were packing food for the trip to Citrine City with Aliyah. I pause my movements and grip the counter to steady myself. Emotions overwhelm me and my head swims. I hunch down over the counter to bring my vision back into focus.

"Enzo, are you alright?" Jade asks, coming into the kitchen.

"Yes. Sorry. I don't know what came over me."

"It's okay. Can I help you?"

"I am just packing some supplies for the journey today. Can you find some of those seeds?"

"Of course. How are you doing? Nevermind, that's a stupid question. Obviously you're not alright."

"I'm fine. We are bringing her back, so everything is fine. I won't have to be without her for much longer."

"Enzo—" Jade starts.

"We are bringing her back, Jade!" I roar.

"And what if we can't, Enzo? Huh?! What then?! How many times do you think we can keep doing this to her?! First the ax, then the pool, and then that day on the battlefield!" Jade yells. "Did you ever think maybe she is better off in whatever afterlife awaits her? Look at everything that has happened! She's gone, Enzo. Go—"

I cut her off as my hand flies around her throat. Shoving her up against the wall, fiery rage begins to cloud my mind. I am squeezing so hard, the sound of choking fills the space around us, but this time it isn't in my mind. It's coming from Jade. I close my eyes and try to let her throat go, but I just can't. The words she was saying...the things she was implying...I won't allow those kinds of thoughts.

"Don't you *ever* say those words again. Aliyah is *not* gone. If I don't bring her back, what do I even have to live for then?" I release her neck and she slumps to the floor, gasping for air on all fours.

"I'm sorry, Enzo. I didn't mean to make you upset. I just wanted you to start to see reason in all of this. There may be a chance we can't bring her back and as your strategist it is my job to help foresee outcomes that favor us."

"If you are to *remain* my strategist, then I expect you to be working on a way to bring her back! I will accept nothing less. Either Aliyah comes back, or I will have nothing and no one to come back to. Do you understand me?"

"Yes. Understood. I'll go find the seeds." Jade walks from the kitchen and out the front door. A heavy breath leaves my lungs at the silence. I busy myself checking over our bags when the next member of my family comes down the stairs. Small arms wrap around my waist from behind me, hugging me tight.

"We will find a way, Enzo. I promise you. I can feel it in my heart, we will find a way. No matter the cost." Liliana's words bring comfort to me and a new string of hope floods my senses. It wasn't there a moment ago, but I feel relief and determination coursing through every molecule of my being. Whether it's from Liliana, which I suspect it is, or from the thought of bringing back my little dove, I don't care.

"Thank you. You may release me now."

"I'd like just another moment please." I feel her smiling at my back.

I huff out a breath and stand there, motionless, as she finishes her hug. "Are you quite done?"

"Yes, I'm done now. Thank you!" She singsongs the words as she makes her way over to her pack. She starts taking out essential items from her bag and placing them in another. I tip my head in question.

"I like to mess with Duncan," she says shrugging her shoulders. "It always confuses him why his pack is so heavy when he swears he is a light traveler." Liliana laughs as she slips her water pouches into Duncan's pack. I shake my head and pull my bag over my shoulders.

Gunnar, Saraphena, and Duncan come down the stairs last. Duncan moves to stand behind Liliana, but makes no move to touch her. She cranes her neck back to look at him and gives him a soft smile. Seeing them together should make me happy, my friend deserves to be loved, but instead all I feel is a pit in my stomach.

I shift my eyes away from them and glance at Gunnar. He is smiling and talking to Saraphena who beams up at him. My mood morphs into irritation and my teeth grind at the amount of love around me that I cannot share with my mate.

The front door swings open and Jade walks in with a bag of seeds in her hand. She throws it into her pack and glares at me. I can see the faint purple finger marks on her neck, clearly healing, but my grip must have been tighter than I thought. I want to feel bad, but I simply don't.

"Come together everyone!" Liliana's cheerfulness is unnecessary at this hour. "Now that we are all here, I wanted to take a moment to pray to the Maker. If anyone can help us bring her back, it's Him. Everyone hold hands!"

We gather in a circle and each grasp each other's hands. Jade steps up next to me and laces her fingers through mine. She looks at me and mouths *'I'm sorry'* before closing her eyes. I bow my head and listen to Liliana's words.

"Maker, thank you for blessing us with this beautiful day. I ask you to keep us safe on our journey and help us find the answers we are looking for," she starts.

As she speaks, a smile creeps onto my face and happiness washes over me. Hope springs up in my chest and determination joins the cause in my mind to bring Aliyah home. I crack open my eyes to find everyone else smiling as Liliana continues in her prayer.

"Finally, I ask you to keep us strong and understand your will may differ from ours, but we trust in you to bring Aliyah back to us. Maker, please, let it be so."

"Let it be so," the group says in unison. As we break apart, I see Liliana wipe away tears from her eyes and see the pulse point on her neck beating rapidly. She leans into Duncan as he walks her over to the couch. Laying her down, Duncan returns to the kitchen to fetch a glass of water.

"Is she ill?" I ask.

"No, just tired. She did not sleep well last night." He claps me on the shoulder and walks back toward her. She smiles at him, but I see the tears leaking from her eyes. Confusion pulls at my mind, but I am dragged from my thoughts when Gunnar approaches.

"So, what's the plan?"

"Bring her back," I reply.

"Right and how exactly are we going to do that? So far our plan is," he starts counting on his fingers. "One, go to Twilight to find a lost relic no one has seen in ages. Two, bring her back. I'm thinking there may be some holes in this plan."

"It's a good thing we have the entire journey to the Twilight Kingdom to think of one," Jade says. She gives me a smile and I nod my head at her.

"If we can't come up with a plan in that amount of time then we should probably retire as the Queen's Guard," Duncan laughs. The whole room goes silent as we stare at him. Duncan almost never laughs. *Ever.*

"What?" he says, looking around at each of us.

Something washes over the room and we all burst out into laughter. It doesn't feel forced this time, but it feels strange to laugh in such a dire circumstance. I don't question it though. I welcome the company in the land of delusion where Aliyah is not really gone.

As we make our way out the front door I glance back at Liliana. She smiles at me, but I note the light purple circles deepening under her eyes.

Glancing down at the sleeve of her tunic, I spot a few drops of crimson on the hem. She quickly tucks it into her palm and rushes forward to catch up with Saraphena and Jade. I stare at her as she finds her way to them.

She looks over her shoulder at me, but quickly averts her gaze when she sees me looking at her. Just as I am about to call her back to me, a wave of calm washes over me and I completely forget why I was concerned. Her footsteps waver, but she loops her arm through Saraphena's and steadies herself.

I walk behind the group feeling lighter than I did moments ago. I should question the feeling, but I can't seem to find a care in the world right now.

Chapter 3

SARAPHENA

S trapping our bags over our saddles, we mount the alicanto and prepare to leave for the Twilight Kingdom. Liliana had sent for Molly, her matched sphinx, as soon as we decided to go to Twlight. Seeing Kaleron last night was more disturbing than I thought it would be. Part of me wanted to be so angry over what happened, but at the same time, we have lost so much already. He is Gunnar's brother. Regardless of the things he has done, he is family.

My alicanto, Daisy, shakes her feathers as I climb aboard. I look across the field of crystals surrounding the stables. I spot Mirage looking back at us. Her once bright feathers have dulled to a reddish- gray color and have lost their luster. Something in my heart breaks watching the alicanto grieve the loss of her matched. *Me too, Mirage. Me too.*

Mirage hasn't been the same since we returned from Twilight. She barely eats anything, and refuses to head to the border of Krystal to feed. It's like she is waiting for Aliyah to come back. I haven't found it in my heart to actually say the words to her. Telling Mirage Aliyah isn't coming back just feels cruel.

Gunnar comes up beside me. "You ready, love?"

"Ready," I smile.

We turn towards the road leading to the Twilight Kingdom. Excitement flares in my chest thinking we will find the fallen star to grant us a wish and bring Aliyah back. I'm trying not to go into this mission with high hopes, but part of me can't help feeling excited knowing we aren't giving up. I want to bring Aliyah back with all my heart, but relying on a lost relic no one has seen in ages feels like a stretch. I'm not certain our group is ready for what happens if we don't find the answers we are looking for. If we fail today, I'm not sure we will recover.

"Let's get a move on people. We need to keep a sharp eye out along the way, but especially when we get back into Twilight. We have no clue what we are facing on the other side," Jade calls back. Our group takes off in the direction of the pillar. It is a straight shot along the north side of Krystal, so we should only have to stop once along the journey. I know Enzo is impatient, we all are, but we are no good exhausted and burnt out, so we will need to rest when we can.

Since the barrier came down around the Banished Kingdom, we have not received any reports they have attempted to come onto Olyrium soil, but if anything, that's more concerning. It means they are hiding in the Banished Kingdom gathering their forces. Krystal isn't ready to face The Kalari this soon after the last battle.

I wish you were here. I try to push the thought down the bond I know isn't there. I instinctively touch my left forearm where our Soul Bond mark used to be. The flat skin feels foreign to my touch. I don't want to believe she is really gone. If anything, I want to believe we can bring her back, but the star has to have limits, and I'm not sure it will accept raising someone from the grave as a wish.

Out of everyone in the group, Gunnar, Liliana and Duncan seem to be the only one's dealing well with Aliyah's death. Duncan I can understand, he lost his first love so he knows how to deal with loss. Liliana can control emotions so it makes the most sense if she is okay. I glance at Gunnar and see a carefree smile on his face. He looks over to me and I give him a soft smile back. *I don't understand you, Gunnar,* I think to myself.

I've been acting like everything is fine, mainly because I am hoping we can bring Aliyah back and I won't have to deal with this irritation at him any longer, but I am starting to get frustrated that he can move on so easily. I push those feelings down, set on dealing with them later. I need to focus on the mission. I can't afford to be distracted right now. I made a promise to watch over Aliyah until my dying breath. While technically my breath ended in the SunSpark ballroom, it doesn't count because Marigold brought me back.

I hope Aliyah has found Marigold in the afterlife. Maybe they can make each other happy until Enzo joins her. I wish I could have saved them both. I am a pretty crappy Soul Guardian at this point. So many times Aliyah almost died and when she needed me most, I was halfway across the battlefield.

"Hey, you okay?" Gunnar asks.

"Why did that woman choose me to be Aliyah's Soul Guardian? She knew nothing about me. I couldn't even do the one job she asked me to do. Keeping Aliyah safe was her *only* request and I failed. What could she have possibly seen in me?"

"Saraphena. My love. You are the kindest, bravest, strongest woman I know. She chose you because you are a good person. You left everything behind to protect a baby you had no relation to. You, Saraphena, are the most selfless person in all the realms. Aliyah knew that. She knew you would do anything for her. I saw it every day in your friendship and you are here now trying to get her back. You don't give up on people. That is why she chose you."

"I love you too you know?" I smile at him.

"I know. But I also know I will always have to share your heart with Aliyah. I'm okay with that." He leans over his alicanto and places a kiss to my head. "We will get her back. I promise."

At his words, my face falls. He can't promise me anything. We have no idea if we are going to get Aliyah back. I try to hold onto his word though. I know he will do everything he can.

Several hours later we stop to rest for the night. It isn't far to the Twilight pillar, but we have no way of knowing what lies in wait on the other side. We need to be well rested.

Gunnar sets up our tent and Duncan and Liliana set up theirs. It is nice to see Lil with him. Duncan had such bad luck with love so I hope he doesn't pass up an opportunity to be with her. He shared his story with me one night after we said our goodbyes to Aliyah as Enzo and Jade took her back to Luar. I think he wanted to bring me comfort saying life does go on after tragedy, but in the moment, it wasn't what I wanted to hear. Still, his story did give me perspective in a different way. Seize every opportunity for love because you never know which day will be your last.

I glance over at Gunnar as he finishes setting up our tent. I walk over and turn him to face me.

"I will love you to the ends of this realm and beyond. I swear to never take a moment for granted and I promise to never leave you again. You are my eternity." I pull him down for a deep kiss and he wraps his arms around my waist picking me up and spinning me.

"Well that was unexpected," he says, breaking our kiss. "Though I won't say I didn't enjoy it," he winks. "You are my eternity too, Saraphena. I know Aliyah will always have a place in your heart, but I am glad to hear you can make room for two."

He pulls me into a hug and breaths in deep as he nuzzles his nose into my long curly hair. I close my eyes and thank the Maker for giving us another day together.

"So, who wants to train?" I ask.

"Oh sweetheart you really don't want to pick that fight right now," Gunnar mocks.

"What do you say, Jade? Care to show these boys how it's done?" I smile.

"I'll take any opportunity to show them how a *real* warrior fights," she smirks.

Taking a seat on the ground, Gunnar, Duncan, and Enzo give a collective huff.

"Is there room for one more?" I turn to see Liliana standing, hoping we will invite her in.

"Always," Jade and I say together. Liliana jumps in excitement and moves closer to us.

"Lil, how exactly do you use your ability in fighting?" Duncan mocks from the sidelines.

Without a word, she blows him a kiss and takes a casual stance.

"The fight begins on three," Enzo calls. I look over to see a smile pull at his lips, knowing what comes next.

"On three or after—" Gunnar starts, clearly goading him.

"ON THREE!" We all shout in unison, laughing together like we aren't on an impossible mission.

"One," Duncan starts.

"Two," Gunnar calls.

"Three!" Enzo shouts.

I instantly disappear and make my way behind Jade, planning to strike. Right as I move to kick out her knee, I burst out into laughter. Jade turns and punches me clean in the face, knocking me back into existence.

"Lil, you dirty little—" I grind my teeth and vanish again. If I'm going to win this fight I need to take down Lil first. Seething anger takes over my body and all logic leaves my mind in a red haze induced fury. I falter my shield and she lands a kick to my leg. Pulling out her dagger she tips up my chin, the point digging into my flesh.

"Gotcha," she smiles.

"I yield, I yield," I laugh. I know it is all just in fun, but it stings to lose nonetheless. Now it is just Jade and Liliana.

Jade circles her, analyzing her movements. Liliana stands there with a smile on her face waiting for Jade to strike. Jade pulls a knife from her holster and eyes Lil up and down. Jade swings at Lil, but tears start pouring from her eyes, blurring her vision. She stumbles and Lil has her dagger to the back of Jade's neck before she can regain her footing.

"And gotcha again," Lil laughs.

"Yeah, yeah. I yield, but only because I wanted you to win. Duncan has been trying to beat me for years and has yet to succeed. It'll drive him mad knowing you beat me without even touching me," Jade smirks.

"Lil I thought you could only feel and siphon another's emotions. I didn't realize you could inflict them as well," Duncan asks.

"The ones in my life who know I can do that are few. If they do know, I have asked them to keep it a secret. Being able to alter another's emotions can be a dangerous ability to have. Some may take it as having influence over another, forcing them to make decisions based on emotions, instead of logic, but I have never used it in that capacity. It's fun for training and combat, but I don't need the elders snooping around wondering if I am influencing our kings and queens. It is more trouble than it is worth," Lil explains.

"Your secret is safe with us," Duncan says. She walks towards him and gives his hand a small squeeze. He smiles softly down at her before she takes a seat in the dirt. "For the record, I am proud of you for beating Jade. At least one of us could do it," he smiles.

"You boys care to train?" Jade asks.

"Not for me. I think I need some rest," Enzo says.

"I'm good too," says Gunnar. "I have other plans for this evening." Gunnar's eyes find mine and tingles rush up my throat. Gunnar stands and reaches for my hand. We walk back to the tent and climb inside as I hear Duncan yelling to us.

"I hope your plans are to sleep!"

I hear Duncan and Liliana talking to each other as Gunnar settles in behind me. He places a kiss to my neck and I turn my head to meet him. He kisses me deeply and passionately. Guilt pulls at my heart and I suddenly feel bad for doing this knowing Enzo is alone.

"Gunnar," I say. "Tonight, let's just be together. That is all I wish."

"At your command milady," he smirks and I roll my eyes. He settles in behind me and pulls me close. Some time later his breath evens out and sleep consumes him. Pulling on my boots, I make my way out of the tent. I walk several hundred yards away from the camp so no one will hear me.

I lay down on the ground and look up at the night sky. I watch the colors dance among the stars and I let the moonlight wash over me. I turn my head to look next to me and imagine what it would be like if Aliyah was here. I close my eyes and when I open them again, there she is laying next to me. She looks up at the stars and a smile graces her face. Her blonde hair is sprawled out on the ground around her head. She turns to look at me, but speaks no words. Tears prick at my eyes as I begin to speak.

"Hey Ali. There are so many things I want to tell you. Things are so different with you gone. Enzo is losing his mind a little thinking we can bring you back. Gunnar seems fine, which is irritating as hell. If you were here I know you would understand why. Then again, if you were here, there would be no reason to be sad," I sigh. "Jade is Jade I suppose and Liliana is trying to take on everyone else's emotions so we don't fall apart, but I see the toll it's taking on her. If she keeps this up much longer I'm going to have to say something. Right now though I need her to keep Enzo in a positive place so he can focus on bringing you back. I miss our bond and the way we could talk without anyone hearing." I close my eyes and tears roll down the side of my face.

"For so long it was just you and me. I thought it so strange watching you grow in Luar. Being glamoured by that enchantress, you aged at such a human rate, nothing like the fae do in Olyrium. There you were, rapidly growing before my eyes and I remember telling myself how strange it would be to watch you grow old and die while I lived on. Little did I know that you would not even get the chance to experience a full life. I thought once the glamour broke you would have hundreds if not thousands of years ahead of you. I thought we had time, Aliyah. I need you back, Aliyah. Please. Come back to me. We have to be together again. 'Til the end." I smile at the words she once spoke to me, and I to her. I blink and when I open my eyes again, Aliyah is gone. The ground shows no indentations of where her body may have been.

I stand brushing off the dirt from my clothes and make my way back to the tent. I feel a little better after talking to Aliyah, even if she can't talk back. *Soon*. I will see her again soon.

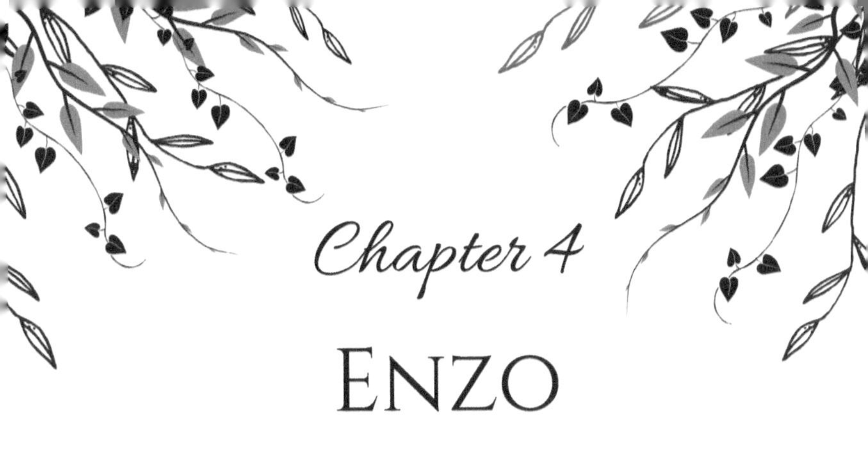

Chapter 4

ENZO

L ight streams into my tent from the outside world. I blink my eyes a few times to clear the fog from my mind and for a few blissful moments, everything is right in the world.

There has been no war. No enemy breaking down the doors to our peaceful world. Aliyah isn't dead. But as those milliseconds pass and I hear the sounds of footsteps in the dirt and low voices speaking of the journey to come, I am reminded of the hole in my chest.

Reality comes crashing in and a feeling of despair wraps itself around me like a black cloak. It weighs me down and I struggle to find the strength to rise from my tent.

Maybe if I don't get up I won't have to face the troubles waiting for me on the outside. Maybe in the safety of this tent I can be shielded from the heartbreak that awaits me beyond these canvas walls.

I shake my head and grumble at the notion I could ever give up on finding a way to bring Aliyah back.

"Enzo, let's get a move on. We need to make it to the Twilight Kingdom before nightfall," Jade calls from beyond my safe haven. Pulling myself from my tent, I stretch my arms above me and twist so my back cracks and pops away the night's tension from my bones. I grip the battle ax around my neck and close my eyes. I exit my tent and stride towards the others.

"Today. Today we will find answers, little dove. I swear it," I whisper to myself. "When we reach the Twilight palace, we head directly for the library. I don't want to waste any time," I address the group.

"At least we don't have to worry about a welcoming party and an entire ball thrown for our arrival," Gunnar winks at his sister.

"Now why would you go and bring that up? How was I supposed to know the ball would go up in flames. *Literally.* Next time you come to SunSpark I'll be sure to let Kaleron know you have no wishes for any fun in your life." Liliana throws her arms up in defeat and huffs as she stalks towards Duncan.

Liliana looks better today, more well rested. The purple circles are absent from her eyes and her spirits seem to brighten the air around us again. Even Duncan is smiling down at her. I avert my gaze as I see them looking into each other's eyes.

Aliyah's gray orbs flash through my mind and I curse under my breath. I take a deep inhale in and out. Packing up my tent, I shove the canvas and rods into my bag and sling it over Ruby's back. Molly comes bounding over to Liliana as the rest of the group mount their alicanto.

"We finish the journey to Twilight today. Stay close and stay sharp." Jade commands the group and I am thankful for it as I am in no mood to give more orders.

The alicanto take off into a sprint and Molly flaps her white wings hard before she begins soaring above us. I look up and when my eyes snag on the sphinx something explodes in my chest.

I wait for the pain to accompany the feeling, but it never comes. Instead I am engulfed with a sense of joy. My heart feels like it is reaching out across the oceans. I look to Liliana to see if she is the cause of this flood of emotion. She looks down to me from the sky and simply smiles.

As the sensation passes over me, I feel a familiar hum in my veins. Determination opens the gates into my soul and I spur Ruby on. *Faster. Faster.* We fly past the group. Crystal mountain ranges blur around us as the wind whips my hair back with force. The rapid beating of my heart only propels me on. The group is far behind me now, but I can't seem to bring myself to stop.

"Enzo, wait up!"

"Stop! We can't keep up!"

"Enzo, look—"

Their voices cut off as an arrow flies through the sky. It misses me by mere inches, but a torrent of arrows now rain down around me. I look up at the mountain of crystal above us and spot The Kalari archers firing at our group from atop the formation. There aren't many, but I don't have time to take them down one by one. Ruby screeches as an arrow impales her wing. Another strikes her leg and two more embed in her back.

A red haze washes over me. I will not lose another thing I love. Without hesitation, I fling my power out around me and obliterate the enemy in seconds. I hop down from Ruby and inspect her wounds. I quickly pull the arrows from her body, hoping the poison has not yet reached her bloodstream. Duncan materializes next to me as the others approach.

"They must have been hiding out after the battle in Twilight. Are you hurt?" he asks.

"No. I'm fine." Blood drips onto Ruby's wing, blending into the color of her feathers. I dab my eyes and find a thin stream of blood lining my cheeks.

There must have been more of The Kalari than I originally saw. I wipe my hand on my pants and slowly stroke the other over Ruby's head. I start to place my hand on her wound, thankful it is not more serious.

"Here, let me. You have exerted too much power already. What were you thinking?" Duncan lays his hands on Ruby and warmth radiates from his palms as he heals her wounds. She shoots up from her spot on the ground and ruffles her feathers before trotting away.

"I was thinking we were getting ambushed. I was not about to lose her!" I practically yell.

"Why did you run ahead of us? We need to stay together, Enzo!"

"Don't you dare yell at me! I am your *General* and you will respect me as such or I will not hesitate to relieve you of your duties!"

Hurt flashes over Duncan's face before he sets his stare into one of cold steal. "You may be my General, but do not forget who helped get you there," he seethes.

"You could have had it for yourself if you hadn't been such a coward and showed up to academy as a child like the rest of us! Instead you were home, galavanting around with your lover!"

Duncan stumbles backward as if I have physically struck him. Liliana comes running up beside him and pulls him away by his arm.

"Enzo, enough. Look at me brother." Gunnar pulls my gaze towards him. "Look at me."

My chest rises and falls as the blinding rage subsides. I blink once and my mind clears.

"Duncan. I apologize. I didn't mean those things. I simply— I don't know what came over me," I say.

"I know you are hurting, Enzo. We all are. You once asked Aliyah why she was pushing you away when she was hurting. You are the one hurting now. Do not push us away," Duncan says.

"I'm sorry. Once Aliyah is back all will be right with the world. I am sure of it." The rest of the group mount their alicanto once again, but Saraphena stops me.

"Aliyah loved you Enzo. Don't let rage cloud your mind. Be the man she fell in love with. The one who protects, not destroys. That is the man she believed in. That is the man she wished you to be."

Saraphena pulls a small cloth from her bag and wipes away the remaining blood from my eyes. I snatch her wrist as she finishes and let my face fall into a stern look.

"Make no mistake, Saraphena. Without Aliyah, it will be *you* protecting the world *from* me. I will burn every corner of this realm so they might feel a fraction of the pain I am in. If we can't bring her back, everyone will suffer as I have suffered."

I turn my back on her, leaving her to stand there shocked by my words. I mount Ruby who seems to be just as pissed off as I am. With a swift kick of my heels she takes off running towards the others.

Enzo. I will always love you. No matter what you do, I will always love you.

My heart stops as Aliyah's faint voice filters into my mind once more. I almost fall off Ruby at the sound. I use her voice as fuel to the fire of my mission.

I'm bringing you back, little dove. I'm coming for you.

We Bridge to the same village we once did not so long ago. The air hangs heavy around us. The bodies which were peeled of their skin and burned still lay on the ground in a slow decay.

Not a single sound ripples through the air, save for our footsteps hitting the dirt as we approach the palace. Twilight palace looks no different than the day we first arrived here. The front doors are hanging off the hinges and there is not a soul to be found.

However, this time there is no impending battle on the horizon waiting for us. We make our way up the steps and breathe in a fresh layer of dust that kicks up as we walk.

"The library is this way," Duncan instructs.

The last time we were here, there was no time to explore or see the palace for what it once was. Now it is just an empty shell. A vessel waiting to be filled by its rightful king. Make that two kingdoms now without a ruler. Twilight was large and vast. While word may not have yet reached the villages on the outskirts of the kingdom, they will soon be in search of a new leader. Someone must rule them to avoid anarchy throughout their kingdom. The residents of Krystal respected the King and Queen too much to ever let that fate fall upon them.

Duncan is in denial of his new role as King of Twilight. He needs to take his place on the throne and regain control of his kingdom before they appoint someone else, or worse, someone usurps the throne and leads our realm into destruction, like Aramot planned to do.

"I am sorry this is what has become of your home," Liliana says to Duncan. She takes his hand in hers and I turn away from the moment. Looking out the window, I gaze across the battlefield where Aliyah was slain. Long blonde hair catches my eye in the distance.

"Aliyah?" I whisper. "Aliyah!" I take off running out the back of the palace and onto the battlefield.

"Enzo!" Gunnar yells behind me. I hear the sound of their footsteps as I break out into a full sprint. There standing on the hill is Aliyah. Just as I crest the top of the hill, I spin around looking for her.

"Aliyah!" I call. "Aliyah! My dove! I'm here!"

"Enzo...she's not here," Gunnar says timidly.

"No! I saw her! I saw her standing out here. She was right here!" I plead. Tears well in my eyes as I turn in every direction searching for her.

"Enzo—" Saraphena begins.

"No! She was here. Do not tell me otherwise. I know what I saw! I know what I saw...I know—" I fall to the ground on my knees as tears flow freely from my eyes. "She was right here. She was— *AHHHHHHHH!*" I scream into the sky as my fingers dig into the dirt beneath me. The world around me disappears as the ground shakes and rumbles under my touch. A wave of power ripples off me as I continue to yell.

As I lean on all fours and take jagged breaths, the world reappears around me. The others are pulling themselves off the ground several hundred feet away. I stand and start walking towards them.

"She was there and I don't want to hear anything different." I stalk past them and back into the palace.

As we re-enter the great hall of Twilight's palace, trepidation sits heavy in my chest. I close my eyes and try to shake away the feeling. Whether it is because I am going mad, or my grief is inflicting hallucinations, I am thankful for the sound of Aliyah's voice. Faint as it may be, it is still the sweetest sound.

Figment of my imagination or not, to see her face again was both blessing and torment. The dark halls of Twilight match the somber mood of the group as we make our way to the library. If anywhere is going to have answers to the questions we desperately seek, it's there.

Chapter 5

LILIANA

My lungs fill with stale air as we sift through tome after tome looking for anything to help bring Aliyah back. Sleep pulls at my conscious, but I shake my head to clear it from the lull. *I can rest later.* This is the same sentence I keep telling myself on repeat the last few days.

Siphoning off everyone's emotions has taken a bigger toll on me than I thought it would. Before I met them, I rarely used my powers. There was no one around worth doing it for. I look over to Duncan who sits slouched over in a chair and flips through pages of an obscenely large book with browning edges and tears in the leather.

He looks up and his eyes catch mine. A wave of anxiousness washes over me as I read his emotion. We are all scared we will not find answers here. I try to siphon off some of his turmoil. I feel my knees begin to buckle and a crushing weight sits on my chest. I try to muster a smile as Duncan's brows pull together in a look of concern. He sets his tome aside and stands, but I turn back to my book, ignoring him. I may be the one who is able to read emotions, but Duncan has the keen ability to catch every small detail in my expression.

He materializes next to me, putting his hand over my book to hinder me from reading on.

"You need to stop doing that. It's going to burn you out."

"I don't know what you're talking about. I'm fine," I smile up at him.

"Lil—"

"I've got something!" Saraphena squeals from across the room.

I push away from Duncan before he can scold me any further. No one chastises him for using his ability! Well except for in the training ring, but never when it's in pursuit of helping others.

"What did you find?" Enzo rushes to her side looking over her shoulder.

"The writing isn't clear, but it looks like the story of how they found the star initially." She points to some faded text on the page.

"Can you read it?" Gunnar chimes in.

"I think so," Saraphena starts. "It looks like a passage written by the king several thousand years ago, maybe even longer. Someone named King Valiton. I've never heard of him before."

"He was one of the first kings in Olyrium. Some say he is the founder of the Twilight Kingdom, but there are not many tomes written back this far. Where did you find this book?" Duncan asks.

"It was in a drawer in the desk at the back of the library. It looks to be handed down through generations of kings and queens based on the list of names in the front of the book," she shrugs. Saraphena starts to read the passage.

"Word has spread throughout the kingdom of a large boom that rippled throughout the night. A great light blast down from above and broke free from the night sky... An island not far from here claims to have found a fallen star... no one dares touch it for fear of what destruction it may hold... sent a group of men to scour the island and bring back the relic for further inspection... may be able to help revitalize our lands for the future of Twilight."

"Is that all?" I ask.

"No, there is another entry several months later referencing the star again," Saraphena confirms. She begins reading the next passage.

"My men were unsuccessful in bringing back the entire fallen star. It proved to be too heavy on their ship and was lost to the sea along with half their crew. All was lost save for one small chunk they managed to carve out before leaving the shores of the island... the key to Twilight's survival. After many failed attempts, I have finally found the key to making the star work in our favor. The Maker has blessed us with the power to grant any wish I ask of it, but the cost of the wish is not one to be taken lightly. The few wishes I have made cost me... To secure the safety of this power, the stone has been carved down... We shall use this star to save the people of Twilight from those who would wish us harm. The relic shall

be passed down through the line of kings and queens to come. We thank the Maker for His blessing of our people."

"That is the last passage written in the book. Some of the writing I cannot read due to age and time, but now we know it came from an island. Maybe if we can't find the relic itself we can find a piece still left on the island?" Saraphena says. She moves to close the book, but Enzo stops her.

"Wait. Look there," he points to the spine of the book. "Pages have been torn out. Hundreds of pages it seems. It is if someone deliberately ripped out any information on the star past it's origin. Why would someone do that?"

"The passage mentions a cost of the wishes. Maybe the price became so great that whoever ripped out the pages was trying to protect anyone else from using it. Unfortunately, there is no way of telling how the relic was lost," Jade says.

I look to each of my friends and see worry pulling at their faces. "We can't give up hope, yet. Saraphena is right, maybe there is more of the stone on the island or maybe one of the inhabitants has more information to help us. We should go there."

"We don't even know what island it landed on. How will we know?" I ask.

"The passage says it landed on an island not far from here. There are three islands surrounding the Twilight Kingdom. It will be a distance to travel to each one, but it may be our only option. Jade, any suggestions?" Duncan adds.

Jade pauses and considers all the information for a moment. I can feel the contemplation seeping off her body in waves. Finally she says, "There is another option we should consider."

Collectively we tip our heads in question, waiting for her to go on.

"We have no clue what the Banished King is planning. As we speak, he could be gathering his army once more or sailing across the sea or waiting to use the pillar to come through Twilight again. We need to take action. Bringing Aliyah back is at the top of our list, but at our core we are still the Queen's Guard. We vowed to protect these lands and we have been neglecting our duties. We shouldn't all go to the islands. It isn't a six person job, anyways. We should divide and conquer."

"You can't be serious," Enzo starts. "We need to focus on bringing Aliyah back!"

I feel the pulse of his rage ripple through the room. I quickly take over his emotions and try to bring him back to a reasonable mindset. My thighs quiver as I take on his rage and I bite the inside of my cheek to mask the force of it all. The taste of copper fills my mouth. Taking several deep breaths in through my nose, I regain my composure.

"Lil, are you alright?" Jade asks.

"I'm fine. Listen, I think Jade is right. We shouldn't all go. Twilight is filled with neighboring villages that were hopefully not touched by The Kalari. Maybe some of their elders will have some information to help us with both the fallen star and with the Banished King. Maybe they will be willing to stand with us against him once more. That way it would at least slow the Banished King down if he does decide to come back to Olyrium."

"Gunnar and I can go to the island. It might be nice to get away for a little while anyways," Saraphena says.

"Liliana and I will visit the neighboring villages. I should check on the people of Twilight to see how they are fairing after the death of their kings," Duncan says. He moves to stand beside me and takes my hand. I welcome the feel of his palm in mine.

"And where does that leave Jade and I?" Enzo asks, anger lacing his tone.

"If the Banished King decided to strike tomorrow we are painfully, and obviously, unprepared to fight a battle. We need soldiers who are willing to fight. I think it might be a good idea to start recruiting again. We will need an army sooner rather than later."

"So we have our plan then. Jade and I will build an army. Duncan and Lil, visit the towns looking for anyone willing to fight and to make sure they are surviving after this colossal betrayal. Gunnar and Saraphena, visit the three islands and try to find any remnants of the star that may have been left behind. We all leave first thing tomorrow," Enzo commands.

"I'll find us some rooms to sleep in for the night," Duncan says. As he moves to leave the room, Enzo calls him back.

"Our first priority is bringing Aliyah back. Do not forget that. I want reports of your progress. Is that clear?"

"I think we can manage," I nod.

"One more thing," Enzo starts. "Thank you all. While it pains me to separate, I have all the faith in the realms this is the best team to find a way to bring Aliyah back. I know you will not fail me."

"Aliyah would do the same for us," Saraphena nods her head. I see the small tears brim in her eyes and I push my power out towards her, but Duncan grips my hand tight and my eyes snap to his. A dark warning is in his gaze and I rescind my power from Saraphena.

"Liliana, Saraphena, and Jade you all held a place in Aliyah's life and I know she would want you to have these." Enzo pulls Aliyah's knives out of the holster on his ribcage. He hands one to me, one to Saraphena, and one to Jade. I look at the clear crystal encasing the colored feathers, reminding me of Aliyah's dress from the ball. I look to Saraphena and smile. I got my best friend back, but lost another far too soon.

We all exit the library and follow Duncan to our rooms for the evening. The halls are tattered and torn, and the paint from massive murals peals down the walls. Every window is shattered and there isn't a single light inside except for the torch Gunnar provides from his hand, illuminating our path. Everyone makes their way into their assigned rooms. As I settle into mine, a knock comes at the door. I open it to find Duncan leaning against the door frame, biceps bulging and a serious look on his face. The wings tattooed around his throat flare with the rapid intake of air, likely caused by his anger at my actions in the library.

"We need to finish our conversation from earlier," he says pushing his way into the room.

"No we don't. There isn't anything to talk about. I'm fine. Everyone is fine. It's all fine," I say waving my hands around the space.

"Lil. You're not fine. You think I don't notice the shift in my mood? I don't think I have smiled this much since— a very long time."

"And couldn't it be because you are happier now with me here?" I smile, stepping into his personal space. His nostrils flare at my deflection and a stern look falls over his face.

"Liliana. You're taking on too much. Your legs shake and you bite the inside of your cheek to stop the pain from taking over. I see it. I see *you*."

"Duncan, seriously. I'm okay. I know how much I can take on. I know how much I can handle." I smile wrapping my arms around his waist. He stiffens for a moment before letting out an exhale and wrapping his arms around me. "I just don't like to see the ones I love hurting is all. I can help them. I can take it on so they don't have to."

"That isn't how it works, sunshine. They need to feel what they are going to feel. It's the only way they are ever going to get past it. You can't take on everyone else's pain. How will there be any room left for your own?"

"There won't be. I guess—" Tears start to well in my eyes. "I guess I figure if I take on everyone else's pain then I won't have to deal with my own. Do I even have a right to grieve Aliyah?"

"What do you mean? Of course you have a right. She was a part of your life, no matter how short a time. Grief doesn't play fair and it certainly doesn't have rules on who it affects. Aliyah meant something to you. If you didn't feel anything, I'd start to worry you're becoming like me," he smiles.

"See, you're smiling and this time it isn't because of me," I laugh.

"Sunshine, my smile has everything to do with you." He leans down and places a soft kiss to my lips. *Our first kiss.* I always felt his affection towards me, even after I covered him in jam and feathers, but he has always been hesitant to show physical affection. His lips are soft and plush. My hands find his dark hair and I run my fingers over his scalp. A deep groan releases from his throat at my touch and I can't help the smile pulling at my lips. He breaks our kiss, but doesn't release his hold on me.

"Who knew the princess from SunSpark would ever be kissing the King of Twilight?" I smile.

His face falls and he pushes out of my grasp. "I am no king. I don't want to be king. The people will choose someone else." He makes his way to the door with his head hung low.

"Duncan, wait. I didn't mean to—"

"Goodnight, Liliana. Get some rest. It will be a long journey before we find a village not plagued by my brothers crimes." With that, he shuts the door and leaves me alone in the dark with only the moon for light. As I climb into bed, the frame creaks at my movement and with each toss and turn, the incessant sound of rusted nails scratches at my mind.

"One step closer for two steps back, Liliana. Good one." I roll my eyes at my stupidity. There will be no rest for me tonight even though Duncan was right. I am burning out my body day after day. Maybe some time away from everyone is exactly what I need.

Chapter 6

ENZO

I *stand in a familiar field of wheat and wildflowers. I scan the horizon, looking for her.*

"Enzo," she calls. I turn and find Aliyah standing in the distance wearing her tattered dress, a smile on her face.

"Little dove!" I yell. I try to move towards her, but my feet will not budge.

"Enzo, I'm scared. I need you. Please." Tears drip down her face and drop off her chin.

"I'm so sorry, Aliyah. I'm sorry I couldn't save you."

"Shhhh. Enzo, it's okay. No one could have known. But Enzo, I need you now."

"I'm sorry, little dove. I can't go to Luar. It's too painful. I know even now in this dream, you are just that...a dream. Maybe I am going mad, but I will happily live in insanity if that is where you exist in my mind."

"No, Enzo. Please. I'm—" Aliyah is pulled into the darkness and I am left standing in the field alone.

"I'm so sorry, Aliyah. Forgive me."

I shoot up in bed as the memory of my dream comes pelting into my conscious mind. My breathing is ragged and my heart feels like it's being pulled across the sea once more. I grip the sheets and try to clear her from my thoughts. I need to stay focused.

Today we head out in our separate directions to try and bring Aliyah back. While I am not thrilled to be going back to Krystal and get recruits for the coming war, I know I can trust my family more than anyone to find a way. I can't help but feel useless while the others go out there scouring the lands for answers, but I know Aliyah would not want me to leave the realm unprotected. Aliyah loved Citrine and I heard her vow to come back one day. I need to keep it standing so she will know I have not failed her once again.

I rise from my bed and pull on my tunic and black leather pants. I feel the cool metal of the ax necklace hanging over my sternum. Somehow, the chain feels heavier today than it has in the past. I bring the silver steel to my lips and kiss the tiny ax before tucking it under my tunic. I slip my knife into the sheath around my chest and finish packing up the rest of my bag. As I finish and slip the bag on my back, Jade opens the door to my room.

"Ready to go?" she asks.

"Yes. I want to get back to Krystal as soon as possible. The sooner we get back and secure the recruits, the sooner we can start looking for Aliyah again."

"I think we should move into Citrine City. They will have the space for a military Korin simply doesn't have," Jade continues as we make our way to the front of the palace. "Once we have the army built maybe we can start looking for the heir."

"Agreed. If we cannot get enough recruits from Krystal, I will travel to SunSpark to see if the new King Kaleron is as generous as he is leading on."

"I know the people of Krystal will stand with you. We can tell them what happened in Twilight and speak of how it's in ruins now. I believe that will be enough motivation for them to rise up once more. We can send letters out with some of our military who still reside in Korin to search other towns for any information about the heir, along with sending recruits our way. With us covering Krystal, and Duncan and Liliana covering Twilight, someone has to know something."

We start heading off in the direction of the pillar. Once we Bridge back to Krystal we can call for our alicanto and make it back across the north side of the mountain pass fairly quickly.

"Did the others leave already?" I ask.

"Yes. They all left together early this morning. The plan was to head in the same direction starting on the farthest side of Olyrium and make their way back towards the palace before continuing to the villages on the other side. Gunnar and

Saraphena need to find a boat to take them to one of the islands to start looking for pieces of the star."

"Hmm." It is all I can manage to say, getting lost in the thought of my dream last night.

"Enzo," Jade starts. "You've been dreaming about her haven't you?"

"What makes you say that?"

"You, umm, well you have a tendency to talk in your sleep. I heard you last night yelling for her when I got up to fetch some water. Do you think it is real?"

"No. I know it isn't. It is just the Maker playing with my mind."

"But you saw her on the field in Twilight?"

"I saw her. Whether you did or not is inconsequential. She was there."

"Do you think she is trying to contact you?"

"I don't have an answer for you. But seeing her face...it reminds me why I am doing all this. To bring her back. There has to be a reason why she plagues my mind."

"I hope we find that reason soon." Jade says the words under her breath, most likely so I wouldn't hear. The rest of the walk to the pillar is in silence.

"Why do we keep moving from one dusty palace to the next?" I ask.

"Bad luck?" Jade shrugs her shoulders.

Citrine City still remains empty. Jade and I had chosen our rooms for the foreseeable future and settled in. We now sit in the dining room feasting on ham, potatoes, and vegetables. She even managed to get the seeds that grow those decadent powdered doughnuts I love so much. A smile graces my face as I think of the night in the kitchen when Aliyah caught me with powder on my face.

"What's so funny?" Jade smiles.

"Just thinking of Aliyah. She once found me in the kitchen with powder all over my face from these doughnuts," I say pointing to the treat. "She could have easily made fun of me for hours, but instead just laughed with me over how a warrior such as myself could possibly eat doughnuts. I wish I could go back to those simple moments with her."

"Sounds just like her. She did always seem to find joy in the little things," Jade says. "I miss her. I think she made us...better. All of us. It's like the last piece to our family puzzle clicked into place. Without her— Well, I hope we don't have to be without her for much longer."

"Agreed." A genuine smile crosses my face thinking about her. I take a bite of the doughnut and let the memory sink in a little deeper.

"So, what's the plan for recruiting?" Jade asks.

"You tell me. You're the strategist, remember?" I wink at her.

"Good to know I still have my title," she smirks. A moment passes between us, our eyes locked on each other before she continues. As she speaks, an unsettling feelings presses on my chest. It isn't painful, but it feels like— anger?

"Enzo. Are you even listening to me?"

"Send word into towns we are putting together an army to fight the Banished King and plan to request a meeting with Kaleron in SunSpark to see if he will join the effort if we cannot get recruits from Krystal," I repeat back her words.

She gives me a side look like she knows I wasn't fully listening. "Correct. I will write out the letters tomorrow and call upon our soldiers still in Korin to make their way here. Will you be alright here by yourself for a few days while I gather them?"

"Of course. Why wouldn't I be?"

"No reason. What are the parameters we are setting for those who want to join us?"

"How do you mean?"

"What is our minimum age requirement? Are they required to have abilities? What of those who served in the first war? Are they to return to fight by requirement or by volunteer only?"

"For now we take volunteers. I don't want to force anyone to join a war they shouldn't even be fighting again. So many were lost in The Great War and it pains me to even ask them to join us again. My hope is they will listen and come to our aid of their own volition."

"They will. I'm sure of it. What of the age requirement?"

I huff out a long breath. I think about how young Jade, Gunnar, and I were when we first arrived here in Citrine. I remember thinking how unfair it was that such younglings would have to learn how to kill so soon. However, if I didn't join when I did, I would have never met my found family.

"We take volunteers. No age limit or requirement. If they want to fight, they can fight, but no one will be forced to fight. At least not yet anyways."

"I'll go start drafting the letters now. Hopefully we will receive our first update from the others by the time I return. Duncan and Liliana have likely made it to a few villages by now. We are one step closer to getting answers, Enzo. We just have to be patient. It isn't like Aliyah is going anywhere." A soft smile crosses her face in her attempt to make a joke.

I smile back at her, but it doesn't quite reach my eyes. I know she is right. Aliyah is lying in her iron grave just waiting for me to bring her back. At least I know she isn't suffering while she waits.

The next morning, Jade heads off towards Korin to spread word to our few trusted soldiers to start looking for the heir and pass along that we are taking recruits. The corridors echo with emptiness as I stalk around the hallways of Citrine. I stand before the painting of Queen Dione and gaze up into her eyes.

"Was it worth it? Knowing the barrier has been broken after your eternal sacrifice, was it worth it?"

"Yes. It was. It kept my kingdom safe for over 25 years. Sometimes, sacrifice isn't about saving someone forever, but buying time until they are ready." The painting before me comes to life as Queen Dione speaks.

"No one has the magic you did. We are sorely unprepared for the coming war. What would you do?"

"The only thing you can do. Fight, General Enzo. You fight with everything you have left."

I blink and the painting has returned to normal. I push the heel of my hands into my eyes to rub away the exhaustion.

"I must be going mad. Here I am talking to a painting. Maybe Jade was right to question if I would be okay for a few days alone."

Chapter 7

LILIANA

"The Kalari haven't stepped foot on these lands in over 25 years. Why would we believe you now?" the village elder, Garmon, asks.

"You truly don't know what happened at the palace? What Aramot did to your people?" Duncan asks.

"The king and queen have not spoken to or visited the far villages in some time. We have not received any news in ages!" Garmon yells.

The tension in the village is palpable. Many are angry at Duncan for just being related to the rulers who betrayed their kingdom, and the other half are angry because Duncan now refuses to take the throne. Duncan stands in the village square on a make-shift stage overlooking the people. This is how it has gone at every village we have visited. Duncan speaks of the coming war, they don't believe him, they yell, and we get no answers.

"Who will take the throne now?" one asks.

"Why didn't the king and queen say anything about the attacks?" another says.

"Why are The Kalari attacking again?" says one.

"Are you a traitor too?" someone yells.

"I don't have answers to your questions. I had not been to Twilight in some time. I was unaware of the situation taking place until we arrived and found the king and queen dead and Aramot conspiring with the Banished King. What we seek now is information about the fallen star and any knowledge of an heir to Krystal, rumor or otherwise." Duncan's voice carries over the crowd and a wave of whispers washes over the tension.

"We know nothing of an heir of Krystal. Maybe you should be more focused on the heir of *Twilight* first," Garmon seethes.

"I am no king of the Twilight Kingdom and I am sorry to say I will never be king. Once the palace has been restored we will gather all the elders from the villages to decide on the fate of Twilight. Anyone who wishes to come and help restore the palace is welcome, but have no expectations for me to take the throne," Duncan says.

Grumbles fall over the crowd and anger taints the air around us. These people have been through so much and now their only leader refuses to take the throne. Duncan would make a good king. The crowd begins to shift away from questions and look towards action. The first village was warm and accepting, but this one seems to be angry at the royal family. I suppose they have a right to be after everything that's happened. I try to siphon off the rising emotions so Duncan can finish his speech. Hopefully I can siphon enough off before someone decides to choose a path of violence. I've had a few days to rest so pulling this many emotions shouldn't be too much of a struggle.

I feel the anger flowing through my veins. The red haze of violence creating a film over my mind. I take a few deep breaths and try to dissipate the feeling. Breathe in peace...breathe out anger....breathe in peace...breathe out anger. The crowd settles as they listen to the final words of his campaign. I quickly wipe away the line of crimson dripping from my nose before Duncan can see.

"Take the time you need to think about joining our cause in restoring Twilight palace. I present you with another alternative as well. Krystal is building an army. Believe what you want, but the Banished King is coming. We are trying to be prepared. If you would like to join our forces, please inquire with me directly for instructions. We will be staying at the local inn. If you have any information about the heir or the fallen star, we will be here for another two days before we must move on. Thank you." Duncan steps off the stage and takes my hand.

"Don't think I don't know what you did out there, Liliana," he whispers to me. Anger is etched onto his gaze. It seems to be the only sort of face he makes at me recently.

"I don't know what you're talking about," I say, a little more winded than I expect.

I see his jaw clench. "Listen here sunshine, and listen closely. I brought you with me because I thought you would be good company, but make no mistake, I will not hesitate to send you to a deserted island where you will have no one's emotions to siphon off. Maybe then you will finally get some rest."

"Is that concern I feel peaking out of your emotions?" I wink.

"Liliana," he says with a bite to his tone.

"Duncan," I smile up at him. He stops us in the street and looks both ways before turning me and pulling me harshly to the nearest wall. The cool stone bites through my tunic, but a smile still creeps up my face. Rage flares in his eyes, but adoration seeps into my senses from him.

"Stop doing that. Stop taking on everyone else's crap. You can't handle it all at once and I will not— I *cannot* lose another person I care about. That is why I will not be king. When you are king, you lose everything, one way or another." He reaches out and cups my face with his strong hand and the warmth that seeps from his palm is a comforting balm to the cool of the stone at my back.

I reach up to wrap my hand around his wrist. "I can't promise I will stop, but I will promise I will never take on more than I can handle."

"Fine, but no more siphoning off *my* emotions. Understood?"

"Understood," I say as he releases my face. He takes my hand again and makes our way to the inn. The rickety sign above the door reads "The Mud Puddle" and my mood instantly sours. Hopefully the sign is metaphorical. Pushing open the door I understand the name. The floor is made of packed dirt with holes of varying sizes filed with water from leaky ceilings. The patrons inside match the aesthetic perfectly. Most of them smell like they haven't showered in a week and the other half are caked in mud with flies buzzing around their heads.

I don't mind roughing it, especially given I grew up in a palace and could use a change of scenery, but this was a different level of rough.

"Two rooms, please," Duncan says to the bar keep. My stomach drops in disappointment. He tosses Duncan one key and points to the back corner of the tavern.

"Only one. Sorry mate, guess you will just have to slum it with the little lady," he says winking at me.

Duncan looks at me in question, trying to sense any hesitation to sharing room with him. I smile and nod towards the hallway leading to a row of rooms. My stomach summersaults back up my throat and nervousness floods my system.

"You sure you're okay with this? It isn't the same as sharing a tent out of necessity. This is a little more cozy," I say.

"I'll be fine." He squeezes my hand slightly tighter. This way is better so we can watch each other's back. Not everyone is happy we are here and now we can ensure we are both safe.

Opening the door to our room we find a single candle lit and one small bed about the size for one person, maybe two if you squeezed in close.

"I'll take the floor," Duncan says.

"Nonsense! This is your village, your people, your bed. Please, I insist."

"If you think I am going to let a princess sleep on the floor, you might be more delusional than I thought," he winks at me.

I scoff. "I am *not* delusional! If anyone is, it's you! I mean after all, I might be a princess, but you are a king!" I try to make my tone sound as if I am making a joke, but clearly it doesn't land.

His face suddenly falls. "Stop saying that. Get that notion out of your head, Liliana. I am not going to have this conversation with you again. I am not what these people need."

"Duncan, you would make such a good king. The people need someone to rise up and give them stability. You could be that person!"

"I haven't been to Twilight in ages! I have no clue what these people have gone through or how to help them! They don't want me!"

"Why are you denying your birth right?! You are meant to take the throne now, Duncan. It is your responsibility! If Kaleron and Gunnar were to ever die, Maker forbid, it would be my responsibility to step up and rule, whether the people wanted me or not. Why can't you see it is the same for you?"

"It is not my responsibility. It never was and it never will be. Krystal is my home. Enzo and others, *they* are my family. All this," he motions around the room. "This is all I will ever be and I am fine with that!"

I try to feel the emotions coming off of him to see if there are any hidden truths. A secret desire to be king that maybe he is afraid to say out loud. All I feel is anger and denial.

"But you can be so much more. Be who your people need you to be! Be their king!"

"No. That's final." He blows out the candle and crawls to the floor, pulling a blanket and pillow down from the bed. I stand there in the dark frustrated and confused.

"Ugh!" I throw my arms up and huff as I crawl into bed. Sleep takes me faster than I expect.

I wake up to moon light streaming in from the window. I rub my eyes and turn over looking for Duncan. The blanket and pillow have been discarded on the floor and he is nowhere in sight. Climbing from the bed I walk over to the door and make my way to the front of the building. Duncan is sitting with an older male who speaks between bites of food. The scent of biscuits and pork wafts from the kitchen and my mouth waters.

Duncan's eyes meet mine as he waves me over. I take a seat next to him right as the bar keep from last night sets a plate of steaming food in front of me. Salted ham and biscuits with a white gravy sit on my plate and I immediately dig in. I close my eyes and moan under my breath when the warm gravy hits my tongue. Opening them, I find Duncan staring at me as I chew and swallow.

"Sorry," I say taking another bite. He fixes his eyes back on the man.

"...brought to the palace by the king after the star had been found. He heard I dealt in rare materials and asked me to forge the star into something tangible. I fastened it into a ring for the king to wear. That was the last I saw of it."

"What did the ring look like?" Duncan asks.

"Oh son, that was ages ago. I honestly can't remember the details, but I know the stone was black as night with small flecks looking to be the perfect description of the stars above," the man says in a raspy voice. I am honestly surprised he is still alive based on how old he looks.

"Thank you, sir. This is very helpful information. Thank you for coming forward," Duncan says.

"Of course, my king. I would do anything to help you!"

"I'm not—"

"Your generosity is noted. Here, take this for your information." I pass him a small bag filled with gold coins. Who knows when this man's last day will be, the least I can do is buy him a few good meals. You can distinctly see his ribcage and I could count the number of vertebrae on his spine through his tunic.

"Thank you. Thank you." The man stands and bows before Duncan, excusing himself from the inn.

"Why did you stop me from informing him I am not the king?" Duncan asks with an edge to his voice.

"He is an old man. Let him have his thoughts. There was no sense confusing him."

"Hmm. Well at least we have some more information about the star. Now at least we know it was formed into a ring. The only problem is a ring is significantly smaller and harder to find."

"True, but it is a good starting point. Maybe your mother left some jewelry behind we could go through. If not her, maybe the king did wear it. We can scour Twilight palace when we get back," I smile, finishing my food.

Duncan stands to leave. "Duncan wait. About last night—"

"There is no need to apologize. It is I who needs to seek forgiveness. I know the things you would do for your kingdom, so I understand why you would say such things. That does not give me the right to become angry at you for expressing how you feel."

"Oh, um, okay. Well thank you for apologizing, but I owe you an apology too. I shouldn't have pushed you so hard. I know you never planned to be king. I do hope one day you come around to the idea. I'd love to see you clad in the finest clothes and a glittering crown," I wink at him.

"The day you see that is the day I would want you to put me out of my misery," he laughs. "Come on, let's get going. I want to spend the day walking around town and hope someone comes up to us with more information. If not, we leave first thing tomorrow."

"Sounds like a plan! After you, Your Highness," I tease. While Duncan thinks I am just teasing him, as evident by his smile, I am hoping if he hears it enough, he will start to see it *is* the title he carries now, whether he likes it or not.

"Oh, and Liliana," he says. "Don't ever make those sounds in front of another male again. I've done horrible things for Enzo to protect Aliyah. Imagine what I'll do to protect someone *I* care about."

On our way out of the tavern, a male and female stop us in the street. They are both dressed in fine weapons and wear leather, almost armor-like, clothing.

"Good morning, how can I help you?" Duncan says.

"We hear there is a war coming and we are prepared to fight," the female says. She has short, light brown curly hair pulled up into leather band and light blue eyes. The male next to her has shaggy blonde hair and hazel eyes.

"It has been some time since we fought, and I think it is time to dust off those skills again. It would be an honor to fight for this realm," the male smiles.

"Do you have names or are you willing to die as anonymous helpers?" I ask.

"Ah yes, apologies. My name is Eilith and this is my husband, Davion. We have been fighters all our lives. We fought in The Great War and were lucky enough to come out alive together. We are happy to fight for this realm once again."

"Eilith, Davion, thank you for your service in the past and in the coming battle. If you head to Citrine City, General Enzo is gathering troops. He will direct you in ways you can assist. Tell him Duncan sent you." They shake hands and with a short head nod, the couple heads off.

"Well, that's at least two! We have fought with worse odds," I smile.

"Yes, and look what happened. We need to be ready this time. Come on, let's get going to see if we can gather some more fighters."

Chapter 8
SARAPHENA

We have spoken to the elders of the villages and they have no information on the heir. They have so many questions for Duncan and we have so few answers. Duncan has been helping rebuild homes and care for the sick along our journey. He would make such a good king. I just wish he could see that. It's kind of hard not to fall in love with him with each passing day. I miss you so much and I hope you are having better luck than we are. We learned the star was fastened into a ring and is black as night, with flecks of silver like the stars. Love and miss you. ~Liliana

Recruiting is going slowly. Very few want to come and fight. They don't believe the Banished King has the forces to take over Krystal. They don't even believe Twilight has been desolated. Our kingdoms have been separated for too long. We need rulers who will help bring them back together. We need hope again. Enzo gets more agitated by the day. His continued inability to bring Aliyah back is starting to take a toll on him. Please find the star soon and come home. We need you back. We need her back. ~Jade

I stand on the shore and let the sand squish between my toes as a wave comes up and washes it away. We have yet to find any fragments of the star. Liliana's description of the star will be helpful so at least we aren't just wandering around looking for any kind of rock. This at least narrows it down.

This is our third and final island to visit. It has been almost a month since we've been gone. I know we won't be here long enough to get comfortable, but the view is too good to pass up. Each day we go out to a part of the island, talk to the villagers, scour the caves and rivers, and come back home empty handed.

We have failed at our task and I can only imagine the anger Enzo is going to unleash upon us when we return.

I stare out into the endless ocean and instinctively reach down and touch my left arm. My sun scar disappeared the moment she mated to Enzo. When I saw it vanish on the battlefield, I was so happy.

But now— Now I wish I could hear her voice in my head one last time. I miss her. I miss her laugh and the way she made me smile. I miss my best friend— my sister. A tear slips down my cheek and washes away with the tide below.

I sit down in the sand and let the waves crash up around me. I wish the ocean could wash up and pull my sadness away into the endless abyss of the sea.

"Things are good here, Aliyah. I saw a pod of dolphins yesterday. You would have loved it. There was this one who kept bumping into another and it reminded me so much of you and I back in Mareen. No personal space," I laugh.

"Duncan and Liliana are doing well. We just got a letter from them this morning, but they have found no one who knew the whereabouts of the star, but they did learn it was fashioned into a ring. Jade wrote too, but things aren't as good with Enzo. He misses you so much. Everyone misses you. Enzo and Jade are training recruits for the military. Let's hope they are ready to fight whenever the Banished King decides to strike. This time we will be ready and you'll be standing by my side. I know it. Well, that's all I have to report today. I'll see you again tomorrow."

"Saraphena," Gunnar calls. "The food is ready."

I look up to the sky and repeat what I always do each morning, hoping wherever Aliyah is, she hears me. "I'm still there with you wherever you are Aliyah. 'Til the end."

As I make my way back up the beach, I see Gunnar waiting for me outside. The islanders have proven to be far kinder than we anticipated. Accepting travelers from the mainland seems like the most exciting thing to happen to them in a millennia.

On each of the islands we have visited someone has offered to house us. I won't deny, it has been nice having others around most of the time. The home we are staying in now, however, was left to us by an elderly couple while they visit their family in

SunSpark. They were ecstatic to offer their home to the prince from their home kingdom. Gunnar has set the table and cooked up some meat and a side of fruit from the island.

"How is she today?" Gunnar asks.

"I think she is doing well. I know she got a kick out of my dolphin story," I smile. I'm thankful Gunnar doesn't judge me for how I am processing losing Aliyah. When she first passed, Gunnar wanted us to take some time away so I could come to grips with everything that happened, but I knew I couldn't leave the others. We needed each other too much.

I can't deny living right on the beach is pretty amazing and I am somewhat thankful for the time apart. The fresh air is good for me, I think. Each morning I go out and give Aliyah a report on all the things I would have told her if we were together. I hope wherever she is, she can hear me.

"Oh, I bet!" Gunnar replies. We eat in silence the rest of the meal and look out over the ocean. I know Enzo is struggling. Jade's report proved he is still dead set on bringing her back. At what point does hope transform into something toxic and become an all-consuming focus?

Duncan and Liliana will have one of the hardest tasks in Twilight. Their king and queen are dead and the successor to the throne was a traitor. All that's left now is Duncan and he wants nothing to do with the throne. At this rate SunSpark will be ruling every kingdom, if only to help hold them all together.

The villagers look to their kings and queens for guidance and protection. These people have no one now.

I look at Gunnar who has a carefree look on his face as he eats. Gunnar is processing in his own way, but I think he is being strong for me. He doesn't know, but sometimes at night I hear him crying in the kitchen. I think he doesn't want me to be sad or see him crumble, because if we both fall apart, who will pick up the pieces?

Chapter 9

ENZO

The last month has been excruciating. Aliyah's ghost continues to plague my dreams, begging me to come and save her. If only I could. There are days when her soft voice filters into my mind, filling my heart with love and joy, only to be followed with silence and the agony that comes with the feeling of losing her all over again.

I am not sure how much more my heart can take. It's as if I am constantly on that battlefield. My heart bursts with affection only to be snapped in pieces, repeating like clockwork.

My attention snaps back to the training circle with just over fifty recruits as Jade explains the rules of living here in Citrine. There are less than I thought there would be.

Many responded to our call saying the Banished King would not dare to cross into these lands again, but little do they know the treachery he may be planning.

The others are right, though. We need to be ready. As I look at each of the faces in front of me, they all seem too young. Most of the recruits who stand before me look to be no more than children. The elders have already fought their war. It is time for a new generation of soldiers to rise up and fight for their home.

Eilith and Davion arrived from Twilight and have been helping to train our new recruits. I had a chance to spar with them both a few times in the previous days, and they are skilled fighters. Neither of them have powers, but their experience in combat is far beyond mine.

They had been fighting in The Great War for some time before my class was sent away to fight. We would have never been placed in the same squad during the battle, so their faces are new to me, but their fighting technique is much the same as what I was taught. They will have valuable skills to pass onto our new recruits.

Jade finishes explaining how their time here will be spent and now I take the reins.

"Recruits! Welcome to your new home. Citrine City will be where you eat, sleep, and breathe. I suggest you take some time to get to know the other recruits as your time spent here will be one filled with grueling tasks. The first is to restore Citrine to it's former glory. You will be cleaning, rebuilding anything broken, and securing the palace. If you cannot protect and restore your own home, how will you protect and restore the lands?"

"Sir, yes sir!" Their response echos in unison. A smile creeps up my face at the memory of being just like them. I was so young back then. I hope some of them find their families much like I found mine in my days of training.

"How many of you have powers?" I ask.

About twenty of the recruits raise their hands. Less than I would have liked, but some are better than none.

"Wonderful. Those of you with powers, you will train with me. You will learn to harness your power, use your power in battle, and learn how to fight without your abilities. Those of you without powers will train with your leader, Lieutenant Jade. You will address me as General or General Enzo. You will address her as Lieutenant or Lieutenant Jade. Is that clear?"

"Yes, General!"

"Let's get started. Those of you who have powers, come with me. The rest of you, follow Lieutenant Jade. She will provide you with further instruction. Eilith and Davion will be supervising you. You will treat them with the respect they deserve and listen to their counsel for they have fought in The Great War. Let's go!"

The twenty-two recruits with powers follow me to the right side of the training field. They line up in poor formation and await my instructions with smiles on their faces. Oh to have the spirit of youth once more!

The memory of Aliyah experiencing Olyrium for the first time shines brightly in my mind and I absentmindedly palm the small ax hanging around my neck.

"Listen up! Each of you will provide your name, your ability, and a short demonstration. After, I will pair you off with a sparing partner to practice while the others demonstrate their ability. I may not be watching you directly, but I will know if you are slacking off. First up," I motion my hand to the first male in line.

"Barley, General."

"Barley?"

"Yes, General. My parents were not very creative I'm afraid."

I smile at his boldness. Barley has short black hair, dark red eyes, and dark bronzed skin. He is lean for his age, but not weak. He is quite tall. He will fill out in no time with the proper training. "Ability?"

"Dominion of crystal formations, General. I can pick them up, pull them from the earth, things of that nature."

"Do you see the large crystal boulder across the field? Demolish it."

The young male closes his eyes and lifts his hands. Stepping forward with one foot and pulling his hand towards his body, the crystal shatters into pieces.

"Impressive, Barley. Step to the side please. Next!" A young female with long brown hair, pale skin and cyan eyes walks up. "Name?"

"Gwynavere, General."

"Ability?"

"Dominion of water, General."

"Demonstration."

Gwynavere steps forward and points towards a dried up fountain in the courtyard of the palace. She shifts her hands like the flow of water and a strong stream bursts out of the fountain, shattering it upon impact.

"Sorry, General! I'm still working on it. I will fix the fountain."

"We are all here to learn, Gwynavere. No harm done. Go with Barley to practice sparring until further notice." The two walk off together and I hear the grunts of their sparring. "Next!"

A female with long blonde hair and cobalt eyes pushes through the crowd.

"Aliyah?" Hope flares in my chest as I see her features clear as day.

"No General. Felicia is my name."

I blink and in front of me stands a girl who looks nothing like Aliyah save for her blonde hair and blue eyes.

Felicia is significantly shorter, she has golden skin, and the shape of her nose is slightly crooked. She wears thick, black leather gloves on her hands.

"Ability?" I say clearing my throat.

"Pain, General. I can inflict pain on anyone with just a single touch, hence the gloves," she says with shame in her voice.

"Do not be ashamed of your ability, Felicia. It is all about how we use the gifts we have. I will not ask you to demonstrate. Step aside, please. Next!"

"Rory, General."

Rory is a young male with fire red hair and green eyes. His skin is pale, with a dusting of brown freckles across his face. I am surprised Rory has not been swept off with the wind. His body is thin and if he turned to the side, I swear he would disappear completely. Every part of his body lacks muscle and he is rather short for his age.

"Ability?" I ask hesitantly.

"Necromancy, General. I can speak to the dead."

"What? Anyone who is dead?"

"Not just anyone. Only those who wish to communicate back."

"Demonstrate. Reach out to a girl named Aliyah. Tell her it's Enzo." I can get a message to her! I can finally tell her I am going to bring her back and apologize for everything I have done. Rory might just be the hero I need.

He closes his eyes and a soft glow illuminates around his body before flickering out.

"I'm sorry, General. There is nothing on the other end. She must not want to be spoken with."

I grit my teeth. Of course she doesn't wish to speak to me. She is angry and upset I failed her. I let her die.

"Go with Felicia, Rory. Spar with the others."

"I'm sorry I failed you, General."

"You have not failed me, Rory. It is I who have failed. Now go. That's an order." Rory stalks away with Felicia. "Next!"

After hours of viewing the recruits abilities and watching them spar, I have a far better idea of where they are in their training.

It'll be a miracle if we win this war based on what I saw. They haven't seen combat and they sure as hell have not trained a day in their life. As I send them off to the barracks where they will be staying, Rory stops me.

"General, who is Aliyah?" he asks.

"Aliyah is—was— my mate. The most beautiful woman in all the realms."

"What happened to her?"

"Aliyah died in battle because I could not save her. But I am going to bring her back."

"I have not heard of anyone being able to bring someone back from the dead."

"Well we are going to be the first then. Rory, do me a favor. Keep reaching out to Aliyah. If she ever responds, tell her Enzo is coming for her. That I'm going to bring her back."

"Yes, General. I hope you do."

"I will. I promised her."

Rory runs ahead to catch up with Felicia, Barley, and Gwynavere. They are all laughing and talking as they make their way into their new home.

Something pulls at my heart as I think about Gunnar, Jade and I as children meeting at this very spot. The bonds you form here are for life, as long as that may be.

"Hey!" Jade says coming over to me. "How did it go today?"

"They show promise, but they need a lot of work. You?"

"Similar. They have no abilities, so they can't even rely on magic to protect them. It is going to be a lot of work, but hopefully we can get them trained up in time for the coming battle."

"Let's hope so. Otherwise, I fear we will lose more than we did in the first war. We were ready then. This time, we are doomed for extinction. The Kalari will wipe us out before we even have a chance to defend ourselves."

"Hopefully the others are having better luck finding the star. At this point, it may be our only hope since we are no closer to finding the heir either."

"Let's not bet on the heir. The missives you put out over a month ago with our village soldiers have not yielded any results. This is starting to turn into a ridiculous ghost hunt. What is the latest update on finding the fallen star?"

"Saraphena wrote just this morning. No luck yet, but I am confident they will find something soon. Any small piece is a step in the right direction. Liliana wrote as well. They spoke to an elder in one of the villages who said he was summoned by the king to forge the star into a ring. It doesn't help much seeming as there are dozens of rings in Twilight alone, but it narrows it down. Whether Saraphena finds a piece of the fallen star, or we find the ring itself, we will bring her back. Just give it time."

"Time is the one thing we never seem to have enough of."

Searing agony rips through my chest. My heart is breaking all over again at the thought of having made no progress in bringing Aliyah back. It is killing me knowing she is having to wait so long for me to find a way. I just have to keep reminding myself that she is in the above, safe and secure, waiting for me to bring her into my arms once again.

Chapter 10
SARAPHENA

"Good morning, Aliyah." I sit down in the sand and start my daily ritual. I listen to the waves crash around me and imagine all my worries being swept away in the sea. "I can't believe it's been over a month since you died. I think I've come a long way in dealing with your death. I wish I could say I had good news about Enzo, but he is really hurting. I wanted to show you my new tattoo. Gunnar took me to get it last night in honor of you. I know we don't have the Soul Bond anymore, but I think having the sun marked on my skin forever will always remind me of what we had. I smile every time I look at it. I think you would have loved it.

"The longer Gunnar and I are away from Krystal and the other kingdoms, the more we joke about staying away forever. I'm starting to think he might not be joking anymore. We have built a mini- life here on this island. We even know some of the other villagers. It's strange to live in a place with nice neighbors and no one hurting another for a scrap of food. This is the last island we have left to visit and we have no more answers than when we first set out on this journey. Anyways, I hope you're doing well. I still miss you more than my heart can bear, but I know wherever you are, you're happy. I love you, Aliyah. I'll talk to you again tomorrow. 'Til the end."

Walking back up the beach, I spot the local letter carrier heading away from the house. Gunnar comes walking out the back door towards me.

"Did you tell Aliyah I said hello today?" he asks.

"You ask me every day and every day it's the same answer," I smile at him.

"You didn't tell her did you?" he laughs.

"Gunnar if you want to say hello you can go out there and talk to her! I'm sure she would love to hear from you." I know Gunnar won't do it.

"I think I just might one of these days," he smiles.

"What did the letter carrier drop off?"

"Nothing. He just stopped by to say hello."

"That's odd. He's never done that before?"

"I mean there is a first time for everything! What would you like to do today?" Gunnar asks, changing the subject.

"I'd like to visit the cave system we saw on the way to the river yesterday. That villager said he heard a rumor that a piece of the star was hidden in one of the tunnels for safe keeping. It's a stretch, but it might be our only lead at this point. It's been over a month since Aliyah's passing and Jade's letters only depict Enzo as getting worse. We need to find something to help him.

I'm afraid if we can't find the star, there will not be much to go back to. Liliana and Duncan are at their last village before they head back to the palace in Twilight to look for the ring. No one has any information on the heir. I'm starting to think it might be a lost cause."

"I think you might be right. We have visited every island and are left with nothing but rumors. It is like the star just vanished. Short of going to the bottom of the ocean to retrieve it, we don't have many other leads."

"Jade says the recruits are doing well, but Enzo is growing impatient. What if we don't find anything? How are we going to tell Enzo we failed him? He trusted us to find a way to bring her back."

"Let's worry about that another day. Pack your bag for a day trip and we will head to the cave system. I don't think it is far from here."

"Fingers crossed we find *something*."

"Do you think it is strange we have had no reports on The Kalari trying to cross into Olyrium?" I ask.

"Strange? No. Concerning? Yes. It gives us zero knowledge on what they are planning. SunSpark isn't exactly being forthcoming with information either. All we can do right now is focus on our own tasks." Gunnar's voice echos off the walls of the cave.

"This is useless. We have been wandering around here for hours and have found nothing. I don't think it is here. It doesn't help that the only information we have to go off of is that it is black with silver- like specks that resemble stars. This whole freaking cave is black!"

"Agreed. Let's head out and get back to the house. We can regroup and talk to some more locals."

"Okay. What a colossal waste of—" My sentence is cut off by a growl rippling through the cave system. "Gunnar," I whisper. "What was that?"

"I'm not sure. Keep your voice down and move slowly. If you see anything coming towards you, vanish." He douses the light from his palm and grabs my hand. My eyes strain to adjust to the darkness of the cave, but nothing becomes clear the farther we walk. The growl sounds again, closer this time. Low clicking sounds reverberate off the walls.

"Crap," Gunnar says under his breath. "It's a quayler. They use echolocation to find their prey and trust me, you do not want to get caught by one. They are huge hairy beasts with thousands of legs and bodies long enough to wrap around an entire palace. They also have fangs dripping with poisonous saliva. I've only come across one in my lifetime and they are impossible to kill. Their hair is sharp like needles and their skin is hard as armor. There is no fighting one, all you can do is run."

Chills run down my spine at the image Gunnar paints in my mind. I hold my breath to not make a sound as we make our way through the caves. We can see the light of the moon glowing just around the corner. Thank the Maker we are almost in the clear. As we round the corner, my foot catches on a rock and sends it bouncing off the cave walls. Gunnar freezes before quickly pushing us against the wet stones. I cringe at my actions and pray I haven't just screwed us.

The sound of a thousand legs comes barreling towards us.

"Run!" Gunnar yells. We take off in a dead sprint towards the entrance. Just as we make it to the opening, I look back to see the quayler behind us. It's sharp fangs snap in our direction and a pool of saliva follows in it's wake. Gunnar wasn't wrong, the beast is huge and gaining on us quickly. It releases a wail right as we shoot out of the mouth of the cave. I think we are in the clear, but the qualyer keeps on us.

"What are the odds we run into this thing lurking about the caves?" I yell, panting.

"You crossed your fingers!" Gunnar yells back.

"What?" I snap my head to look at him and will my legs to move faster.

"You freaking crossed your fingers praying we would find something in the cave. Well, here is your *something!*"

"I didn't mean this! I meant about the star! Are you seriously making jokes as we run for our lives right now?!"

"Just trying to lighten the mood before we die!"

My legs burn as we race across the terrain. We sprint toward the village hoping to hide. We are too exposed out here making it easier to track us, but if we can make it into the village, the echo will bounce off too many objects. As we near the village, I see a man standing at the edge waving at us. We fly past him and hear the sounds of an ear piercing screech.

I turn to see the quayler burst into a thousand pieces. Blood sprays across every building in sight and legs fly through the air, landing in piles across the ground. I catch my breath as the male turns to us.

"Having a little fun in the caves, are we?" he says.

"Oh my gosh! That was crazy! Thank you! How did you do that?" I ask.

"Hemokinesis. I control blood," he shrugs. The male has white hair and frosty blue eyes. His skin is dark and his muscles have muscles.

"Well, thank you, again. What's your name?" Gunnar asks.

"Nyckolas, but you can call me Nyck." Bright white teeth shine with his smile.

"I'm Saraphena, and this is Gunnar." I stand straight, finally catching my breath. "It's nice to meet you."

"And you. You two are the one's looking for the fallen star, yeah?"

"Yes. Do you know anything about it?"

"Unfortunately, no. My family has been here for generations and we have heard nothing of the star here. I'm sorry you traveled all this way for nothing," Nyck says.

"If your family has been here for generations, maybe they know something about the heir of Krystal Kingdom?" Gunnar asks.

"Hmm. I'm not sure. My great grandfather lives near by. We can stop and ask him if he knows anything. Why do you seek the heir of Krystal?"

"It's a long story," I laugh.

"I'd love to hear it sometime. I have never left this island, so I am always seeking a good story from the lands beyond these," he says.

"For another time," Gunnar smiles, clapping him on the back.

"I would love to host you for dinner. Please, you must let me give you something to remember the island by, and I'll say, our food is the best!"

"I thought you said you've never left the island?" I ask.

"Exactly," he says winking at me. "It's the best I've ever had!"

We make our way through the village and stop in front of a run down home with no windows and a caved in roof. Nyck doesn't bother knocking on the door and walks into the home.

"Grand Papi! I have guests!" he calls.

Shuffling comes from the back of the home before a short, hunched over man, comes out. He has bright white hair like

Nyck and the same dark skin, but with significantly more wrinkles. His eyes are frosted over like a window on a cool night.

"Grand Papi, these two want to know about the heir to Krystal. Do you know anything about an heir?"

"Oh yes, yes. I know lots about the heir to Krystal Kingdom. Please sit down. Sit, sit. I insist," he says. The man stumbles into several objects as he finds his way to the chair. I move to help him, but Nyck shakes his head at me.

"What do you know about the heir?" I ask.

"She was beautiful young girl. She was the best of the rulers to come through Krystal and quite the powerful enchantress. Oh the stories I heard of her still get my heart racing. She had that mate of hers, the king. A good strong male he was. They were so happy together."

"Sir, I think you are mistaken. You speak of Queen Dione. We are asking if she had a child," I correct.

"Ahh yes, the queen's heir! I remember rumors being passed around about a child. The future of this realm some said. The child would have been the first ruler after the war. It's a shame their rule never came to pass. Queen Dione held many secrets about her life and her abilities, but when you drain your entire power— a shame it was to lose her. There is no coming back from that sort of sacrifice. It is likely for the best though. Now she can be with her mate forever in complete paradise."

"Grand Papi, the child. You were saying something about the child?"

"A child?" The old man quirks his eyebrow and rubs his chin as if he has forgotten our conversation from just moments ago.

"Yes, Queen Dione's child," Nyck continues.

"A beautiful baby girl she was said to be, but lost after the war, never to be seen again." A tear slips down the man's eye.

"You're certain of this? A baby girl?"

"As certain as an old man can be! The mind...the mind you know can be a fickle thing. It can twist and turn over time," he laughs. "But I think I would remember an heir. I heard the rumor from an old love of mine. Mari— Tari— Cari— something was her name."

"Marigold?" I ask. Hope flares in my chest that maybe Marigold knew more than she let on.

"Yes! Marigold. That was her name, from SunSpark Kingdom. She was the one who got away," he smiles. "I wonder what ever became of my sweet Marigold. The last I had heard from her, she was traveling the kingdoms in search of adventure."

I don't have the heart to tell him she died helping Aliyah. I used to think Olyrium was vast and wide, but maybe it is smaller than I think.

"Thank you, sir. I appreciate your time," Gunnar says standing.

"Come back any time, young man. Any chance I get to hear the voice of such a beautiful lady, I will take."

I smile at him and place a small kiss to his cheek. "Thank you for your time, sir."

As we exit his home, I can't help but feel a little hope in getting our first semi-real answer.

"Sorry he couldn't be much help. Seems you keep hitting dead ends at every turn," Nyck says with a frown. "Please, join my wife and I for dinner. We would love to have guests."

"He was more help than you could even know," I smile.

Gunnar takes my hand and we follow Nyck to his home. He opens his front door and two small children crash into his legs, hugging them tight.

One has white hair and green eyes and the other has short curly brown hair with deep purple eyes. Their skin is lighter than their father's, but still a beautiful shade of golden brown as if kissed by a sun that doesn't even exist in this place. The boy peaks around his father's leg and flashes a smile at me before darting back into the house. The little girl comes up to me and tips her head.

"Can I touch your hair?" she asks.

"Nadya, do not ask such things," Nyck scolds.

"It's alright. Of course you can," I say. I squat down so I am eye level with the girl. She reaches out and strokes her hand gently down my hair from root to tip.

"Beautiful," she whispers. "One day, I want to have hair like yours." She turns and runs back in the direction of her brother.

"Saraphena, Gunnar, meet my wife, Jennipher."

"Welcome to our home!" she says. Jennipher's creamy white skin is a stark contrast to her shoulder length dark brown hair in tight curls, just like Nadya's hair. Her turmeric colored eyes are warm and inviting. We sit down at the table filled with different meats, cheeses, and vegetables. Our conversation is light while we eat and a sense of normalcy washes over me.

Nadya and Nolynn, whom we learned are twins, clammer on about their adventures in the village today and all the cool rocks they found along the way. I glance at Gunnar and his smile brightens as he shows off his fire powers to Nolynn who "oo's" and "ahh's" at each new trick.

"Do you have powers too?" Nadya asks me.

"I do! Would you like to see?"

"Very much so, miss." She bounces up and down in her seat waiting to see what I can do. When I vanish, her eyes go wide and she claps her little hands in excitement. She looks under the table as if to see if I simply went under there and then reaches her hand out in my direction. Her small palm rests on my leg and she jolts back when I reappear.

"Wow! That was amazing! So much cooler than Gunnar's power!" Nolynn says.

I smile at Gunnar who crosses his arms in denial that I am apparently cooler than he is to the children.

"Father says we are not to use our abilities. That without proper training we could hurt someone," Nolynn scowls.

"He is likely right. While all abilities are beautiful gifts from the Maker, some powers untrained can unintentionally harm someone. Maybe when you're older you can come to Citrine and I will personally train you myself." Gunnar ruffles the hair on Nolynn's head.

"Can I dad? Can I go to Citrine one day and train with Gunnar? Then I can fight in a real battle instead of just having to pretend battle with Nadya." He rolls his eyes.

"Maybe when you're older," Nyck smiles. We finish up dinner with some light conversation and excuse ourselves to head home.

"Gunnar, hold up!" Nyck calls. "If what you say is true, and there is a war coming to Olyrium, send for me. It would be an honor to fight by your side. I know there are others in the village who would follow. If the time comes, we will stand with you."

"I'm going to hold you to that," Gunnar says with a smile, shaking Nyck's hand. Nadya and Nolynn wave from the doorway as we make our way out of the village. Our walk back is silent as we ponder the events of the day.

"Gunnar," I start. "Is it bad having dinner with them felt...normal? Maybe even *nice* for once not to be thinking about bringing Aliyah back or dealing with Enzo's pending rage? Like The Kalari didn't even exist?"

"I don't think it is bad at all. It was a nice change of pace compared to our normal," he laughs.

"Can I admit something to you?"

"Of course."

"I kind of don't want to go back. We have almost no leads on the heir front, beside the fact it *might* be a girl, and no leads on the star front. What if it is just a dead end? What if we can't bring Aliyah back? This was the last island we had to visit and I'm not sure I can deal with Enzo and the wrath he is going to inflict on the realm."

"I wish we could stay away forever, but this war is coming whether we like it or not. We can't leave our loved ones alone to fight. Aliyah would have wanted us to save as many as we could."

"I know. It was a nice thought though," I smile. "A brief moment of peace was nice, but I know you're right. Enzo needs us now more than ever, especially when we break the news we haven't found the fallen star."

Chapter 11

GUNNAR

"It feels a little strange to be doing this." I sit in the sand outside our small temporary home and let the waves come up and crash around me just like Saraphena does every morning.

"Saraphena is at the market this afternoon getting supplies for our trip home, so I figured I would take my opportunity to be alone while I could. I miss you, Aliyah. Saraphena misses you so much. We all do really. No one has been the same without you, not even Jade. Maker, this feels so weird to be talking to the sky, but Saraphena is convinced you are out there listening. I hope she's right. Even if you aren't there, she finds you in the beauty around us. I'm a little nervous to go home if I'm being honest. She is in such a good place right now and I'm afraid going back will just make her sad again. If you are really out there, keep an eye on her for me alright? Don't stop listening. If you can help bring some peace to Enzo, please do. He is so lost without you. Enzo is to me what you are to Saraphena. I need my brother back."

I take a deep breath knowing what I need to do next.

"I know you once thought of Saraphena as family. I know she still thinks of you as a sister. She's lost everyone now. Her parents and you. Both times she didn't get to say goodbye. I want to bring her happiness forever. After everything happened..."

Tears brim in my eyes, catching me off guard.

"Gosh, I didn't expect this to be so hard." I clear my throat. "I know you are Saraphena's family, and I'd like to be that for her now. I know of all the people she cares about most, you are at the top of the list. So, if you're up there listening, I'd like your blessing to marry her. I know she will be crushed you can't be here for her, but if you give your blessing, I know you will be the first one she tells. Thank you Aliyah for bringing her back to me. I'd like to keep her forever now, if that's okay with you?"

In the distance, I look out and see a dolphin jump into the air before diving back under. I think back to the story Saraphena told me about the dolphins she saw, reminding her of Aliyah. I take this as my sign.

"Thank you, Aliyah. I promise I'll take good care of her for you."

Chapter 12

SARAPHENA

Gunnar and I finish packing our things. This mission started out as a journey of hope to bring Aliyah back, but now we are going home with so few answers. I look down at the sun tattoo on my arm and smile. Hopefully when we return I can see the places Aliyah once stood as a happy memory instead of a sad one.

"I think that's the last of it," Gunnar says. Walking over to the window, I look out across the vast ocean.

"I'll just be another minute," I say. Walking out of the cottage, I make my way down the beach to my usual spot. I don't sit today, because I know Gunnar is waiting for me.

"I guess this is our last talk here on the beach. It's going to feel so strange not coming out here every morning. I'm sure Gunnar will miss the peace and quiet. It's time to get back to reality though. I'm not going to stand here and say I'm not scared, but I know you'll be with me every step of the way. Enzo needs us now more than ever. Jade's last letter proved to me it is time to go back. I hope he can find the same peace I have. I love you, Ali. We'll talk soon."

Turning, I find Gunnar kneeling. "Saraphena, from the moment I met you, I knew you had ruined all other women for me. When you left, I never thought we would get another chance. I know you miss Aliyah, and I know she was your family. But if you'd give me the chance, I'd like to be your family now."

"Oh, Gunnar. You were always part my family. Married or not," I laugh. "But the answer is yes. Always and forever, yes."

He jumps up and throws his arms around me swinging me around in the sand. For the first time in what feels like forever, the tears I cry are ones of joy. As Gunnar sets me down, he pulls a small box from his pocket.

"When did you get that?" I ask.

"Remember the day the mail carrier stopped by to say hello?" Gunnar laughs.

"I knew it! He never just stops to say hello," I laugh. "You're always full of surprises."

I look at the ring he holds. It is a dark purple triangle cut stone in the center with three small diamonds on each side of the band. It's absolutely breath taking. As he slips it on my finger, my eyes meet his. Something deep pulls in my heart and for the first time, it doesn't feel like I'm sad anymore.

A burst of bright light flashes between us showering us in golden rays. I feel that invisible tether snap in place between us. As the light fades, there in front of me stands Gunnar. *My mate.*

"I knew it! Yes! I knew it all along! I mean don't get me wrong, mate or not, you were mine for life, but this just seals the deal!" Gunnar yells.

I laugh as he wraps his arm around me. When I look over his shoulder, I see her. Aliyah stands in the distance, smiling at me. I blink, and the vision of her is gone. Pulling back from Gunnar's grasp, tears fill my eyes.

"Saraphena, did you not want to be my mate?"

"No, no, it's nothing like that. I promise. It's just— Now that you and I are mates, it means my connection with Aliyah is for sure broken. I knew it was that day on the battlefield when she mated with Enzo, but part of me hoped— Being her Soul Guardian meant I couldn't be mated until our bond was gone. It just makes it feel more real. I assumed it hadn't snapped into place before I left for Luar because we both know how unpredictable it can be, and then when I was Soul Bonded I accepted that I would never find my mate. This is one of the first moments I have truly felt happy since Aliyah died. I think my heart was just waiting until I was ready."

"Aliyah will always be a part of you. Mates or not, you will always have a connection to her."

"I love you, Gunnar."

"I love you, Saraphena."

"Let's go home. Our real home."

PART II: ANGER

Jane Rose Publishing, LLC

Chapter 13

JADE

*B*lood *drips onto the dirt beneath me as I clutch my stomach when the boy lands another kick to my ribs.*

"Is that the best you've got?" My voice doesn't come out as strong as I wished it had.

"How does it feel to be a poor little orphan? Your parents deserved what they got and you should have died right along with them." Spit hits my face as the boy finishes spewing venom into my soul. I knew what my parents were, but I am not them.

The boy lifts me by the collar of my shirt and my little legs kick off the ground, scrambling for purchase. I grip his wrists trying to pry his fingers off my clothing, but his hands won't budge.

"Looks like the Maker decided to let me punish you instead." The wicked grin on his face widens as he brings his fist back, ready to connect it with my face. I close my eyes waiting for the blow to land.

"You have your entire life to be an idiot Leyon, why not take the day off? Put her down." My eyes crack open at the sound of another

boy's voice. Two boys come up behind the group of bullies, challenge gleaming in their eyes.

"What are you gonna do about it? You're smaller than she is!" Leyon snorts.

"Size isn't everything, douche wad. A sentiment you'll be hearing the rest of your life from every female in the realm, if you're so lucky to even make it to third base." Another boy steps up behind Leyon and pins him with a stare. I crumble to the ground with a groan on my lips as Leyon releases my tunic.

"This isn't over, Enzo. Don't think because your father is on the Queen's Council you are untouchable." Leyon and his goons back away slowly, never breaking eye contact with the newcomers. I don't dare get up for fear of what these new boys might want with me. I've been a punching bag for every jerk who thinks they crap out gold bricks. One day I'll be stronger than them all.

The boy with short brown hair and chocolate eyes reaches his hand down, waiting for me to take it. I smack it away and hold my side as I roll to stand on my own.

"I don't need your help. If you're here to get your licks in too, at least have the decency to not pretend to care. If you're going to beat me, you'll beat me standing up." I glare at the pair before me who simply smile at each other before breaking out into a fit of laughter.

"She's got more fire in her than you do, Gunnar." Enzo's smile brightens as he sticks his hand out in greeting. I stare at it cautiously before reaching my own hand out and take it. "The *name's Enzo, and this here is Gunnar." Gunnar's short blonde hair glistens in the sunlight as he steps forward to greet me.*

"I think she is going to do just fine here. Stick with us and we'll keep you safe." Gunnar nods his head at me.

"For the record, I never thought you needed saving. I just like giving Leyon a reminder he isn't all that." Enzo's eyes shine as he looks at me. I think this is the first time anyone has actually looked at me here. Since day one no one has spoken to me, let alone intervened when getting my butt handed to me.

"I'm not going to thank you if that's what you're waiting for. I didn't need your help." Another drop of blood runs down my nose and over my lips. I lick it away quickly not wanting any more evidence of my pain.

"As I said before, I never thought you needed saving. However, there are strength in numbers around here. Maybe together we can keep each other safe? We could use someone with your tenacity by our side," Enzo smiles.

"You don't want to hang around me. No one does."

"How come? Because you're a girl? We don't care about that!" Gunnar's laugh.

"My parents were—" I hesitate with my words, afraid my potential new friends will desert me just like all the others. "My parents were traitors in SunSpark. I was sent here after their death."

"Trust me, there are parents out there who have done worse. The only difference is they do it amongst the shadows and under the

guise of their own sick desires. You are not your parents." Enzo reaches out and places a hand on my shoulder. The warmth of his palm melts the icy exterior I have built in the attempt to survive in this place. Maybe I am better off with them. Enzo may be little, but at least he wasn't going to back down from a fight.

"So," Enzo starts. "You got a name?"

"Jade. My name is Jade."

"Welcome to the family, Jade. I think we are going to have a bright future together." Enzo holds out his arm for me to take. I hesitate for a moment, hoping this isn't some trick. Against my better judgement, I loop my arm through his as Gunnar extends his next. The three of us walk back into Citrine City and for the first time, I think I might have found exactly where I'm meant to be.

I stare at Enzo sitting across from me at the dining table. The purple crescents under his eyes have grown darker, and I can tell his body is starting to give up on him. I haven't seen him like this since his father was alive. He's endured so much, but losing Aliyah broke whatever shred of good was left over from what his father broke.

My once brave hero now broken in pieces over a girl who promised she wouldn't break his heart. An uncomfortable feeling seeps into my heart as I wrestle with trying not to be angry at Aliyah for breaking her promise. The logical part of me knows she never meant to hurt him, yet my heart is furious at what her death has caused.

I watch Enzo mindlessly place food on his tongue and chew it as if he has to force it down his throat. A large bottle of amber sits before him, not a cup in sight. He picks up the bottle and takes three large gulps before setting it back down. This is his third bottle today. I shake my head and look down at the food being pushed around my plate, my appetite lost.

Enzo saved me that day in Citrine from a lifetime of torture from my so- called peers. It is a debt I thought I was never going to be able to repay, but looking at him now, I know this is my chance to save *him* from a lifetime of torture. Enzo needs me more than ever. I'll do whatever it takes to make him whole again. Enzo pulled me out of a dark place once, and now it is my time to return the favor.

I can be the reason he has a future again. I will be the light at the end of his dark tunnel. Enzo has been and always will be my future. I thought I lost my chance at happiness with him when Aliyah came along. I won't make the mistake again of pushing my feelings aside after the debacle with Enzo's father. He may not have forgiven me fully for what I did, but we have spent hundreds of years together. If we can survive all of that, I know we can find a future together. I just need to find a way to heal his heart first.

Chapter 14

LILIANA

Sweat coats my brow as I work to hammer nails in the wall for the new paintings I picked out. Duncan smiles down at me from atop the ladder as he fixes the chandelier in the entry way. I'm happy Duncan asked me to come with him to Twilight to rebuild his home. He could have easily sent me back to SunSpark, but I am not ready to face my family yet. I think in his own way Kaleron is grieving Aliyah too. I don't think any of us were ready to see her die.

Almost two months ago we started on a journey to find the fallen star from Twilight. Each of us have failed. Duncan and I work to rebuild the palace during the day and rip apart each and every room at night looking for the ring. Jade's letters are getting darker and darker as more time passes. Saraphena has written they are coming home, and I won't deny, I am excited to see her.

It has been far too long since we have all been together. Enzo needs all of us now. With Twilight almost being fully rebuilt, we can focus on getting him better. I've tried to listen to Duncan these last few weeks about not siphoning off his emotions. I suppose I need to start accepting maybe the best thing to do is feel whatever it is he needs to feel. We have been in this bubble now for far too long, however. When Saraphena and Gunnar get back I am afraid of what Enzo is going to do when reality crashes in that we can't bring Aliyah back.

"Slacking off down there, Lil?" Duncan teases. I hadn't realized I stopped hammering, getting lost in my own thoughts.

"Only a little," I smile up at him. I focus back on my work and think about everything we have been through in the last few months.

When things get too overwhelming I walk out to the spot on the battlefield where Aliyah died and scream into the darkness. I let every emotion pour out of me and into the air. My ability to siphon off other's emotions is like powering up a magical reactor to full strength, but never setting it off. All that pent up emotion has to go somewhere. Screaming at the stars is my reactor exploding into the night until I have nothing left.

I knew Aliyah the shortest amount of time, but seeing the impact she had on this family— no one can ever replace that. Enzo will never recover from this, and I fear the realms will suffer for it.

Duncan steps down the ladder and makes his way over to me.

"What are you thinking about?" His eyes sparkle in the starlight glimmering in from the open windows. Twilight looks good on him.

"Aliyah." A solemn smile crosses my lips before Duncan places a soft kiss on them. "What was that for?" I laugh.

"I don't like to see you upset. There are enough frowns to go around, so if I can help it, you will never frown in my presence," he smirks at me.

"That seems like a bold challenge." I loop my arms around his waist and place my chin on his chest, looking up at him. "Do you miss her?"

"Everyday. I think in a different way than everyone else though. Aliyah and Enzo didn't have enough time. Much like Zorellya and myself. Finding your mate is the most special thing to happen in one's life, but to lose them before you have even had time to experience what it is like to be with them is another form of tragedy few will ever understand."

"I didn't know she was your mate. Will you tell me about her?"

He huffs out a sigh and lays his chin on top of my head, wrapping his arms tighter around my body. I feel love pouring off him in waves as he thinks about his first love...his mate. It's hard not to be jealous because I will never have with him what he had with Zorellya. It makes me wonder what I would do if I found my mate. Would I leave Duncan for him? Would I deny my mate to stay with Duncan?

"Zorellya was a free spirit. Far more than I ever would be. I guess that's why I fell in love with her so quickly. To see someone so passionate about life and who gave everything she had to everyone else, it was truly magnificent. Our love was fast, and reckless. From the moment I laid eyes on her I was consumed by her presence. We spent every waking moment with each other. She took me to places in Twilight I hadn't known existed and showed me what it would be like to live a care free life. With Aramot in line for the throne, I thought I could ignore my responsibilities, so I did. Zorellya was not High Fae, but I didn't care. I loved her more than I ever thought was possible.

"When the mate bond snapped in place, I thought we would have eternity to spend together. I finally mustered up the courage to bring her home to my father and introduce her as not only my mate, but my fiancé. I thought he would be overjoyed. I thought having the mate bond sealed our fate from harm. How wrong I had been. I was foolish to think my father would ever see a lowborne fae as something other than scum on the bottom of his boot," he sighs.

I tighten my arms around him and our eyes meet before he continues.

"I cost Zorellya her life that day. My mother tried to intervene, but my father's word was law. He ordered me to kill Zorellya so a more *well suited* female could be my wife. When I refused, he locked her in the dungeons with a special spell to prevent my magic from working there. I had no way of freeing her. Every day he would bring me down to the dungeon and command me to kill her. Every day I refused. She was so strong. She took every ounce of torture my father threw at her, but everyone has a weakness. Zorellya had a younger brother who was everything to her. When my father brought him in, the choice was made clear; kill Zorellya or he would kill her brother. She begged me to kill her. It broke me. I can still hear the sound of her neck breaking in the silent moments of the night."

"Duncan, I am *so* sorry." Tears drip down my face at everything Duncan has had to endure. It was not just his father killing his mate, but forcing Duncan to do the job for him. No wonder dread hovers over him like a dark storm cloud everywhere he goes. My poor King of Shadows.

"It was a long time ago. After that I left for Citrine to join the military. There I met Gunnar, Enzo, and Jade. They became my family. Part of my heart will always belong to Zorellya, but maybe...maybe there is someone out there worth sharing it for again." Duncan's eyes are lined with tears I have never seen before.

I reach out and wipe a fallen drop away with my thumb.

"If you gave me your heart, I would keep it safe until the end of my days. My heart is yours Duncan, and I would be honored to hold a piece of yours."

"Who said anything about you?" he teases.

I lift onto my tiptoes and place a kiss to his lips. Passion flows through his emotions like a tidal wave, drowning me in all that is him. I scrunch my fingers through his long black tresses and a groan slips from his throat. His hands trail down my spine and leave shivers in their wake. He walks us towards the wall until my back hits hard stone. He steps back from me, the heat in his eyes palpable. He grips the back of his collar and pulls his tunic over his head. Panes of muscle and ink tense before me in restraint.

I unlace the top of my tunic so the soft curve of my cleavage shows just slightly. When I look back up, my eyes snag on his as I pull my bottom lip into my mouth. Duncan's demeanor changes from my sweet shadow to something primal, as if I am to be his prey. He steps into my body, leaving no space for air between us.

I grip his arm muscles as they flex under my touch. I work my way down his jaw line with soft kisses and light nips of his flesh. My lips cascade over the multitude of tattoos that cover his body. The wings on his throat, the tribal lines on his chest, down the swirls of ink over his heart. I let my hands explore his body as his chest rises and falls.

His fingers stroke my hair and my breath catches in my throat at his touch. Suddenly he disappears before me and I gasp, turning to find where he has gone. Down the hall, a throat clears and I whip my head in the direction of the sound. There, standing in the middle of the hallway, is Duncan, a cocky grin on his face.

"Hey! Not fair!" I march my way down the hall towards him, but right as I reach him, he disappears again. Frustration boils in my veins and I start to lose my patience.

"Lil." His voice sounds again, echoing off the walls around me, but he is no where in sight.

"Alright that's it! Two can play at this game! But just know, you started it!" I push my power out in every direction, searching for him.

"*Pst.*" His voice comes from behind me right next to my ear. I whip around and connect my fist with his jaw. My power slams into him and anger ripples off me like a boulder dropped into a still lake.

Duncan doubles over in hysterical laugher inflicted by my power. I don't stop there though. Fat, wet tears drip off his chin as grief consumes him. A second later, agony shreds through his demeanor. He staggers back as the tears dry on his face and he grips his chest in anguish. I don't let up. I cross my arms over my chest and tap my foot on the ground.

Happiness overwhelms his senses causing a smile to crack his face in two.

"Lil, stop! I yield! Ouch! My cheeks hurt from smiling this much! I don't use these muscles often enough to warrant this kind of abuse!" He laughs, pushing his hands down his face to try and force the muscles to relax.

"Are you done with the disappearing act?" I quirk an eyebrow and push my hip out to the side.

"I'm done! I'm done! I swear!"

"Good." I harness my power and stand there while he massages his jaw.

"Gosh, remind me not to make you upset any time soon," he smiles.

"Emotions are a weapon only the finest warriors can wield. Don't push me, or I will push back...*hard.*"

"Noted." He walks up to me and wraps his arms around my waist, but I make no move to drop my crossed arms and irritated facial expression. "Liliana, please forgive me."

"What are you willing to do to gain my forgiveness?" I tease, picking at my nails as if uninterested in his words.

He withdraws his arms and I stare at him as he lowers himself to the floor. I send out my power to sense his emotions and while nervousness slips down the line, love overpowers the feeling. He kneels before me and places his hands on the back of my thighs before looking up at me.

"Liliana, Princess of SunSpark, wielder of emotions, and keeper of my heart. I am yours. I give you my heart. Every broken, jagged, rigid piece, I give to you. All I ask in return is for your word you will keep it forever."

I kneel on the floor in front of him and place his hands in mine. He leans forward so that our foreheads are touching. I close my eyes and smile.

"Duncan, King of Shadows, master of all things dark and mysterious, I am yours. My heart is yours from now until my dying breath. All I ask in return is no matter what happens, you will allow me to remain by your side."

"Forever my sunshine."

"Forever my shadow."

His lips meet mine and he pushes on my chest as I lay back on the cold floor.

"Don't disappear on me this time, shadow."

"I'll never leave your side again."

His kiss is deep and consuming. My heart feels like it is going to burst out of my chest. We may not be mates, but Duncan is my forever. Even if I were to find my mate in the future, Duncan is the one I would choose. No more doubts.

"Oh my Maker! Gah! Get a room you two! Geez we leave for a few short months and suddenly making out on the floor in a public hallway is acceptable?!" Gunnar's voice floats through the air and happiness pours from my eyes.

"Saraphena!" I fly up and race down the hall, throwing my arms around her neck as Duncan comes up behind me and claps Gunnar on the back in welcome.

"How are you, Lil?" Saraphena asks.

"I'm good! I have missed you so much! Welcome home!" I say. She pulls from my embrace and I look to Gunnar who puts his hands up in surrender before slowly backing away. "Gunnar, now where do you think you are going?"

I run towards him and throw my arms around him in an air stealing hug. He wraps his arms around me and laughs.

"Nice to see you too, sis! I'd like to breathe again now, if that's okay?"

"It's nice to see you both again. Sorry to hear you couldn't find the star, but good work on figuring out that the heir might be a girl. That absolutely narrows it down," Duncan says sarcastically.

"Hey! That's more than you got! You found out the star was made into a ring! Only like a hundred thousand of those in the entire realm," Gunnar teases.

"Oh screw off Gunnar. So we all failed! There is only one small problem with that." Duncan looks around the group and pulls his lips back into a firm line. "Now we have to tell Enzo we have no way of bringing Aliyah back."

"Do you think he'll be mad?" I ask.

"No. I think he will be happy we tried our best and thankful for all our efforts," Gunnar replies.

"Are you serious?" Saraphena quirks an eyebrow at his response.

"No. I think he is going to be royally pissed. I just hope we aren't in the blast radius."

Chapter 15

ENZO

"Again!" I yell at the recruits. Eilith and Davion are over working with Jade and the other recruits who do not possess abilities.

We are almost at the point where they can practice fighting side-by-side and have an even match in skill level. With Jade, Eilith and Davion all training them, the recruits have come a long way.

Gwynevere and Barley spar in the circle before me. Barley has grown into his abilities well with his training and can now pull giant crystals from deep in the ground before hurling them through the air. Gwynevere can not only wield water, but she uses it now to demolish the crystals being thrown at her.

"Good! Good! Keep up the good work you two!" The pair smile at each other before continuing their wielding practice. I walk over to where Felicia and Rory are seated, eyes closed and legs criss-crossed in front of them. "What do we have happening here?" I ask.

"Meditation, General. Rory is trying to contact more than one spirit at a time and I am working on not touching anything by accident," Felicia smiles.

"Rory, any luck with your personal assignment?" He has been attempting to contact Aliyah with no luck.

"No sir. I apologize sir. I promise I will keep trying."

"Try harder, recruit!" Anger snaps in my tone before I can stop it. I pull out my flask and take a large swig of amber, praying its effects take quickly to numb this feeling.

Tears well up in Rory's eyes as he looks at the ground. A few fallen tears slip into the dirt beneath him. "I'm sorry, General. I will try harder."

I huff out a breath trying to regain my composure. It isn't the child's fault he cannot reach her. It is my fault she does not wish to be spoken to. The anger she must feel towards me.

"See to it that you do. Wipe your tears, boy, there is no room for tears in battle."

As I stalk away to check on the other recruits, I see Felicia leaning over towards Rory and place her arm around him, but she does not touch his skin. I hear her whispering everything will be okay and I didn't mean what I said.

I wish I could say it is true, but I do need Rory to keep trying. If fear of failure is what pushes him to keep going, then so be it.

I look out across the training grounds and see four figures exiting the palace. Duncan, Liliana, Saraphena, and Gunnar come into view. Liliana waves and starts running towards me.

I put my hand up to halt her assault, but she leaps at the last second and flies into my arms, tackling me to the ground. She places kisses all around my face and I pretend to gag at the contact.

I push my power out and Liliana flies through the air, a scream combined with laughter tears from her throat before landing right in Duncan's arms as he materializes beneath her.

"Long time no see, grumpy pants! How have you been?" Liliana clears her throat as Duncan sets her safely on her feet.

"I was good until you got dirt down my pants. Thank you for that." I grumble while shaking the dirt from my pant legs.

"I figured you could use one of my famous hugs since you haven't had one in so long!"

"And still I could have gone longer." I give her a side smirk as she rolls her eyes. "Duncan, do try to keep your woman under control. I can't have these recruits thinking I can't stand on my own two feet against someone as...tiny...as her."

"If I had *any* control over this woman, don't you think I would have used it by now?" Duncan's smile is genuine when he speaks about Liliana. I see him looking at her and her at him.

Love, clear as day, beams from their eyes as they look at each other. Before we left on our missions, Duncan barely touched her. Now he can't seem to *not* touch her.

"And here I thought I could always count on you to brood with me. Don't tell me you've gone soft, brother. I need my most trusted exterminator to be sharp and cold, not turned to mush," I say glaring at him.

"Recruits!" Duncan calls. The younglings run over forming a circle around us to hear Duncan speak. "My name is Duncan. This here is Liliana, Saraphena, and Gunnar. We are *far* superior warriors compared to this old sap," he points a thumb to me.

Irritation boils under the surface at the shear fact he would so casually degrade me in front of the recruits.

"I don't know, Mister. General Enzo has been pretty scary in his time with us! I've seen him best every recruit here time and time again!" Rory pipes up from the crowd and smiles at me.

Pride flares in my chest. Even after my harsh comment towards him, he would still speak back to a commanding officer.

"Oh young one, you have been bested because you are no match for the *General.* But we are here now! We will show you what it means to be the best!" Duncan winks at me as he puts his arm around Liliana's shoulders, pulling her in close.

"I don't think you have it in you, sir! I put my money on the General," Barley teases. I flash him a look and he quickly adds, "respectfully, sir."

"What do you say, guys? Up for a little sparring?" I ask.

"I thought you'd never ask," Gunnar smirks.

The recruits sit down in a semi-circle around us and bounce in anticipation of the coming fight. Jade joins the group and sits down next to Saraphena and Liliana. I hear them exchange brief pleasantries and hugs.

Rory, Felicia, Barley, and Gwynevere sit right at the front of the circle. My star pupils. I give them a quick wink as the others take their stance.

"Don't embarrass yourself too much, General," Jade calls from the crowd. The younglings clap and cheer as we begin circling each other.

"Let's not have a repeat of the library, okay Enzo?" Gunnar teases.

With that, Duncan disappears and Gunnar throws a fireball in my direction. I throw out my power and pull his feet out from under him, smacking his head on the ground.

Duncan appears behind me and reaches for my neck, but not before I swerve and grab his arm, flipping him forwards over my shoulder. He lands with a thud on his back and looks up at me with a smile.

"So you're suddenly using your powers in training now, huh?"

"No sense in hiding them now," I smile. In a way, it feels good fighting with my brothers again. I'm actually having...*fun.*

My chest feels lighter and my head less clouded with dread. It's like we are back in the training academy ourselves. My mind wanders to simpler times.

"You guys! Wait up!" My short legs push harder off the ground as I run after Jade and Gunnar.

My cheeks hurt from being in the sun all day and I know I will be scolded later for not putting on my protective lotion. Jade and Gunnar dip behind crystal formations out of sight as I finally catch up to them.

"You're it, ZoZo! You'll never catch us now! You're too slow!" Jade teases.

I jump around each crystal formation looking for them. I hate that nickname. I know I'm smaller than they are, but teasing me about it is simply unnecessary.

"Gotcha!" I jump around another formation only to find it empty. "Ugh! You guys, come on! This isn't fair!"

I hear the shuffling of feet and giggles coming from behind a giant purple crystal. I tip toe around the crystal and jump behind it with my fingers spread out like talons.

"Rawwwwrrrr!" I leap forward and tackle Gunnar to the ground. "You're it, Gunnar!"

I jump up and run as fast as I can away from my friends, knowing I need the head start if I am going to remain 'not it.' I turn back to see Gunnar trying to catch up with Jade. She runs beside me and grabs my hand.

"Come on, ZoZo! Faster! He's gonna get us!" she squeals. A smile pulls at her cheeks and her hand pulls me along with her. I look at her face as we run and her eyes meet mine as a fit of laughter breaks out between us. Jade is my best friend.

Even though we are training for a war, she makes sure I have happy memories to look back on. She is always there to comfort me after my father makes me do horrible things. I hope we are best friends forever. I look back to see Gunnar gaining on us. I know I won't be able to out run him. If I can just make it back to the—

"Oof!" I fly backwards as my body connects with the legs of a stone wall. As I clear my head, I look up to see my father looming over me.

"Play time is over, son. Our next training assignment is ready for you. Do try to make this one quicker, I have a council meeting with the queen for dinner. I can't have you hesitating every time." He picks me up by the forearm and drags me away from my friends.

Tears pour from my eyes as I look back at them. I know they can't save me. No one can save me from what I'm about to do.

"General Enzo, watch out!" Rory's voice snaps me back to reality as a stream of fire comes flying in my direction. I duck at the last second and it hits Duncan in the chest behind me.

I glance at the kid and give him a wink as I throw out my power and knock both Duncan and Gunnar on their backs. I hold them on the ground with nothing but my ability and walk towards the recruits.

"You see, having the ability to fight with your fists is a skill every warrior needs to master in the event their powers fail them, but for demonstration purposes, I will continue to hold down my brothers until they yield. A lesson in not challenging their leader, again." I smirk back at my brothers on the ground and laugh when I see them struggling to get up. "Would anyone like to come and try to challenge my brothers in a spar?"

Three recruits raise their hand, including Rory. He is quickly becoming one of my favorites here. He isn't afraid to get his hands a little dirty to prove himself.

"It seems only fair we even out the odds of this fight! Jade, care to join?" Jade rises from the crowd and takes her stance in the ring.

"Alright, ZoZo," she teases. "Time to let the boys up now."

Releasing Gunnar and Duncan, the three recruits immediately pounce on Gunnar, holding him down with their body weight. The recruits laugh as Gunnar rolls in the dirt trying to push them off of him, but they hold firm.

All fifty recruits burst into action and race to pile on top of my friends. All of them are pinned to the ground with younglings crawling all over them. Laughter fills the air and turns what used to be a place of nightmares into something better— something far more magical.

My heart beats with joy and happiness floods my senses. I thought this place would only spark pain in my heart, but seeing these recruits laugh and play with my family has brought on immense joy. This one happy moment gives me hope in finding a way to bring Aliyah back once more.

Enzo, please. I'm alive. I need you! Please come to Luar!

I shake my head trying to force the sound of her voice out of my mind. I try to block out the sound of her as to not ruin this happy moment. I cannot have the reminder that she is no longer on the other end of that bond haunting me all hours of the day.

The tiny ax around my neck feels like an anvil chained to my person. I need it off. I can't take the weight. I grip the chain and pull it from my neck, shoving it into my pocket, the weight disappearing with it.

Go away! Enough of this torment! It isn't real. It isn't real. It isn't real.

I repeat this over and over to myself until the sound of her voice fades from my mind.

Chapter 16

JADE

Shivers run down my spine as the chill from the ground beneath me seeps into my bones. The sky is lit up with ribbons of green and blue as the moonlight bounces off the crystal mountains surrounding us. I look over and see a smile gracing Enzo's face as he looks up at the night sky. Colors dance off his features as his eyes find mine. His jaw has sharpened with age, his body now corded with muscle from years of training. With each passing year, my love for him grows.

"Do you regret it?" he asks.

"Regret what?"

"Being forced to come here?" Uncertainty laces his tone as he searches my eyes for an answer.

"No. What I have found here is far better than anything my parents could provide for me. Here I have a true family. I have...love." I reach out and grasp his hand in mine. He doesn't pull away from my touch and his smile grows brighter than any star above.

"Me too. I don't know what I'd do without you, Jade. My father...well, I don't know how I would survive him if I didn't know you'd be waiting for me on the other side. You're my best friend in all the realms. Don't tell Gunnar though, he might not take it well." A laugh passes between us before tension sits heavy in the air.

Our eyes lock for what feels to be eternity, both of us waiting to see what the other will do. We've come so far together since we were first children here. Enzo is stronger now, both physically and mentally, and I have learned to survive in a world without powers to defend me. I know we have a long and uncertain road ahead of us, but one thing I know for sure, is that no matter where that road leads, Enzo will be there to walk it with me.

Rumors have spread throughout the kingdoms of a threat looming, but war is not yet upon us. We have time. We are still but young adults in the eyes of mortals. Enzo and I will have hundreds of years left together before we are expected to fight in any war.

Enzo leans in and I let my eyes slip shut, stealing my breath waiting for his lips to meet mine. I feel his breath on my face and the rapid beat of my heart, dangerously close to bursting from my chest. His hand tightens around mine and my chest constricts with the feeling.

"SON! Enough of this nonsense!" Enzo is thrown back from me, slipping from my grasp as his father's booming voice shatters the peace surrounding us. I hear Enzo gasping for air as General Felix's power chokes him from afar.

"No! Please stop! Don't hurt him!" I yell.

"The only one who will hurt him is you! He has no time for this foolishness! You will only ever be a liability to him!" His father drags him away by his throat, still gasping for air as the tendrils of his father's power rob him of oxygen. I cry on my hands and knees watching my tears drip into the dirt as I watch my best friend be dragged away from me.

I know what his father will do to him. It's the same thing he has done to him over and over again since we were small. I slam my fist into the ground and plead to the Maker to protect Enzo from what is to come. The tears stop flowing, but the anger that sits heavy in my chest flows freely out of my pores.

Enough of this. Enzo has suffered for far too long. I am no longer that weak girl who couldn't protect him. Leyon may have been my bully, but Enzo's father is his. I know he will never stand up to him. This is what years of abuse does to the mind of someone innocent. It convinces them they are powerless, weak, and unworthy of love. Enzo may be strong, but around General Felix a switch flips and he is that scared little child again, and who could blame him? Parents are supposed to be the ones who teach us what it's like to be loved, yet here we both are, robbed of what unconditional love means.

I'm done sitting back and letting Enzo feel like no one is fighting for him. His abuse ends today, no matter the cost.

My knuckles crack as I continue my jabs on the straw mannequin before me. The rough burlap sack covering the body of my immobile opponent cuts into my fists as I think about that day with Enzo's father. *The day that changed everything.*

I feel the beads of sweat dripping down my back with my determined pursuit to get those images out of my mind. *Enzo's screams. Liquid crimson covering the floor like splashes of paint.* Every second of that encounter lives in my mind, digging its relentless claws into my present.

Enzo changed after that day, more so than he had in the previous months. His father had officially broken him into the pliable weapon he so desired. I thought I could save Enzo. Instead, I lost him in the only way that mattered. From that moment on, I was only his friend...*his strategist.* I was no longer the woman he might have loved. Part of me wishes I could take it all back, but the other part knows I did what I had to in order to set Enzo free.

Chapter 17

SARAPHENA

I look around the table and feel such joy at the first time we are all together again. Seeing everyone laughing earlier in the training ring was a much needed change of pace. I was expecting Enzo to get right down to business and bombard us with questions about our progress. The table is laid out with the finest meats and cheeses to grow on plants and the wine is from the special cellar in Citrine. Memories pull at my mind of Gunnar sneaking me down there the last time I visited him before he left for the war.

"So where are we with finding the ring?" Enzo asks taking a large gulp of amber from his glass.

Well there goes our good mood.

"Liliana and I have searched the entirety of Twilight's palace and have found no sign of any ring that can grant a wish," Duncan replies.

"How would you know if it was the right ring?" Gunnar mocks.

"We made a wish on each one! Obviously," Liliana smiles.

"What did you wish for that many times?" I ask.

"I wished for the sun to shine, just once in Twilight," Duncan says.

"I wished for some strawberry shortcake with the whipped frosting I love so much from a bakery back in SunSpark," Liliana laughs. "When we didn't see either of those things happen, we would toss the ring into a bin and move on to the next."

"Speaking of rings," Jade starts. "I see that Saraphena has added a new accessory to her wardrobe."

All eyes turn to me and Gunnar. My cheeks flush at the attention, but I can't help but smile when Gunnar grabs my hand. The purple stone glimmers in the candle light above us.

"What in all of Olyrium would possess you to want to spend the rest of your life with *Gunnar*?" Liliana teases.

"He isn't so bad," I say. Gunnar reaches over and places a kiss to my knuckles before turning to the one we feared most finding out.

"Enzo?" Gunnar asks. Enzo has his eyes closed and his knuckles turning ghost white as he grips the edge of the table. His rapid breathing comes in and out in short, forced heaves.

"Enzo," Jade starts. She gets up cautiously and makes her way over to his side. She rests her hand on his forearm and squats down beside him. "Breathe, Enzo. It's okay. You're safe."

I look around to the rest of the table and gauge their reactions. Worry pulls at everyone's faces and I see Liliana struggling the most. From her nose drips a steady stream of dark red blood. She clutches Duncan's hand under the table and I see him lean over and whisper something in her ear. I turn to Gunnar who is cautiously pushing his chair back from the table.

"Saraphena, we need to go now." He moves to grab my hand, but I pull my arm away.

"Enzo. Talk to us. Don't shut us out," I plead.

Enzo's grip tightens on the table, and a small chunk of wood breaks off in his hand. His eyes are still closed as he reaches up and grips his heart. Pain laces his face as he pulls away from Jade's grasp. I flick my eyes back to Liliana who keeps wiping her nose with her sleeve. The once white tunic is now a deep shade of red, a clear indicator of how much blood she is losing. Duncan is begging her to stop under his breath.

Tension laces the air around us and anger flares in my chest seeing Enzo putting us all in danger instead of talking to us. Liliana falls out of her chair and into Duncan's arms. He swears under his breath and teleports out of the room. With Liliana no longer holding off Enzo's emotions, the table in front of us explodes into a million shards.

Jade flies back from where she was kneeling next to Enzo. Gunnar and I shield our faces from the blast. Fire lights in Gunnar's palm prepared for a fight.

"Enzo, please. Just talk to us," I beg.

"Talk?! *Talk?!* What is there to talk about, Saraphena? Congratulations on your engagement!" Ridicule fills his tone as he wields malice like a weapon towards us. "It's so *wonderful* to hear while you were away you had such a *grand time!* While the rest of us were here suffering, agonizing, on how to bring back *your Soul Bonded,* you are just out there having the time of your life! How absolutely *wonderful* for you!" Sarcasm drips from Enzo's voice like the poisonous saliva dripped from the mouth of the quayler.

"Stop it! Don't you dare speak to her that way. You have no idea how she has been processing Aliyah's death. Maker forbid I try to give her an ounce of happiness!" Gunnar yells.

"That's just it, isn't it Gunnar! You both get to be happy while I what, sit here and suffer? Watching you galavant off with your new wife and give up on bringing Aliyah back? Why do you deserve happiness more than I do?!" Enzo screams. Glass from the chandelier above us shatters and rains down upon the broken shards of the table that litter the floor beneath us.

"Stop it, the both of you!" I whip my head back and forth between Gunnar and Enzo and place my hands between them. "It isn't about who deserves to be happy more than the other. We *never* meant to hurt you Enzo. Please know that we would never give up on trying to bring Aliyah back. You deserve to be happy, too. I wouldn't dream of getting married without Aliyah there, so we have to find a way to bring her back. I wouldn't have it any other way. So please, just please, calm down."

Enzo's breathing is erratic and shallow. He closes his eyes and shakes his head as if clearing some sort of fog from his brain. "Get out of my head! Get out! Get out! Get OUT!"

I duck at the last second and cover my ears as power bursts off Enzo's being and shatters whatever is left in the room. The three glass pillars holding up the ceiling come crashing down as paintings and decorations break into smithereens. Enzo's roar ripples throughout the space until Jade's voice drowns out the rest.

"Enzo, it's okay! It's me! I'm here! You're safe now!"

I look around as the dust settles and see the carnage that Enzo's power has caused. He kneels in the center of the room with every broken item surrounding him as if the room reflects everything that is broken inside him. I turn to Gunnar to make sure he is alright and I find him pushing off a piece of the ceiling from his leg. He brushes off his pants and makes his way over to where I stand.

Enzo has his head hung low as Jade kneels in front of him, cradling his head in her chest. Her arms are wrapped around him as she rubs his back in soothing circles. I take this moment to check Gunnar for any injuries, but he seems to be in one piece.

"I had no idea—" My sentence is cut off as I hear Jade's next words.

"It's okay, Enzo. I'm here. It's me...Aliyah. I've got you now. You're safe."

"Jade what the—" Gunnar is cut off when she flashes him a glare and shakes her head.

Well that's new. I reach down the bond to Gunnar as total astonishment crosses his face.

What in the hell has been going on since we left?

I have no clue, but we are going to have to discuss this with Jade. You heard her too, right? She called herself Aliyah.

I heard.

"Aliyah. You're safe. I'm so sorry, little dove. I'm so sorry." Enzo wraps his arms around Jade's body and holds her close. His heavy sobs fill the room as Duncan reappears beside me.

"What in the hell happened in here?" he asks.

"Enzo just lost it. But that isn't even the craziest part," I whisper. "I think he is hallucinating again. Jade called herself Aliyah and he latched onto her. Did you know about this?"

"Not a clue." Duncan's face is impassive as he looks between Jade and Enzo holding each other.

"How is Lil?" I ask.

"Fine. She just took on too much. She thought she could hold him off. She is resting now. I will check on her later."

"What are we going to do?" Gunnar asks.

"He can't go on like this. Someone is going to get hurt," I add.

"Right now, let's just get him to bed. We can figure out what to do after that. Gunnar, can you go and check on the recruits to make sure no one saw what happened here? Saraphena, you go with him and track down any kids who might be out of bed. I'll help Jade get him back to the bedroom," Duncan instructs.

"What do we do about the room?" I ask.

"We tell them we destroyed the room as a training exercise. We need to see how quickly they can fix up a completely destroyed room because part of serving in the army means helping rebuild homes after battles. Play it off. Do not let them know this was Enzo's doing."

With that, Gunnar takes off toward the exit and I follow in his footsteps, trying not to step on any broken glass. I slip off the ring on my finger and place it in my pocket. Looking back, I see Enzo fall limp in Jade's arms, completely passed out. Hopefully Enzo won't remember any of this in the morning.

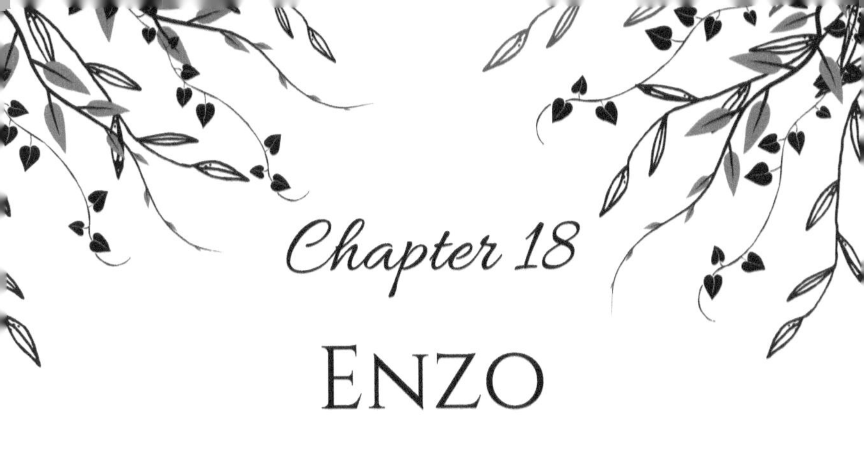

Chapter 18

ENZO

My feet pad barefoot across the cool marble floors. The empty halls match the void inside my heart that Aliyah once filled. As I walk into the kitchen, memories of that night with her flash through my mind. I cringe at the memory and take another swig of alcohol. It is the only thing that numbs the pain. As I sit down at the island, Aliyah's voice flashes through my mind.

Enzo, please. Please help me. I need you. I can hear her faintly like my memories are mocking my pain. I throw the bottle at the wall and it shatters into pieces.

"Get out of my head!" I scream. Her voice cripples me during the day and her soul tortures me at night in my dreams. I walk over to the shelf to get another bottle of amber, ignoring the glass on the ground cutting into my feet. I feel no pain now. Nothing can ever hurt as much as losing her that day. I hear footsteps behind me and I already know who it is without looking.

"Did you have another nightmare?" Jade's voice fills the space.

"I can't get her out of my head, Jade. I hear her even now pleading for me to help her. Begging me to save her. I failed her, Jade. She is dead because of me."

"It isn't real, Enzo. You know it isn't really her in your mind. You have to try and block it out. What can I do?"

"You can leave me be. Send everyone home Jade. There is nothing left for them here. I'm losing my mind, Jade. Pieces of my memory are blocked out. I don't even know how I got to bed tonight. The last thing I remember is eating dinner with everyone and the next thing I know I am waking up in bed."

"Sometimes when we grieve it can feel like we are just going through the motions. I am sure your brain is just trying to combat the pain you're feeling. I wouldn't worry too much over the lost memories, but I'm not going back to Korin, Enzo. Even if you don't talk to me, I will be here anyways. You shouldn't be alone."

"But I am alone!" I scream at her. My fists connect with the island I once laid Aliyah on top of and shatter it in two. "Without her— without her I will always be alone."

Jade comes up behind me and turns my chair to face her. She wraps her arms around me and my head falls onto her chest. Heavy sobs pour from my body as my arms wrap around her waist. I know I push her away, but I am thankful she stays, if only so I would not drive myself to madness without someone to pull me back into reality again.

"Why? Why did she have to leave me? Why couldn't I save her Jade?" I sob.

"You did everything you could Enzo. We all did everything we could. This isn't your fault."

"But it is. It is my fault. That mate bond awoke in her and she got distracted. If that had never happened— if I wasn't her mate, she would still be alive."

"You know that the bond snaps into place at any given time. There was no way to predict that." I know Jade is right. In my mind I know the mate bond works in its own way, but in my heart— in my heart I know it was my fault.

"What am I going to do without her?"

"The only thing you can do. Live. Move on like she wanted you to do. Enzo, she would want you to be happy. She would want you to live a happy life."

"How can I ever move on from her? She is my everything."

"You don't have to move on right now and no one can ever replace her. But in time your heart will heal. I promise." She stands to leave, but I grab her wrist before she makes it too far away from me.

"Jade—"

"Yes?"

"Nevermind." I release her wrist and put my head down in my hands. She leaves me in the kitchen to think through my actions.

I hear soft footsteps pad into the room before they abruptly stop.

"Oh my! I apologize General! I wasn't aware anyone else was awake! I was just getting a snack, but I'll leave you alone. Apologizes again!" Rory's small voice makes my heart break at how afraid of me he is.

"Come in Rory. Get what you came for." His little feet connect with the floor as he makes his way over to the shelves filled with snacks for the recruits. He pulls out a powdered doughnut and places it on a plate. As he makes his way around the kitchen, he makes no mention of the broken island. He sits down in a chair across from me and balances the plate on his legs, a huge smile pulling at his lips as he looks at the treat. His eyes snap up and catch on mine.

"Oh, um, would you like one?" His voice cracks at the end.

"No. Tell me about yourself Rory."

"There isn't much to know General Enzo. My parents are both High Fae. They used to work here in the palace when they were younger, but when they married, they found themselves a small cottage on the outskirts of Krystal. They own a small farm that helps feed some of the other villagers close by. That's where I was born."

"And they were fine with you leaving to come here?" I ask.

"Oh yes sir! I was so happy to see the letter arrive in our village square that you were seeking recruits! Boy, oh boy, was I excited! After a ton of begging and doing almost every chore imaginable, they told me I could come. To be trained under you is an honor, sir! I mean you are one of the *Queen's Guard!* I couldn't have asked for a better teacher!"

"I am not a good man Rory. I have pushed you in ways no recruit deserves to be pushed. You are doing your best, and I keep letting my grief cloud my mind. You don't deserve that." Tears well in my eyes at the thought of who I am becoming. *My father.*

"Oh, General Enzo, please don't cry." He gets up from the other side of the broken table and walks around to sit next to me. "I lost my nona a few years back. She was the nicest lady in all the realms. She taught me how to garden and take care of the animals. She even taught me how to ride my first alicanto! My nona was everything to me. When I lost her, well, I felt like I lost everything. Grief— grief makes you do funny things. I know you don't mean to be cruel. Sometimes, when bad things happen, our bodies just gotta protect themselves, you know? We form this outer layer to protect us from the world. We push people away, because it's easier to be alone than to open ourselves up to being hurt again. But you know what is worse that being hurt?"

"What?" I look him in his little emerald eyes, filled with so much love and emotion.

"Never loving at all. Love means giving a piece of yourself to someone else and hoping they keep it safe. The trouble is, the more pieces you give out, the more chances you have of getting hurt, so you gotta be careful who you give it to. That is what makes love special. You just gotta find the ones worth giving a piece to. Sure, it's a risk, but the reward is so much greater when they give you a piece of themselves back. When you give a piece, and they give a piece back, it's like you are whole once more. Did you give a piece of yourself away, General Enzo? Is that why you're so sad?"

"By the time I met her, I only had one piece left to give."

"It seems like a lot of people here love you, General Enzo. Maybe if they give you enough pieces of their hearts, they can make you whole again." Rory smiles up at me before collecting his plate and walking off towards the recruit's wing.

"Rory," I call. "How did you move on? From your nona's death I mean."

"I don't think we ever truly move on. I think we just grow until the grief doesn't take up so much space in our hearts anymore. I've spent all my life talking to people who have died, and you know what I've learned from them? Life is too short to hold onto anger. Sometimes, you just gotta let things go and accept what we can't change."

He leaves me alone in the kitchen to stare at a broken island that was wrecked by my anger. I wish I could move on, or grow out of this grief, but growing means letting Aliyah go. I'm not ready to do that. Deep anguish rips through my heart and I grip my chest at the feeling. I reach for the bottle of amber and chug down its contents— I need to feel nothing.

Chapter 19

GUNNAR

Dinner is painfully quiet as each of us sit in silence, not quite knowing what to talk about. Ever since Enzo's outburst, which he conveniently doesn't remember, everyone is too scared to say anything for fear of setting him off again. Saraphena hasn't worn her ring since, and while I don't blame her, it makes my stomach clench knowing I can't yell from the rooftops through all of Citrine that I am engaged to her.

The clinking of forks and knives is the only sound in the room and my ears ring with the lack of steady sound. "Okay, that's it. I can't stand this silence any longer!"

"Gunnar, are you okay?" Saraphena's hand reaches for mine, but hovers above before her gaze shifts to Enzo and back. Pulling her hand away from me, irritation settles heavy in my soul.

"No. I'm not okay. Frankly, none of us are okay. I miss the old us. The group who knew how to have fun! Dancing at Adryanna's, placing ridiculous bets on each other, and just being able to freaking *smile!* I want the old us back, even just for a night."

"I agree!" Liliana chimes in. I can always count on her to encourage having a good time.

"We need a night out!" I declare.

"A night out? No way. There is too much to do around here," Duncan adds.

"See! Even Duncan is back to his old self! Rejecting fun and only worrying about the boring stuff. Who's in?" I look around the table, praying they will agree.

"I'm in!" Liliana raises her hand. "And so is Duncan!"

"I am?" He looks at her with an *'are you kidding me'* look.

"It'll be fun. I promise!"

"It could be good for us to get out of this stuffy palace for the night," Jade adds.

"Yes! That's five!"

"Five?" Saraphena asks.

"Yes, five. You were an assumed yes."

"Oh am I now?" she laughs. "I guess I'm in then."

"Enzo?" I muster.

"You all go ahead. I think I'm going to turn in for the night." He pushes the food around on his plate, not taking any bites.

"Are you sure you don't want to come with us, Enzo? I promise it will be fun! I know this great little tavern not too far from here. Some of my friends back in SunSpark raved about it when they visited Citrine!" Liliana's voice perks up. "They have these amazing musicians there who can play any song you request and they said there is a small makeshift stage that people get up and sing on!"

"Thanks for the offer, Lil, but I think I am going to turn in for the night." Enzo stands and heads out of the dining room. When I'm sure he is out of earshot, I get my friends on board with my master plan.

"That simply won't stand," I say. "Enzo is coming out with us, whether he wants to or not. He *needs* a night out, and we need to show him that he can still have fun! So here's the plan..."

"Liliana I swear if you step on the back of my shoe one more time, I'm going to kill you." My voice is just above a whisper as my sister walks far to closely behind me.

"It was an accident, *Gunnar.* Don't get your panties in a wad."

"My panties are perfectly straight, thank you very much," I whisper- yell. "Don't screw this up, *Lili.* You have one job. Don't let him get mad."

"Don't let him get mad? Seriously? My only job here is not letting us get *killed!* I can handle him not getting mad just fine, but you know he isn't going to like this."

"I only need a few seconds for it to take effect."

"This is the stupidest idea you have ever had and you've had a lot of stupid ideas."

"Stupid, or genius? Only one way to find out!" I hold the rag in my hand and dump some of the clear liquid onto the cloth. *He's not gonna know what hit him.* I laugh an evil genius laugh to myself before I ease open Enzo's door. He is fast asleep on the bed, which makes this task slightly easier because I don't have to trick him into letting me get close to him. *You just need a few seconds.*

"Ready?" I ask.

"Ready."

You all set? I ask Saraphena down the bond.

All set. If you get yourself killed, just know...I told you so.

I shake my head. How can they not have faith in this plan? It's full proof!

I tiptoe over to the edge of Enzo's bed and lean over him like the sneaky thief in the night that I am. *I am stealth!* I reach my hand out to place the cloth over Enzo's nose and right as I cover it, Enzo's eyes shoot open in anger before seeming to settle. Once I am confident my plan has taken effect, I pull the cloth away and thrust my fist into the air.

"Hazah! I knew it would work! You doubters! I am a genius!"

Saraphena materializes before me after Duncan teleported her in here previously to make sure Enzo was in here. When she had given me the all clear, Liliana and I put our plan into motion. Duncan pops into the room a moment later with Jade by his side.

"So he's out cold?" Jade asks.

"Colder than the frostiness of Duncan's heart!" I quip.

"Very funny, Gunnar. Let's just get him out of here before that stuff wears off. I'll meet you all at the tavern." Duncan moves to scoop Enzo's large frame off the bed and throws him over his shoulder, just like Enzo did to Aliyah that first day. *Oh how the tables have turned, my old friend.*

"Meet you at the tavern! Enzo is in for the night of his life!" I rub my hands together like the evil genius that I am.

Duncan disappears into thin air and the rest of us make our way to the door.

"You do realize this is kidnapping, right?" Liliana asks.

"It's kind of a staple in this group. I mean who hasn't kidnapped someone at least once, am I right?" I smile.

"You better hope Enzo feels the same way when he wakes up," Saraphena laughs.

By the time the night is over, Enzo will remember what it is like to have fun, again.

Chapter 20

ENZO

My vision swims as light streams through my cracked eyelids.

"Where the hell am I?" My tongue is heavy in my mouth as I try to speak. Music fills my ears and the room comes into focus. I'm no longer in my bed at Citrine City, but in some seedy tavern instead.

I glance around the table, my mind still muddled from Gunnar's attempted kidnapping. Though now I see it wasn't an attempt at all, but highly successful. Fae of all sorts dance around the tavern, and there are singers on a makeshift stage that sound completely out of tune. Liliana, Jade, Duncan, Saraphena, and Gunnar all sit at the table with a drink in their hand.

"Oh good you're awake!" Gunnar claps me on the shoulder.

"Gunnar. What in the hell did you use on me?"

"Chlorofae! I figured that would be the fastest way to get you to comply!"

"CHLOROFAE! You used *CHLOROFAE* on me?!" I throw out my power, splitting his chair right down the middle causing him to crash to the floor. All he can do is muster up a laugh.

"There's the old Enzo! Here, have a drink." Gunnar passes me a cup full of mead and I scowl at him.

"How do I know you didn't spike my drink too?"

Gunnar simply smiles at me before lifting the mug to his mouth and taking three large gulps.

"Ahhhhhh. Delicious! Next round is on me!" Gunnar stands and makes his way over to the crowded bar, pushing through several other groups of fae to get to the front. My senses have fully come back, along with my full potential for rage.

"Did you all know about this?" I ask, glaring at my so-called friends.

Liliana's cheeks blanch and Duncan simply shrugs. Saraphena claps a hand over her mouth before turning away, clearly stifling a laugh. Jade is the only one brave enough to admit her role.

"Sorry, Enzo. We really thought you could use the night out, though. I promise it'll be fun." Jade gives me a reassuring smile.

"I highly doubt that. Where even are we right now?" I don't recognize the tavern, though it is giving me the same welcoming feel that Adryanna's Tavern did back in Korin.

"A tavern just a few towns over from Citrine. We debated going back to Korin, but it was difficult carrying you the whole way here, let alone on a half-day journey. Gunnar would have had to use more chlorofae and frankly we didn't want to risk it a second time," Jade says.

"Betrayal. All of you. So much for being my most trusted friends. No...my most trusted *family*. You are all dead to me now." I cross my arms over my chest, resigning myself to a night of misery.

"Man that barkeep took forever!" Gunnar drops twelve glasses of amber on the table in small glasses. "Two for each of us! I find a little liquid courage goes a long way during times like this."

"Times like what?" I question.

"You didn't tell him?" Gunnar smiles.

"Tell me what?" My teeth grind together waiting for the answer.

"Um...our song is up next," Saraphena mutters.

"Maker," I say under my breath. "I'm going to need a lot more than twelve of these."

"Well actually those were supposed to be for—" Liliana pipes down as her eyes snag on mine.

My glare bores into her soul as I down each and every last one of the shots before me, the burn barely registering in my throat.

A small man walks out onto the stage as the group finishes their song. His voice barely reaches over the crowd as he announces that our group is next.

Liliana grabs Jade's hand, who in turn grabs Saraphena's. To my surprise, Duncan's has a face-splitting smile across it as he claps Gunnar on the back, making his way to the stage. My whole family is alight with joy, waiting for me to join them on stage.

I shake my head and make no moves to get up. The band begins their song and the crowd cheers, recognizing the classic tune. Gunnar and Duncan stomp their feet and slap their hands across their knee in time with the music, while the girls spin and clap center stage. As much as it pains me, my foot begins tapping to the beat of the song. It used to be one of my favorites. The upbeat tempo of the tune has the entire tavern clapping along as Gunnar starts the song.

"From shore to shore, we fight once more!"

"But I'll come home with tales of Joan!" Duncan bellows.

Liliana slaps him on the arm before picking up the lyrics. "I'll spend time more away at war, but my love is with myyyyy doveeeee!"

"Hey, ho, soldier! Hear my call! My love for you, it will not stall! And while you're gone, I'll wait for you, my darling soldier boy!" Saraphena yells at the top of her lungs.

Together they sing, arms wrapped around each other. "From shore to shore, we fight once more! But I'll come home with tales of Joan! I'll spend time more away at war, but my love is with myyyyy dovvvveeee!"

Jade picks up the song next. "Hey, ho, soldier! Hear my call! I'll be your love forever more, and while you're gone, I'll pray for you, my darling soldier boy!"

I stand and push my way through the crowd as the musical interlude takes over. The five idiots on the stage sway with the music before spotting me walking towards them. The stage creeks under my footsteps. Standing before my friends, their smiles seem to be contagious— either that or the alcohol is finally hitting— because when I look at their faces, I can't help but smile too. Before I can stop it, the lyrics come blasting through my lips with the crescendo of the song.

"From shore to shore, we fight once more! But I'll come home with tales of Joan! I'll spend time more away at war, but my love is with myyyyy dovvvveeee!"

Arms wrap around me as we finish out the song together, swaying in time with the music, belting the lyrics at the top of our lungs. My mind flashes back to my small home as a child. My mother's hand in mine, and my father's in the other, spinning around our living room, singing this song together. My smile today is as genuine as it was back then.

I'll never tell Gunnar this, but maybe getting chlorofaed was exactly what I needed.

Chapter 21

LILIANA

The sun beats down on my back as I stand behind Enzo who commands the recruits before him.

"No one should have to be awake this early," I whisper to Duncan who stands beside me.

"Enzo believes in breaking the recruits. This is how we were trained. Early to rise, late to bed. It breaks them mentally. War doesn't allow for much time to sleep and they need to be able to practice at peak performance under distress," he replies.

"But then why do *we* have to be awake this early?" I smile.

"I promise you the best nap you have ever had later. Especially after last night. Don't think I missed the spot of crimson on your shirt, Liliana. I thought about yelling at you for taking on another's emotions *yet again*, but I can't deny that it was nice to see the old Enzo back. Even if it was just for a night." He takes my hand in his as we listen to Enzo spew instructions for the day.

"Today you are going to pair off again into those with abilities and those without. Jade will be taking those of you without abilities and working on predicting the next move of your opponent. It happens to be her speciality. The rest of you will come with us and work on using your ability on a larger scale. Some of you need some more work in that department. Gwynevere, if you destroy one more fountain, all of Citrine will be without water."

Gwynevere's cheeks flush at the mention of her third destroyed structure. Barley gives her a pat on the leg and bumps her with his shoulder. I reach out with my ability and feel the affection the boy has for Gwynevere and it makes me smile.

The group breaks off in two and we follow Enzo to our half of the training field. Rory runs up next to Enzo and beams up at him. He clearly looks up to him based on the pride radiating off his little body as he speaks with his General.

"Can I practice with you today, General Enzo? I would like to try and reach out to Aliyah again today if that is alright with you?" Rory questions.

"Any time you want to reach out to Aliyah you are free to do so, you do not need my permission. Please let me know if you make contact with her." Enzo looks down at the boy, no taller than his elbow. His innocence pulls at my heart as I watch the two of them speak about Aliyah.

"Will you sit with me when I try to reach out to her? I think knowing you are there pushes me harder so I don't fail you." Rory's smile could light up an entire kingdom.

"I will sit with you, but you will never fail me Rory. I know you are doing your best." Enzo ruffles the child's hair with his hand before putting an arm around him and walking off towards the outer ring, away from where recruits have started sparing with their powers.

"Do you two mind if I join you?" I ask.

"Not at all! That's okay, right, General Enzo?" Rory asks.

"Lil you are always welcome," Enzo replies.

As we walk over towards the training field, my eyes catch Saraphena's hand and notice she isn't wearing her ring. She looks at me before hiding her hand in her pocket.

"Why aren't you wearing it?" I ask.

"I don't want to upset Enzo. He has enough going on inside his head right now. I don't want to confuse him," she says. She looks down at her boots as they kick up dust with each footstep.

"Give it time. I'm sure he will come around to the idea. Once we get Aliyah back, I'm sure he will be alright." I try to give her a reassuring smile, but even I don't believe it.

"Lil, can I ask you something?" Saraphena's features morph into a conflicted state.

"Of course, what's up?"

"So, the other night, after you...left...dinner. Enzo kind of had a small, um, explosion."

"I wondered what happened to the dining room," I laugh.

"Well, afterwards, Jade was comforting him, but I don't think he knew it was Jade."

"What do you mean? Like he thought it was someone else?"

"He thought it was Aliyah."

"What? Why?"

"Because Jade said she was Aliyah," Saraphena whispers.

"Girl, shut up! No she did not!" I say slightly louder than I mean to.

"Shhhh! Keep your voice down. It seemed to calm him down, so I'm less concerned with her calling herself Aliyah. I mean, desperate times, you know? But I think Enzo might be hurting more than he is letting on. Do you think he is still having hallucinations? I mean think about when we got to Twilight. He thought he *saw* Aliyah in that field. What if it is getting worse?"

"I don't know what to tell you. I mean if Jade calling herself Aliyah in those moments brings him any semblance of peace, would it be worse to take that away from him? I mean who is it hurting if he thinks she is Aliyah in those moments of torment?"

"I guess. I just worry about how badly this is really affecting him. I don't want her to be gone either, but I'm really getting worried about how his grief is manifesting itself. I don't want anyone to get hurt."

"I think someone is already hurt. Enzo. He is going to process however he is going to process. All we can do is try to help him along the way. From trying to help bring her back from the grave, all the way through when it is time to let her go for good."

"You don't think we can bring her back?"

"I think it has never been done before in the history of all fae. Well at least I have never heard of it happening. But miracles happen every day. So, do I think we can bring her back? Honestly, no. But I've been wrong before," I smile.

"Just...keep an eye on him for me, okay? If his emotions ever feel like they are getting out of control again, don't try to stop him all by yourself. I know you think you can take it all on, but don't do that to Duncan. He has lost so much already. He needs you." Saraphena squeezes my hand before walking off with the other recruits.

Enzo, Rory, and I settle onto the ground and try to get comfortable. Rory closes his eyes and pinches his eyebrows in concentration. A soft glow forms around him as he throws his power out into the spirit world. It abruptly flickers out before he opens his eyes.

"I'm sorry General. I couldn't reach her. Let me try again." Rory's emotions are spilling off him in buckets. Disappointment. Frustration. Anger.

"It's okay, Rory. Don't burn yourself out." Enzo comforts the child by taking his hand and giving it a light squeeze. Rory smiles at the contact and closes his eyes again while the soft glow illuminates him once more.

I sense the hesitation in Enzo's demeanor. I try to siphon off some of the emotions, but a large boom sounds behind us. Rory's eyes snap open as we see Barley covering his eyes and apologizing to Saraphena for losing control of a flying crystal. Enzo tells Rory he will be right back and leaves to check on the situation.

"I can do it. I know I can do it," Rory whispers under his breath. My eyebrows pinch in at his continued determination to please Enzo.

"You heard what the General said, don't burn yourself out." I take Rory's hand as Enzo did and give him a soft smile.

"Thanks, lady. I know I can do it though. He needs to get her the message. I can get her that message." Rory closes his eyes again and the soft glow around him brightens to a white light extending further past his little body.

"I can do it. I can do it. I can—" Rory's breaths become more forced.

"Rory, stop. That's enough. You're going to hurt yourself." I try to shake his hand, but he pulls it away.

"No I can do it! I said I could do it! He needs me to do it!"

"Enzo!" I call to him and he races back over to where we are seated.

"Rory, enough! Let it go! It's okay! You are burning too much power!" Enzo shakes Rory's shoulders, but Rory doesn't give up.

"It's okay! I can keep going!" Rory grinds his teeth and the white light around him expands further, consuming Enzo and myself.

"RORY! Stop! Please stop!" Enzo is screaming now.

The other recruits have run over to where we are, but Saraphena, Jade, Gunnar, and Duncan are keeping them at a distance. Rory's tiny body is shaking now and he begins to lift off the ground away from us as the white light surrounding him starts to pulsate. It starts to sputter out before dimming completely. Rory falls to the ground in a pile of loose limbs. His skin has a grayish hue to it and his breaths are shallow.

Enzo races over to where he has fallen and scoops him up into his arms.

"Rory! Rory, wake up!" Enzo shakes the boy. I reach out my power and feel Rory's pain. I siphon it off as quickly as I can and his eyes open ever so slightly. I double over as I feel everything Rory feels. Blood drips into the dirt below as I clutch my stomach. Bile churns in my throat threatening to make an appearance.

"General...I....I did it...I got through to her. She's beautiful, sir. Just like you said." His smile is weak and his voice soft.

"Shhhh. It's okay Rory. You did good kid." Enzo looks to me. I shake my head as tears start to pour from my eyes. Enzo cradles the child to his body and begins rocking back and forth.

"She loves you a whole lot, sir. She— she said— she's waiting for you to—" Rory coughs and he grips Enzo's tunic to pull him closer. "She's waiting for you to go get her. She needs you."

"Rory we can talk about this later, okay. Just rest now. You did great, kid. I'm so proud of you." Enzo rests his forehead on Rory's before brushing back his fire- red hair. "You did great."

"Don't be sad, mister. I'm gonna be with my nona now. She's gonna watch over me. You're gotta go get Aliyah back now. Promise me you'll get her back, sir. She's worth that piece of your heart, I just know it. Thank you for letting me fight for you. Tell my momma I love her and my papa too—"

Rory's eyes close and his chest stops moving. Enzo places his body on the ground and slams his fists into the dirt.

"NOOOO!" Dirt explodes around him and crystal formations burst in every direction. Rory's limp body lies in front of Enzo as anguish rips through the air. I turn to see the recruits all in tears. His small group of friends hold each other tight and turn away from the scene. A young girl who wears black leather gloves over her hands walks over to Rory's body.

She kneels down in the dirt beside him and slips off her gloves, laying them nicely beside her. She reaches out and takes ahold of Rory's hand. She looks at him as a single tear falls from her eyes. The girl rises and walks back toward the palace without another word. The world falls silent around us as we process what just happened. Enzo picks up Rory's body, and just like with Aliyah, he begins to carry him home.

Rory's parents stand over his small iron coffin and carve their names along with a few runes to help his body pass into the next life.

His mother turns in preparation to address the crowd. Everyone from Rory's village has come to say goodbye to him for the last time. There isn't a soul here who didn't love this boy.

"Rory is— Rory *was* one of the sweetest boys. He was kind to everyone he met and always left a piece of himself with them. When Rory asked to join Citrine's army, I wondered how such a sweet innocent boy would want to fight anyone. When I asked him why he wanted to go, his answer was simple. He said, so many fought for him to grow up in a peaceful world, and now it was his turn to fight to keep that peace. My sweet, sweet boy—" The mother's words end in a choked sob. Rory's father wraps her in his arms and walks her back to their seats.

A moment of silence passes before Enzo rises and makes his way to the coffin. He lays his hand on the iron before carving a small heart onto the top. He turns to face the crowd with his head hung low. I reach out my power and pull some of the dread from his mind. He looks up and his eyes meet mine. His head dips in a short nod before beginning to speak.

"Thank you all for coming today. I only knew Rory for a short time, but the impact he had on me will last for a lifetime. One of my last conversations with Rory, he told me that life is too short to hold onto anger. I hope— I hope that in his death he can find it in his heart to forgive me. Rory was knowledgeable about things well beyond his years and his ability to love far surpassed many older fae that I know, myself included. Rory told me that in life, we find who is worth giving a piece of our heart to and pray they keep it safe. I know he will keep this piece of my heart I give him today safe for all eternity."

Enzo walks back to his seat and I take his hand in mine, resting my head on his shoulder.

"Thank you," he whispers. I see him pull a small chain from his pocket and wrap his hand around the small ax. With a deep sigh, he loops the chain over his head and closes his eyes as he tucks the pendant under his tunic.

"I don't know what you're talking about," I smile. His shoulders shake with a light laugh. As the funeral comes to a close, Rory's body is laid to rest to join his nona and our Maker in the afterlife. As I watch them fill in the hole with scoop after scoop of fresh dirt, I can't help but wonder how many more friends we are going to lose before this is all over.

Chapter 22

SARAPHENA

The fireplace roars in front of Gunnar and I as we flip through our books. I swear I have read this paragraph three times already and I still have no clue what it is about.

I look over to Gunnar to see him smiling at whatever he just read. Something pinches in my heart at how calm he can be after coming back from Rory's funeral.

What are you reading about? I ask through our bond.

The enemies are about to become lovers. Gunnar looks over and winks at me before closing his book and placing it on the table beside him.

"I couldn't help but notice you reading the same paragraph a few times over now. Something wrong?" Gunnar walks over to me and lifts me up before placing me back down on his lap as he settles into the wing back chair.

"How can you be so calm all the time?" I ask.

"What do you mean?"

"I mean, first we lost Aliyah, and you were fine. Then we didn't gain any leads while we were away on the island, and you were fine. Now we lost Rory and you're just...fine."

"Who said I was fine?"

Anger slithers across my skin as irritation engraves itself into my very bones.

"Because you act fine! The only time I have ever seen you break down is in the kitchen at night when you finally let yourself cry! Why don't you cry in front of me? Why don't you cry *with* me? Why don't you let me in?" I yell.

I fly off his lap and pace in front of the fireplace while I wait for his response. I know he is going to have some sort of snarky comment like he always does. That is Gunnar, never serious, always joking.

"You're right."

I stop pacing. I turn to look at him and he holds his head in his hands. When he looks up at me, tears brim in his eyes and his bottom lip quivers.

"What?" I walk over to him and kneel before him and clasp his hands in mine. "If you aren't alright, then why are you pretending you are?"

"Because I didn't lose her like you did. Saraphena, my love, you lost your best friend. You lost your *Soul Bonded*. You have lost far more than I can even comprehend. How can I be sad, when I know you are going through all that loss? Who will be strong for you if I break down too?"

Tears flow freely now from his eyes as he reaches out and cups my chin with his hand. I sit up on my knees and wrap my arms around his head, pulling it into my chest where he lets out heavy sobs.

"Oh Gunnar. I am so sorry if I ever made you feel like you couldn't grieve around me. We *all* lost Aliyah. It isn't a comparison of who was closer to whom. I may have lost my Soul Bond with Aliyah, but in doing so, I was able to gain my mate. Don't hide from me Gunnar. I want to see all of you. Every broken, scary, funny, beautiful part.

"This relationship isn't going to work if we can't be our true selves in front of each other. If you don't want to cry in front of the others, I understand, but *never* hide what you are feeling from me. I love you, Gunnar."

I place kisses on the top of his head as he wraps his arms around my waist and pulls me on top of his lap. I straddle him in the chair as his lips meet mine. His kiss is frenzied and all- consuming. As if he can't stand to breathe air not shared by me. His hands grip onto my backside with force as if to never let me go.

"Saraphena, I lost you once, almost twice, already," he starts. "I never want to lose you again. Seeing the way Enzo is grieving the loss of Aliyah...I never want to feel that way. I know what my life was like without you in it. I will never hide from you again."

He picks me up and places me on my feet in front of the fire. He takes a few steps back from me and pulls the back of his collar over his head exposing his bare chest to me.

"What are you doing? This is a public library! Anyone could walk in!" I whisper.

"Let them see. I have nothing to hide. Not from them, and certainly not from you. You said you wanted to see every piece of me. I figure the outside is the easiest to start with," he winks.

He kicks off his boots and unlaces the top of his pants before slipping them off as well. Gunnar stands before me, naked for the whole world to see.

"To anyone listening," he yells. "I love this woman! Saraphena, I love you until the last star burns out! Until the sun ceases to shine! Until the Maker takes the breath from my lungs, I will love you!"

"Gunnar! *Shhhhh!* Someone is going to come in here!" I laugh. I race over to him and throw my hand over his mouth before he can speak again. Our eyes meet and he smiles beneath the palm of my hand. My own smile breaks across my face.

He tips his head down so his forehead connects with mine and he closes his eyes. He pulls my hand away from his mouth and whispers, "In this life, and every life to come, I am never letting you go again."

His lips crash to mine and he picks me up by the back of my thighs and my legs instinctively wrap around his waist, shielding him from potential intruders. He begins to walk us toward the library doors.

"Gunnar! You can't go out there! You don't have any clothes on!"

"You asked me not to hide anymore," he smiles.

"That is *not* what I meant!" I tip my head back in laughter as my arm holds firm around his neck. My body covers most of his front, but his entire backside is exposed as he walks down the hallways to our room.

Duncan and Liliana come walking around the corner from our wing of the palace and stop dead in their tracks.

"Liliana cover your eyes! You don't want to see this," Duncan laughs. He places his hand over her eyes and she grips his forearm trying to pull it down. I see him back her up to the wall as we pass by, shielding her from view. "He may be your brother, but I will not let you to succumb to that level of torture."

"Oh so we can't make out in the hallway, but you can walk around butt naked, Gunnar? Gross! No one wants to see that!" she teases.

"I'm not doing anything inappropriate, *Lil!* I am simply taking my woman to bed!" Gunnar calls back. He pushes open the doors to our bedroom and throws me onto the bed. I let out a small scream as I fly through the air before landing on our soft mattress. He kicks the door shut behind him and stalks towards me.

When his body encases my own, the world falls away. My problems don't seem as large, my worries not as crushing. It is as if Aliyah is right down the hall with Enzo and everything is right where it should be. I'm going to spend forever with this man, however long forever may be.

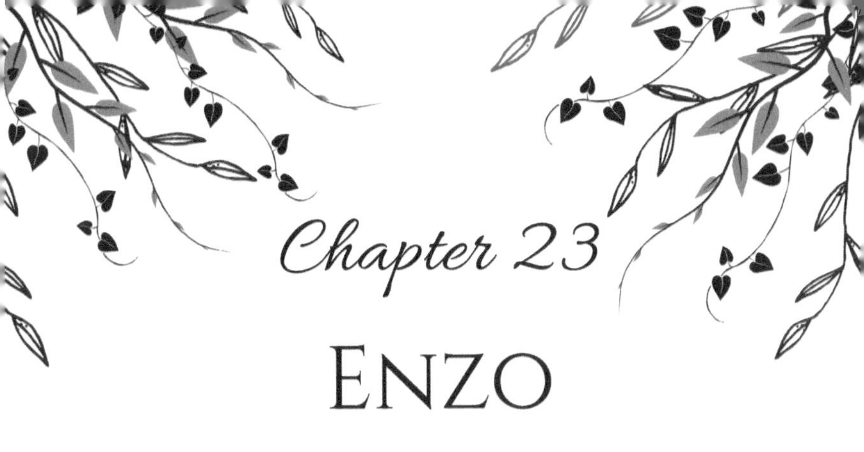

Chapter 23

ENZO

"Rory said she was ready for me to bring her back. This is the last way I can think to do that. He has great magic, you know this. How can I not exhaust every possible option before giving up?" I say. I palm the small tumbler of amber before me and throw it back in one large swig.

"Enzo, this is madness. You can't trust him! And put the stupid alcohol down! It's barely even morning." Jade stabs a piece of ham before putting it in her mouth.

"What other choice do I have? We have made no progress on finding the fallen star, both a piece or the ring, and we have no leads on finding the heir. I've failed her so many times, and now I am just adding to the list of failures by not doing the one thing she wanted us to do. The heir is nowhere to be found. For all we know she is dead and that is if it actually is a girl!"

"What are you two yelling about this early?" Gunnar asks coming into the kitchen and grabbing an apple. "And what in the hell happened to the island?"

The island still lays in two pieces at the center of the room. I didn't have the energy to replace it or to clean it up for that matter. I don't even see why we needed an island when we have a perfectly good table.

"Enzo wants to go and try to make a bargain with the Banished King," Jade says.

Gunnar chokes on a piece of his food, coughing and slamming his fist to his chest. "I'm sorry. I must have misheard you. Enzo wants to do *what?!*"

"I want to go to the Banished Kingdom and try to talk to him about a spell to bring Aliyah back. If he can create those creatures out of nothing, he has to have something to bring Aliyah back," I say.

"You're mad!" Gunnar yells.

"Who's mad? What is all the yelling?" Liliana rubs the sleep from her eyes as she joins us in the kitchen.

"Enzo wants to go to the Banished Kingdom and try to *reason* with the king to try and bring Aliyah back," Gunnar says.

"Enzo that is beyond stupid! There has to be another option." Liliana sits down across from Jade and gives her a soft nod and smile.

"What's stupid?" Duncan asks, joining us.

"Enzo wants to—" Liliana starts.

"Hold on! Don't you dare repeat it one more time before we know that *everyone* who wants to hear is present," I say. Just as I finish my sentence, Saraphena walks into the kitchen and sits down next to Gunnar with a smile. She looks around the table and sees the looks of shock on everyone's face. "Okay, now you can say it."

"Enzo wants to go see the Banished King!" They all echo in unison.

"He *what?!*" Saraphena's face matches the rest. Duncan shakes his head and sits down at the table without another word.

"Ugh! Yes, I know it is crazy. I've been informed. But I'm not asking for your permission to go. I'm going."

"Enzo you can't tru—" Saraphena starts.

"Yes I know! I can't trust him! It's stupid. I'm mad. I get it, but this is the only other logical thing I can think of as a way to bring Aliyah back," I finish.

"Logical, my—"

"Jade, enough. I know what you think about the plan and as my strategist, I appreciate the input, but it does not change my course. I wouldn't forgive myself if I didn't try every possible way to bring her back. Rory said she is ready to be brought home. I owe her this one last try." I rake my fingers through my hair at the thought of even going to see Tyros, but it may be my last hope.

"And you just, what? Expect us to stay here while you go on a suicide mission?" Jade asks.

"This idea is something I must pursue alone. I will not risk my entire family on this mission. If this goes sideways, there has to be someone to stay behind and prepare for the coming war. Thoughts?" I ask.

"Liliana and I can stay here and train the troops. They are going to need all the help they can get. Eilith and Davion can't manage it all on their own. Plus they don't have powers, so the recruits won't be able to practice wielding without guidance," Duncan adds.

Small footsteps come flying into the kitchen as a young boy, Jamison I think his name is, comes crashing into the room out of breath.

"Pardon me, but a letter came for Liliana and Gunnar, sir." The young boy hands a small folded up piece of paper to Gunnar and exits just as quickly as he came.

"What does it say?" Liliana asks.

"*King* Kaleron is requesting our presence in SunSpark," Gunnar reads.

"That's it? He didn't write anything else?" Liliana asks.

"No, just that he needs to see us as soon as possible," Gunnar replies.

"Change of plans then I guess. Duncan and I will stay here and keep training the recruits with Eilith and Davion. Gunnar and Liliana, you okay to go to SunSpark together?" Saraphena asks.

"Yeah! Siblings trip! Gunnar won't that be so fun! It's been ages since it's been just the two of us!" Liliana claps her hands and smiles. I look to Gunnar knowing his reaction will not mirror hers.

"There is a reason for that Lil! You're terrible to travel with! You talk the *entire* way and you always steal all the snacks!" Gunnar crosses his arms in a huff.

"I do not! Duncan, tell him! I am a *great* travel buddy!" Lil yells.

"Duncan doesn't count! He has to say you are a good travel buddy because you two are...ugh. I can't even say it."

"What Gunnar! Say it! Say it! You won't! Duncan and I are what?!" Lil yells.

I see Duncan slowly slide down in his chair as if to hide from the rest of the table. Saraphena has her chin rested on the heel of her hand, watching the two of them, smiling as if this is the funniest entertainment in the world and Jade wipes tears from her eyes from laughing so hard. I can't help the smile that creeps up onto my face watching the interaction.

"I'm not going to say it, Lil! You can't make me!" Gunnar yells.

"Say it! Say it! Say it!" Liliana yells.

"Alright! Alright! Enough you two," I laugh. "You can fight on the road when we aren't around to hear it. Liliana and Gunnar to SunSpark, Duncan and Saraphena here in Citrine, and I will go to the Banished Kingdom. It's settled."

"Care for some company?" Jade asks.

"I thought you'd never ask," I smile. It feels like the first genuine smile I've had in a long time. I was hoping Jade would want to come with me. I hadn't realized it before, but I have grown to appreciate how she always has my back. Maybe I dismissed her too harshly back in the day. She has always been by my side and I should start to appreciate her more for that, especially now. I'm not sure I could have gotten this far without her.

Crushing agony rips through my heart once more. I grip the edge of the table as my smile falls, taking my stomach with it. My intestines twist and anguish rips through my mind. Unfiltered pain courses through my limbs before subsiding. I pull my lips into a forced smile, not wanting to spoil the others fun. I look to Liliana to ensure she does not sense my pain. Relief comes quickly. I don't see Liliana wince and she continues to have a smile on her face. I make a mental note to speak with her once more about not taking on my emotions.

PART III:
BARGAINING

Jane Rose Publishing, LLC

Chapter 24

KALERON

I stare at the three long mirrors before me, reflecting back the image of a king. "Ow!" I flick my eyes down to the tailor who has just stuck his king with the sharp end of the pin he holds.

"My deepest apologies, Your Magesty!"

I release the furrow in my brow as Mother comes up behind me. "Today is a big day, my sweet boy."

"No need to remind me." I close my eyes and try to keep from grinding my teeth together at the reminder of today's events. *Today I am to pick a bride.*

"There is a lovely selection of ladies waiting to meet you in hopes of being selected to be your queen." Mother's tone is nothing but poised.

"You would know, Mother. You selected them," I say rolling my eyes. I glance back at myself in the mirror, taking in the heavy gold and white tones swirling over the fabric of my jacket. The matching gold pants do nothing to pull this outfit together. "Must I wear this? There has to be something in this palace that isn't gold."

"What would you prefer to wear, Your Majesty?" the tailor asks.

"How about something with grays and blues? Maker knows we could use some variety in this place."

"Right away, sir." The tailor scurries off, leaving me alone with Mother.

"You need to remember a few things today, my son. First, you must remember to pick someone that not only makes this kingdom look good, but that makes you look good as well. Someone who is strong, but remembers their place. Someone who can engage in conversation, but knows when to keep their mouth shut. Someone who can—"

"So basically someone completely opposite you then?" I quip.

"Kaleron—"

"Yes, yes. I know what to look for in a wife."

"But she is not just a wife, Kaleron. She is the *queen*. She will rule by your side."

"Were you as subdued when you first came to SunSpark as a new bride?"

"I was. I was the perfect match for your father. But over time I realized he needed...help. Your father was not the strongest leader of our time and without me pulling the strings in the background this kingdom would have burned up under our very sun."

"So what you are saying is that who I choose today may not be the same woman in a hundred years?" I wink.

"Tsk, tsk, my son. I have selected girls whom I can ensure will not threaten your authority. The last thing you need is someone going behind your back to plot and plan your demise."

"Very well," I huff. The tailor returns moments later with a gray-ish blue silk jacket, a black shirt, and black, tailored pants. Familiar gray-blue eyes flash through my mind and I am reminded of the woman of my dreams. *There would be no better queen than her.*

As I shrug on the jacket and swap out the ugly gold pants for the black ones, I gaze once more in the mirror and am refreshed by what I see. "Better."

"I'm glad you are pleased, Your Majesty. Is there anything else I can help you with?"

"No that will be all. Thank you."

The tailor dismisses himself and I follow Mother from the room, each footstep leading towards my ruin. This was not supposed to be my future. Being king of course was always to be my fate, but picking some hoity-toity, prim and proper, high born bimbo was simply *not*.

"These girls are some of the finest in SunSpark and would make the ideal match. Let me remind you not to offend them during your rejections. Their families are still highly influential in your reign and you will want their support during any future conflicts. Their backing could mean the difference between keeping your reign or securing your downfall." Mother's words were pointed and laced with warning.

"Don't offend the pretty little wannabe rulers. Got it," I mutter.

The doors swing open to the large ballroom with small tables circling the outer perimeter. A girl stands behind each table, a small notecard placed on each indicating their name, age, title, wealth, a list of hobbies, and questions my mother wishes me to ask each one. It would be easier if they just fill out the card and I draw one from a bowl at random rather than go through this tedious process of getting to know someone I have zero intention on being satisfied with. *My desired woman would eliminate all these other birdbrains instantaneously. If she were in this ballroom right now, I would dismiss every other girl without a second thought.*

I clear my throat and throw on the mask of "brutal king" so these airheads will understand who they are dealing with. "Sit." At my command, they all take their seats and prepare to wait however long it takes for me to make my way to each of the tables.

"I'll leave you to it." Mother turns on her heel and leaves me alone with these vultures. All they want is a place on the throne. They don't want me or my love. I sit down at the first table and the petite redhead sitting before me beams as she waits for my first question. I could have sworn I saw some drool slip from her mouth as I flexed my muscles, picking up the card before me.

Heidi. 469 years old. Duchess. Extremely wealthy. Likes to knit and embroider. Ask: What do you believe makes a fine ruler?

I could just vomit. There is no way I'm going to keep all of these girl's names straight. I need a system. "So Heidi," I start.

"Yes, my king! I'll answer anything you ask of me!"

"Okay Heidi, calm down." I think I found my system. *I'm going to call this one Hoity Heidi.*

"My apologies, Your Majesty! I meant no disrespect!"

"Enough." My eyes roll so far back into my head I'm surprised they didn't get stuck. "Moving on. Heidi, if I were to threaten you into attending a ball with me, what would you do?"

"You would never have to threaten me, Your Majesty. I would be honored to attend any event with you. There would be no need for threats."

"Err! Wrong answer. You're dismissed." I stand, moving onto the next table, leaving a tearful Hoity Heidi as she sprints from the room, a sob breaking through the air.

The next girl is just as plain as the rest. *Betsy. 287 years old. Heiress. Semi-wealthy. Likes to paint. Ask: What is the role of a queen in regards to her king?*

"Betsy, what a pleasure to meet you." I lean in and place a kiss to the back of her hand.

"And you, my king."

"So I see here you like to paint. What is your favorite piece?"

"I recently did an oil painting of an exquisite rock from the stream near my home." Betsy's face showed not a single ounce of joy as she spoke of her favorite painting.

"A rock?"

"Yes, Your Majesty. It was quite a fine rock. Soft gray edges and yet the tiniest bit of roughness too. I found such beauty—"

I stopped listening as Boring Betsy droned on about some rock in the stream. *How can these be the best single women we have in all of SunSpark?*

"Betsy, let me stop you right there. I find this conversation to be duller than speaking directly to a rock. You are dismissed."

Boring Betsy's mouth hangs agape as I make my way over to the next table. The other women in the room sit in their chairs, spines ramrod straight, shifting back and forth anxiously as they watch me dismiss girl after girl. I need a girl with *fire!* A girl with wit, and stubbornness, someone who can quip back at me as fast as I can dish it out. I can't stand this any longer. I have only spoken with two women and yet I would consider taking a nap on the sun less painful than this.

"Ladies, we need to expedite this process. Please stand and make your way to the center of the room."

"But Your Majesty," one pouts, "we were informed we would get individualized time with you."

I look at her pointedly. "Dismissed."

"Wha— What?" The woman blinks her eyes a few times as if she didn't quite hear me.

"Dis...missed, or do I need to spell it out for you?" I turn back to the rest of the ladies who have gathered in the middle of the room, ignoring the crying girl as she exits. "Let's continue, shall we?"

I walk down the line of ladies, taking a moment to study each and every one looking for *anything* that might catch my attention. I try not to notice the fact that Mother has not picked out a single blonde woman for this line up. As if any of them could even compare to *her* if Mother did select a blonde.

Stopping at the end of the line, I stare at the first girl.

Too short. "Dismissed." I walk to the next, and the next flipping through their note cards as I go.

Too simple. "Dismissed."

Too fancy. "Dismissed."

Too cross-eyed. "Dismissed."

Gone. Gone. Gone. Gone. Gone.

Standing before me there is only one final girl left. Her breasts are spilling out of the top of her too tight corset. Her dress is a horrid shade of vomit yellow and her hair is stacked so high, it towers over even my head.

"So, am I to be your queen then?" She beams up at me, waiting for my confirmation.

"My dear, you are simply too much of *everything*. Dismissed."

I won't be satisfied with my choice until...I...have...*her*.

"You dismissed them all?!" Mother's shrill voice comes crashing through my peaceful evening. The door to my bedroom flies open and she strides in, hellbent on ruining my evening.

"None of them were good enough. Honestly, Mother, I don't know where you found those girls but they were simply all horrid."

"Those were some of the most suitable ladies in all of SunSpark! What would you have me do, Kaleron?! You need to find a wife. A good, suitable woman who will bring honor and *wealth* to this kingdom! If not any of those ladies, then who?! Your brother has found Saraphena and thank the *Maker* she is a respectable woman and one day Liliana will be required to find a suitable match as well. Why do you have to be so difficult?!"

"I will find the right woman, Mother. I just need a little more time."

"Time for what?! Who do you expect to just come waltzing in through the front door?! It isn't like your future wife is just lying in wait somewhere, hoping you *happen* to come across her! That isn't the way it works for royals, my love."

I scowl at the notion that I have to even marry in the first place, but that it can't even be for love. *A suitable match.* That is all that matters to my mother. She found no love in her marriage since she was shipped off here from Twilight, but a small part of me had always hoped for *more*.

"I'll know her when I see her." The vision the Reflecting Pool showed me all those years ago flashes through my mind and a smile pulls at my lips. I know one day she will choose me.

"You have three months. If you have not found a suitable woman by that time, I will select a woman for you. Deal?"

Three months?! What if that isn't enough time to find a way to—

"UGH! Fine. Make it six months and we have a deal."

"Five months. Final offer."

"Five months."

Mother holds out her hand, waiting for me to bind myself to this deal. The moment my palm connects with hers, magic snaps into the air around us, sealing my fate.

The hourglass of my life has officially tipped. I can no longer wait to find the answer to all my problems. I'm a king now. I must take matters into my own hands. Starting with finding any information I can on this fallen star.

Chapter 25

DUNCAN

What is this woman doing to me?

Liliana's soft lips part mine with each kiss and her tongue lightly prods at my mouth. I open for her with almost no hesitation. Any restraint I did have goes out the window as she runs her fingers through my hair. I can't help the groan that slips from my lips and her accompanying smile sends joy ricocheting through my heart.

After Zorellya, I thought my life would always have this dark rain cloud hovering above me for all eternity. But then *she* came crashing into my life and cast away all my dark days. *My ray of sunshine.*

"Promise you won't forget me while I'm gone?" she asks. Her eyes beam up at me and hell if I don't want to melt in her arms. But I have a reputation to uphold. I can't have her thinking she is making me into some sort of softy.

"Liliana who?" I tease. She smacks me in the chest and smiles before pulling me back in for another kiss. Her hand wraps around the back of my neck and pulls me closer to her so there isn't an inch of space between our bodies.

"Forever my shadow?" she asks.

"Forever my sunshine?" I reply.

"You sure you're going to be alright without me here? I know how absolutely dull your life can be without me around," she winks.

"I'm sure I will find something to pass the time. These recruits won't train themselves."

"Don't be too hard on them, shadow. They are only children."

"Children who signed up to fight in a war. Showing any kindness will only make them weaker."

"Why— Why would you say that? Kindness doesn't make you weaker, Duncan."

"Aliyah tried to be kind to me that day on the battlefield. She didn't kill Aramot because he was my brother. Look where that got her."

"Aliyah didn't die because she let your brother live. Her kindness towards your brother didn't somehow make her weaker. She died doing what she thought was right. His fate wasn't her's to decide." Liliana's face contorts into one laced with frustration.

"Lil, it's time to go," Gunnar calls.

"I guess I'll see you soon then." Liliana looks down at her shoes before turning away from me.

"Lil, wait. Don't leave like this."

"If I stay, you might start to consider me *weak.*" Liliana starts walking down the hallway towards the exit.

"Lil!" I yell after her. "How do I always manage to screw things up?" I ask under my breath.

By the time I catch up to her, she is mounting Molly and preparing to take off.

"Lil, stop. Don't leave things like this. I didn't mean what I said."

"That's the thing though, Duncan. You did mean it and that's okay. That's how you see the world. You see kindness as weakness. Maybe when I get back, you'll have changed your mind."

She takes off and soars into the clouds, Molly's white wings blowing my hair back with every beat. As I look up, dark storm clouds gather overhead. My ray of sunshine is gone and I'm left standing in the storm.

I make my way back inside the palace and teleport into my room. I turn and smash my fist into the wall, creating a large hole in the material. Dust engulfs me and I choke on the particles invading my lungs.

I slide my back against the wall and sit on the floor with my head in my hands. When I look up, I see a small note sitting on the nightstand by my side of the bed.

Getting up, I walk over and unfold the parchment.

Dear shadow,

Try not to miss me too much while I am away. But if you do, remember this, I won't be gone forever. I'm coming back to you. I promise. I know we will never be mates, and I know I could never replace Zorellya, but I want you to take some time to consider what I am about to ask you.

I was too afraid to tell you in person, and I figured the time away would let you think about what you really want. I found the Soul Bond spell. If you'd ever consider it, and if we could find someone powerful enough to perform it, I would be honored to be your Soul Guardian. Then we could protect each other until the end of time. I know it is a lot to think about and I didn't want your answer influenced by my presence. Forever my shadow.

Love, your sunshine

There, scribbled at the bottom of the page, is the incantation for the Soul Bond. I had no idea she was even looking for the spell. Dare I say it, but tears prick behind my eyes. *She would consider being Soul Bonded to me?*

The thought hadn't occurred to me before, but she was right about one thing; It was a lot to think about. I'm not sure I could bond my life to hers. What if her mate finds her in the future? We would lose our bond and I'm not sure my heart could handle being crushed like that. I would respect her choice, of course, but I would hate to be the reason she rejected the mate bond.

Even worse, she is on the side of the bond that cannot find her mate while we are connected. She would miss out on the greatest gift the Maker can offer us in this life.

Plus, what if Kaleron and Gunnar do die. She would become the next ruler of SunSpark. She would either have to abdicate, or her mother might call her to marry another for the sake of their kingdom. I wouldn't want my daughter being bonded with someone whose family was as monstrous as mine. They would never allow her to marry the brother of a traitor.

I've spent a long time now thinking about the future of my people. I didn't see it before, but Rory's death opened my eyes. He was so willing to do anything it took to reach Aliyah because it mattered to Enzo. It's my responsibility to step up now, whether I want to or not. My people need a leader. They need a *good* leader. I may not be who they want, but maybe in time I can show them that I am not my father.

Liliana was right, I need to stop seeing kindness as weakness. I was being a coward. Maybe now I can try to make a difference, be a different kind of ruler. Liliana is the princess of SunSpark. That is her home. She will always have obligations there and I know the life of a king.

I saw what happened to Zorellya. My father used the one thing she loved most against her and it cost her her life. If I become king, Liliana would be my downfall. If an enemy used her against me, I would chose her time and time again over my own kingdom without hesitation.

I would rather lose her now and know she is safe, than to lose her to the same fate as Zorellya. We are about to go into a war we have basically no chance of winning. Enzo has already lost Aliyah. If the Banished King ever got ahold of Liliana because of me, I would never forgive myself.

Being Soul Bonded to Liliana would be a dream. But it is just that, a dream, nothing more. When Liliana gets back, I need to let her go. She is going to hate me, but I'm doing this *because* I love her. I need to end things before we are in too deep, and I fear I already am. I know it will crush her, but one of us has to be the responsible one now.

Chapter 26

ENZO

"Well, well, well. If it isn't our little broken general," the Banished King mocks. His appearance has altered since I last saw him on the battlefield. Half his face is now tattooed to resemble a skull, the sides of his head are shaved back with intricate designs etched into his hairline, and his inky black hair is slicked back on top of his head. I can't deny, it looks as if he hasn't aged a day in the last 26 years. He stands a bit taller than I and has seemed to keep himself in peak condition during his time in banishment. His sapphire eyes sharpen as he focuses in on Jade and me.

"Excuse me?" Jade says. "He is not broken." Jade speaks through her teeth as she sneers at the Banished King.

"He is broken. Let me enlighten you. Enzo, sweet, sweet Enzo. Losing the love of your life. You finally found your mate only to have her broken in two, quite literally, because of your bond. Imagine what would have happened if she hadn't been so distracted that day."

"Enough," I grit my teeth.

"Don't worry Enzo, you keep good company. Duncan had his first love slain just for being with him. He understands what it is like to lose." The king's voice drips in sarcasm.

"And Gunnar," he continues. "Gunnar, has to live with the fact that his own brother tried to kill his love. How unfortunate that must be for him. And Liliana, knowing that she will always come second in Duncan's life. He will never love her the way he loved Zorellya. She was his first love for Maker's sake, his *mate*. Liliana will always be a consolation."

"Bite your tongue! You will not speak of my family in this way!" I yell.

"Touchy, touchy," he tsks. "And lastly, Jade. Poor poor Jade. Bound to love someone who will never love you back. You will always be worthless to him," the king sneers.

"Listen here, Banished King. We—"

"Such formalities! Please, do call me Tyros. The Banished King is such an...ugly...name."

"Fine, Tyros. We didn't come here to chat about how broken each of us are. We will all be put back together with your death in time," Jade spits.

"Oh my child. You will not kill me today. You do not have the power to do that. And the one who did ceases to exist. So please, do your worst."

Tyros power comes from the most wicked of places. His father passed down the ability to sense, and create, another's innermost fears. He has been around ages longer than any other fae I know. From what I recall, Tyros used to live in Olyrium with his father, Mytrous, who worked for Queen Dione's mother, Queen Lauryl. They were well liked by every kingdom. I've heard their family was so favored the Queen of SunSpark at the time allowed him to visit the Reflecting Pool. To this day, no one knows what the pool showed him.

But Mytrous believed in conquering all the realms. He believed that Queen Lauryl should seek to move our forces against the other kingdoms. When the queen would not hear of such treason, she cast Mytrous out. She banished him from Olyrium for daring to suggest they upset the balance. Years went by before Tyros came back with an army of The Kalari. His father had died in exile, and Tyros turned on the kingdoms because of it. Along with his affinity for creating nightmarish hell, he also is a well known master of spells and enchantments.

"You know not of the pain you have caused us, Tyros. The suffering we have endured at your hand!" I yell.

"My hand? I have not stepped foot in Olyrium in ages! It could not have been me that caused such...discomfort," he smirks.

"Enough of this. I came here for a bargain. You are clearly skilled in the art of spells, seeing as you have created an entire army using one. We seek information to bring back my mate. Do you know of any such spell in which this can be done?" I ask.

"Perhaps. However, what would I gain from bringing an inconsequential female back into this world?"

"If Aliyah is so inconsequential as you say, then allow me to use the spell to bring her back!"

"I do know of a spell, but the cost is high to work such magic. What are you willing to pay to bring back *one* female?"

"Anything. I will pay any price. Name it."

"*Anything?* You would so willingly pay any price? You do not know the words you speak. But no matter. If it is *anything* you will do, then the price of the spell is death."

"Whose death?" I hesitate.

"There is a town in Twilight. It is filled with murder and crime. A town of outcasts who were not deemed fit to live in society. Seems a simple task to eliminate them from this world as a price for their crimes, does it not?"

"What is the name of this town?" I ask.

"Enzo. Wait. You can't make this deal. Murderers or not, they are still people. You are not the Maker. You don't just get to decide who lives and who dies. It isn't who you are," Jade pleads.

"Sweet child, the males are talking. This is Enzo's decision. How far is he willing to go for the one he loves *most*?" Tyros smiles wickedly.

"What is the name of the town?" I ask again.

"Kastoff," Tyros answers. "There is one condition to my deal. You must not use the pillar to bridge into Kastoff. You must bridge only to the pillar in Twilight and walk the rest of the journey."

"Why?" I ask.

"You said you would do *anything* to bring Aliyah back. Murdering criminals is such a high price to pay, surely walking the whole way is not such a feat. Plus, it will give your companion and I time to get to know each other a little better," he smirks.

"Consider it done. You swear you have a spell to bring Aliyah back?"

"I swear it on my soul. You have one week to complete the task and return here. As a show of good faith, Jade must remain here until you return."

"What? No—" Jade starts.

"Deal," I say without hesitation. Jade will understand one day.

"Enzo. You can't just leave me here!" she pleads.

"As your General, I command you to remain here. I will return for you Jade. I swear it."

Tyros' outstretched hand sparks as he snaps his fingers and metal bars rise from the ground, surrounding Jade where she stands. She grits her teeth at me and swears in my direction.

"If you don't come back for me—"

"I will. I need the spell for Aliyah. I will be back." I turn and head for the pillar to take me to Twilight. A village of criminals is a small price to pay for bringing back Aliyah. I will be wiping out a village of filth to bring back someone far more deserving of life.

My heart explodes in my chest and I remind myself who it beats for. *I'm coming for you, little dove. Just hold on.*

Once again I find myself in the Twilight palace. Duncan and Liliana have created a vastly different experience than the first time I found myself here with Aliyah. The halls are patched, fine paintings hung, and each window has been replaced with beautiful stained glass. The front doors are no longer off their hinges and the sconces are lit to illuminate the once black rooms.

Villagers from every town they visited have come to stay at Twilight palace as payment for helping restore the place to its former glory. The floors are no longer covered in dust, but instead are adorned with lush carpets and polished tiles. The great hall is filled with fae who celebrate the rebuilding of the palace, but I have no interest in celebrating anything until my task is complete. Music pours from the room as fae dance on tables and spill ale over the side of their cups with each turn.

Lovers have found their way into dark corners, lit only by the stars that sparkle in the sky through the glass ceiling of the room. Their affection pulls at something deep in my stomach and I feel my dinner trying to make a second appearance. Duncan once described this place as a mausoleum filled with living souls. His father instilled fear instead of respect, order instead of freedom. I can only imagine what these people had suffered when Aramot took over the throne and aligned himself with the Banished King. My blood boils at the reminder of his actions.

A blur of blonde hair catches my attention as it disappears down a hallway.

Come find me Enzo.

Aliyah's sweet voice fills my mind as I follow the path of the blonde- haired beauty that is my dove. My heart bursts with energy the closer I get to where she disappeared. When I turn the corner, my dove is no where to be found.

Where are you little dove?

I'm right where you left me in Luar. I want to come home now.

You can't be in Luar, little dove. I just saw you. Why do you hide from me?

I'm not hiding, Enzo. Please. Help me.

The silence in the hall is broken by soft groans coming from behind one of the doors. I stalk down the hall, placing my ear to each door listening for the source.

"Yes, baby. You like that don't you?" A male voice comes muffled behind the door.

Enzo. Please help me.

Blinding rage obliterates reason. Aliyah is in trouble and I have to help her! Stepping back, I throw out my power and shatter the wooden door.

"This room is taken, unless you'd like to join." The male hovers above my dove, her face hidden from me, but her blonde hair spills across the pillows. I pin the male against the wall with my power and expose his naked body for all to see. I can't bear to look at Aliyah with what I am about to do. I can't see the look of fear on her face cause by this piece of scum.

"If she was with you I swear I had no idea!" He sounds exactly like the man from the bar, back in Korin. He will suffer the same fate for what he has done to my dove. I didn't get to kill the man who raped Aliyah on that post, so I will take my revenge now. I raise several sharp pieces from the floor and let them sail through the air, embedding them into the male's body.

A scream splits through the air as Aliyah takes off from the bed. She is clearly terrified and fleeing on instinct. I snag her wrist and quickly pull her into my chest.

"Shhhh. You're okay now, little dove. I've got you. He can't hurt you anymore. I'm so sorry I couldn't get here sooner, but I promise no one will hurt you ever again."

She pushes at my chest, trying to get away from me. "Get off me you freak! You disgust me! Let me go!"

"Oh my dove, I know you're mad at me. I'm so, so sorry. I understand why you would hate me, but I'll spend eternity making it up to you I promise." I stroke my hand down her hair and tighten my iron grip around her so she can't get away from me again.

"I loved him! You killed the man I love! Why would you do that!?"

"You didn't love him. You love me. You told me so. I know I didn't say it back, but I love you Aliyah."

A knee connects with my groin and pain shoots up my spine from the impact. *Well this takes me back.* I smile as I remember the day we met. She always did like to fight.

"I am not Aliyah!" She bites into my flesh hard and pulls a chunk of my pec out in her mouth as she rips her teeth back from me. I release my grip on her and she immediately pushes from my chest.

Blood gushes from my wound, soaking my shirt in crimson. The girl before me trembles as she tries to cover up her body. Green eyes flash up at me filled with panic.

"You're not— You're not Aliyah." Realization dawns on me as I take in her features. This fae looks nothing like her.

"No kidding you psycho!" She freezes as she takes in the sight of her lover behind her. I turn and examine the carnage I created. The naked man is pinned to the wall with several wooden spikes protruding from his body including both of his eyes, one in the throat, and one in the groin along with several others holding him to the wall. Blood streams out along the protrusions and onto the floor beneath him. The girl races over and kneels in the pool of blood beneath her lover as sobs take over her body.

"I'm so sorry. I don't know what happened. I thought—"

"Get out you monster! I hope whoever this Aliyah is knows just how much of a monstrosity you are! I hope she never forgives you!"

I stagger backwards out the door as realization washes over me at what I've done today. The woman's words sink into my flesh like her teeth did not moments ago. A mixture of anger and shame fill my blood and pump through my body like a disease. I know once I get her back this will all be fixed. *I'll* be fixed. She can heal this monster I've become. My love for her is greater than all of the mistakes I've made along the way. She will see that. She *has* to see that.

Chapter 27

JADE

The cool metal bars shake under my grasp as I try to pull them apart.

"It is no use, child. Those bars will not be removed unless at my command," Tyros says.

"Then release me. Where am I to go that you will not be able to find me?" I grit my teeth.

"True. I suppose it is the least I could do." The bars slowly lower back into the ground as he whispers something under his breath.

"Why make me stay here? You know Enzo will come back for the spell to save Aliyah. There is no purpose in my presence here."

"On the contrary, my child. We have much to discuss," Tyros smiles.

"I am not a child."

Tyros just smiles and continues talking. "Join me for dinner tonight. We can chat about some history. I am very interested to hear all about your life. It has been some time since I have spoken to another living being. The Kalari are not known for their...conversational skills."

"And if I refuse?"

"Then it is back in the metal cage for you. I have accommodations being made for you as we speak, but if you prefer—"

"No. No more cages." I need to keep up my strength in a place like this and sleeping on rock will only lead to exhaustion. I need my wits about me.

"Delightful. I will see to it that you are escorted to your temporary home and please do let me know if there is anything else I can do for you," Tyros smiles. "I will see you for dinner this evening. I will send one of The Kalari to fetch you."

Tyros disappears down a hallway and four skeletons appear in his place.

"Follow." Their voices sound like sharp glass scrapping across the steel of a sword. My ears cringe at the tone.

I walk behind them, taking in my surroundings as I go. I note the exits and halls leading out from the heart of the throne room. I may be trapped here, but knowing your surroundings is better than being oblivious. The Kalari lead me to a door with a crown etched into the wood.

"Room," The Kalari speak.

I open the door and take in the space. Everything is black with accents of dark green. The walls and floors are black with a black bed frame and black curtains over the windows. I shut the door behind me and flip the lock. I walk over to the window to see if I am close enough to the ground to escape if need be.

Looking out over the edge of the window sill, a cool breeze blows through my hair and the smell of sea water assaults my senses. I am too high up. The ground feels like miles beneath me and even if I did make it to the bottom, there are spikes jutting up towards the sky to impale anyone who might dare escape.

"Great," I huff.

I fling myself on the bed and feel the soft silk sheets under my touch. I guess this might not be so bad. It's temporary. If I just stay in this room for the time being, maybe I can keep my sanity. Exhaustion pulls at my mind and as I slip into darkness, I pray to the Maker that Enzo returns soon.

A knock comes at the door a few hours later. The sun outside my window is setting over the water as I stare out over the rocky shoreline. If it were any other situation, the view might even be considered beautiful, but the ugly truth of where I am comes reeling back in as another knock sounds at the door, harder this time.

I huff out a breath and continue looking out the window. If Tyros wants me to come have dinner with him then he can come get me himself. I will not be summoned like one of his creatures.

I turn towards the door intent on telling off whoever is on the other side, but as I turn, Enzo is there in front of me.

"Enzo! You're back! When did you get— Enzo?"

"Jade. Help me." Blood splatters across my face as Enzo coughs.

As he pulls his hand away from his side, I see three distinct wounds ripping open his flesh. He is bleeding too quickly. Blood spurts out over his hand and drips onto the black floors. My heart thrums in my ears as I rush to his side.

"Enzo, it's going to be okay! Help! I need help in here!" Enzo's blood now covers my hands as I push them into the wound, trying to stop the incessant bleeding. "Why won't it stop? Why can't you heal?!" I yell.

Enzo's eyes meet mine as I lay him on the floor and hold him in my lap. He looks me straight in the eyes, but his words cut like a knife to my heart.

"You'll never be worth what Aliyah was to me. I'm happy to be rid of your presence." His eyes close and his hand goes limp in mine, but a devilish smile sprawls across his face, almost in a snicker.

The door flies open and Tyros strolls into my room, casually.

"You ignored my call for dinner," he says.

"How dare you bring up dinner when Enzo is—"

As I look down, Enzo is gone from my arms. There is no blood on my hands or anywhere on the floor. The picture of horror has been completely erased from before me.

"What did you do to him?" I yell.

"I have done nothing to Enzo. He has not yet returned from Kastoff." Tyros picks at his nails, looking entirely bored with the whole situation.

"He was just here!"

"Was he? Or was it all just in your head?" he smirks.

"He was— Tyros, you son of a—"

"No need for such aggression, my child. I simply wanted to *show* you what would happen if you ignore my call for dinner again, or any other request for that matter. When I call, you will answer, or that is the fate for Enzo upon his return. What was once a fabrication will become your reality entirely too quickly. Now," he claps his hands together with a smile, "dinner?"

I stand, gritting my teeth, and follow him out the door. He leads me down several hallways made of black carved-out stone. Etched into the walls are drawings depicting what appear to be a story line.

"Why do you have these on your walls?" I ask.

"That is history. It is so those who live here never forget their meaning...their purpose."

"I didn't realize The Kalari were so sentimental" I roll my eyes.

"Hmm," his only reply.

I scan the drawings as we walk. There are several faded figures around a large table, then what looks like a woman turning her back on a man. The man is standing next to a smaller figure. A child, maybe? The next picture is of a grave site and the smaller figure before it. The next is a larger man standing above the rest in a commanding demeanor.

Clearly it is The Kalari as depicted by their skeleton features. Then there is a man and a woman together, with another man farther away. Then it is clearly drawn out, The Great War. The banishment of Tyros and The Kalari. The final image is of a single figure that appears to be female.

"Who is the last figure on the wall?" I ask letting curiosity get the better of me.

"A child whose future is yet to be determined. Hence why the drawings end there."

"So the child is alive?"

No answer.

We round the last corner and enter into a large dining room. The roof is missing several pieces, opening itself up to the night sky. The walls are crumbling and the dining set has seen better days. I take a seat as he points to a chair. He settles down next to me and moments later a few of The Kalari enter the dining room with trays of food.

"Where do you find all this food on the island? From the looks of it, it is mostly ruins."

"We certainly have no shortage of supporters that still linger in Olyrium. You would know a little something about that, wouldn't you?" he says making eye contact.

"Indeed. Though clearly their fates are far less painful then other's," I say under my breath. Tyros shifts in his chair almost like he looks uncomfortable.

"Tell me about your family, Jade." He pops a potato into his mouth and my own waters at the sight of food. It smells so good, but is it wrong to give in and eat it? I need to keep my strength. I cut a piece of meat on my plate and chew it before continuing.

"My mother and father were traitors of the crown. You might know them in fact. My parents were spies for your cause. They sold secrets from SunSpark right to you. Though, if your supporters are not so few, I would be surprised if you knew them at all. I am certain everyone is just a pawn in your game."

"On the contrary. I knew your mother well. Much more than your father, that is. Elloiena was quite a woman."

"I'm surprised you know her name." My eye brows shoot up in surprise. "Tell me, how did my mother and father come to be in your service?"

"Your parents believed that Queen Lauryl was cruel to have exiled my father from her service for suggesting that we unite under one ruler. They were some of the first supporters in our cause. This was long before The Great War, and predated your birth. Your mother especially found my situation to be quite dire and often helped...counsel me through my troubles. She gave me more than you could ever know."

"My parents were no saints. I'm not surprised they took pity on you," I spit. "But I am nothing like them. Your sob story will not change the things you have done."

"No, it may not change them, but one day you will find that *pity* may transform into something else entirely. Familial blood means more to me than anything else in this realm."

"I'm sure your mother would be ashamed of your actions."

"You will never speak of my mother!" he yells and I jump slightly in my seat. He returns to his calm temper almost immediately. "She left after my father was exiled. I have not seen her since, nor do I wish to. At this age, she is most likely dead and gone. One less disappointment of a person in this realm."

"So what? Your dad was exiled for wanting to commit treason and your mother left because she wanted no part of it? Boo-freaking-hoo. Get over yourself, Tyros. You can't justify your actions as a full grown fae because you had crappy parents. My parents were traitorous, poisonous people. My father *never* loved me, that much was clear. But I do not let their actions define who I am! No wonder you created an entire army of mindless creatures, because no one could ever love you by choice," I spit. I stand to leave and shove the chair back behind me.

"Your mother did."

"What did you just say?" I stop in my tracks.

"Your mother loved me. And I loved her the same."

"No. She would never. Despite it all, she loved my father. I'm sure of it." Tears start to well in my eyes at his words.

"She may have loved him, but she was *in* love with me. Why do you think it was so hard to send her back to SunSpark to be my spy? Why she risked her life, time and time again, to funnel me information? *Love.*"

"No. You lie! You're a liar!"

"As you just said, your father hated you. Did you ever stop to consider why that might be? Why he had no care for you? He knew you were mine and that your mother loved *me.*"

"Shut up! Shut up! Shut up!" I grip my ears to cover them from his words, but every moment with my father flashes through my mind. I feel Tyros' presence behind me.

"My child—"

"I am *not* your child! Even if I was, what do you expect me to do?" I whip around to face him and slap him across the face hard.

The blood drains from my face when I realize what I have done. The things he can do to me. I am powerless here. I may have the ability to sense his next move, but he has power to create things in my mind I cannot combat.

"Yes. You are. I've been waiting for you to come back to me."

Anger flashes in my chest. "If you are my father, why didn't you come for me when my mother was hung for her crimes? If you loved her so much, why didn't you come to defend her against the SunSpark queen? I don't need you. I have a family.

A family who spoke up for me, *saved me,* when I was thrown into that military academy in Krystal. *They* are my family. Not you. If you expect me to join you now, you are *dead* wrong. I will never leave my real family."

I turn to leave the room once again, not wanting to hear any more of his lies or any more truths.

"Not even for the chance to have real powers?"

I don't stop walking. I follow the drawings on the walls back to my room. I glare at them with a whole new understanding of what they really mean.

I push through my bedroom door and crawl under the covers as if they can shield me from whatever harm lies outside these soft sheets. I curl up on my side and let the tears fall freely. Enzo needs to come back so this nightmare can end.

Chapter 28
SARAPHENA

I make my way out of the palace and walk out towards the bridge leading away from the palace doors. I get about half- way out onto the bridge and swing my legs up and over the crystal wall, dangling my legs over the water below. The training grounds are a nice place to sit and think, but with the recruits setting up for their assignment today, I needed a quiet place to talk to her.

I close my eyes and feel the air around me. A warm breeze blows my hair back and I tilt my face up to the sky. I breathe in and it is in this moment that I feel her with me. I open my eyes and look to the right. Sitting there beside me is my best friend. Aliyah turns her face up to the sky and I take this moment to study her profile. The soft slope of her nose, the smile that graces her lips, but most of all, I study the peace that washes over her. Seeing her like this, I can imagine her happy somewhere in the afterlife.

I turn my eyes to the sky and let them slip shut once more. Tears well in my eyes as I think about what I need to do, but I know it's time.

"This is my last update for you, Aliyah. I wish so badly for you to be here with me, that we could find a way to bring you back, but maybe the Maker called you home for a reason. Maybe—" I choke on my words. "Maybe it was just your time. Maybe He had to take you away because your work in this realm was done. You came crashing into my life at the most unexpected time, but if I could go back and do it all over again, the only thing I would change is not being there with you in the end.

"I know you took those lashes from Cyrus when we both knew it was my turn. You always made sure I was away when he came. You asked me to stay with you in Olyrium when you could have easily begged me to take you back to Mareen. You let me be...happy. You gave me some of the greatest moments life has to offer, and you became the sister I never knew I needed. I love Gunnar with all my heart, but you will *always* have a piece of me.

"However, I think I need to start accepting that you're not coming back. I don't— I don't want to give up on you Aliyah, but by holding onto something that isn't mine to keep is only hurting me in the end. With the coming war, who knows, maybe I will see you sooner than I think, but until then, save a piece of chocolate cake for me, will you? I have to let you go now, but know that if given another chance, I would stay with you...'til the end."

A sob wracks my body as I open my eyes and see Aliyah looking at me. She reaches out and cups my face with her hand, and I place mine over hers. As tears drip from my eyes, Aliyah's figure slowly slips away, until I'm left staring at an open bridge leading to the place she might have called home.

I sit here a while longer until I hear sounds approaching from behind me. I look down at the glassy water and stare at my reflection as another one joins mine. Mirage lays her now graying head on my shoulder and nuzzles into my neck. Tears drip from my eyes and hit the water as small ripples blur the image before me.

"She's not coming back, girl. I'm so sorry. I'm sorry I couldn't save her and I'm sorry your time together was so short."

The coo that comes from the alicanto is filled with sadness. Daisy's yellow feathers glisten off the water as she approaches carrying something in her mouth. Swinging my legs around the ledge to watch their interaction, I see Daisy drop two large crystals in front of Mirage. Both crystals shine with a deep red hue that slightly shifts to blue with the reflecting light. Daisy rolls them over to where Mirage stands, as if begging her to eat. Mirage is showing obvious signs of withering away as her graying feathers fall out in tufts on the bridge around us.

Daisy squawks and flaps her feathers at Mirage. Slowly, Mirage bends her head and picks up both crystals in her beak.

Forcing them down her throat, she finishes every last piece and the color is already starting to return to her feathers. Daisy coos in approval and nudges Mirage in the direction of the crystal fields. Reluctantly, Mirage starts walking that way. She turns back to me with a sense of unease about her.

"It's okay, girl. I'll be here when you get back. I'm not going anywhere." With that, Mirage turns and takes off running with Daisy by her side. If I didn't know any better, I'd say that they were best friends, too.

"Hey," Duncan's voice comes from beside me. "They are all set up. You ready?"

I watch as the two alicanto run away together until they are out of sight. I know they will be back, but at least I know they have each other, just like I had Aliyah.

"Yes. I'm ready. Let the games begin," I smile.

"Recruits! Gather around for instructions." Duncan's voice demands the attention of every recruit standing before us. I know many of them are still grieving Rory's death, a few of them even left after he died, but the majority still wished to fight.

"Today you will be playing a game as your form of training! It will teach you teamwork, strategy, use of your ability in unknown circumstances, and most of all, it will remind you that sometimes it's still okay to have fun. Something Duncan here, sorely needs reminding of," I smirk.

"I am plenty fun, thank you very much!" he scowls.

"Case and point," I say pointing to his scowl. The recruits laugh under their breath before Duncan cuts them a glare and they immediately drop their smiles.

"Saraphena," one girl asks, "how do we win?"

"The game is simple. You have all assembled a series of obstacles you must face while trying to be the first one across the finish line. Fail to complete an obstacle? You're out. Fail to complete the course in enough time? You're out. If you start an obstacle, you cannot go back and start again," I reply.

"That doesn't seem so hard," one boy chimes in.

"Ah, but I didn't tell you the best part! Duncan and I will be completing the course ourselves. If we beat everyone, you all have extra chores this week," I add.

A collective groan rings out through the recruits at the thought of adding extra chores to their plates.

"Saraphena, that isn't fair! We haven't been training as long as you both have," Barley says.

"Do you think the enemy cares you have not been training as long as them? That you have not seen battle yourself? Do you think they will show mercy because you lack the skill to survive?" Duncan questions. Barley shakes his head stepping back into the cluster.

"We will give you all a two minute head start before we begin our course. If you do not complete the course by sundown, or you get out for not completing an obstacle, pick up a bucket and cloth from Eilith and Davion who are spending their evening rebuilding another fountain. Gwynavere, make sure you thank them...again. Good luck, recruits! Begin," I yell. Each recruit breaks off into a dead sprint towards the first obstacle.

"So what's the wager on the winner? I'm betting you five silver coins they try to sabotage each other first chance they get," Duncan smirks.

"I bet you five *gold* coins they fail to even complete the course!" I laugh.

"I'll take that bet!"

"You're on! How long has it been?"

"Long enough. First rule of battle strategy, the enemy never does what they say they are going to, and they *never* give you a head start." Duncan disappears into thin air and I shield myself from sight. I make my way towards the first obstacle and find two recruits stuck in the netting. The first obstacle is a large frame in the shape of an arrow head. They must climb up the netting to the top, hoist themselves over, and climb down. I am so going to win this bet. I shake my head as I watch them fight the netting for another few moments.

Climbing the steps to the beam lofted high above the ground, I watch as another recruit falls from the beam, hitting the ground with a hard thud on their back. I pause to see if they died on impact, but the groan and string of curse words that fall from his mouth tell me he is going to be just fine. I look up and see a small girl smiling down at him, clearly having pushed him. Coming up behind her I jump on the beam and watch her lose her footing as the wood shakes beneath her.

"Boo." I appear out of thin air.

"Ah!" The girl startles backward and falls off the beam, right into the arms of the recruit she pushed. He catches her, but immediately drops her body into the dirt with a thud.

The two walk off together bickering back and forth on their way to find Eilith. I shake my head and smile before disappearing once more.

I spot a group of five recruits flying past me, arguing about how to complete the next task. Looks like Duncan and I were both right on this one. I was surprised when Duncan came to me last night with the idea of playing a game for training today. We spent most of the night brainstorming what elements we wanted to include and what skills it would teach. Duncan's mood has seemed to shift lately. He appears more like a leader. He is taking initiative with the recruits and has even been guiding us in what to do when things seem to go awry with Enzo. Liliana is right, he would make a fantastic king. Hopefully she can convince him to reconsider his position, sooner rather than later.

Lost in my thoughts, a recruit runs clean into me, knocking me to the ground and dropping my shield. He pushes past me and jumps over the large body of mud we created. He snags the rope and swings, ready to latch onto the next one. I watch him complete the task with ease.

I know I need to pick up my pace if I am going to win. Duncan will never let me live it down if the recruits beat me. I sprint towards the rope and feel the burn of my palms as my hand slips before grasping the next one. Aliyah and I never trained like this, so clearly I am out of practice. It's going to be a long day.

Several hours later I stand in front of the last obstacle before the finish line. The sun is setting low in the sky and the ribbons of color provide light to the final recruits who have made it. I look up at the giant wall before me. I'm too short to reach the first ledge by myself, so I pray Duncan hasn't already finished. Mud cakes my body and my muscles burn with a fire I haven't felt in ages.

"Need a boost?" Duncan's deep voice appears behind me. I turn and cock out a hip before crossing my arms.

"What makes you think that?"

"You're about two feet shorter than the first ledge and we created this obstacle so the recruits would be forced to work together or not finish at all," he laughs.

"How do I know *you* don't need a boost?" I take in Duncan's large frame and compare it to my own, knowing there is no way in hell I would ever be able to boost him over this wall.

"Funny." Duncan moves out of the way as the only surviving three come up to the wall next to us. Felicia, Barley, and Gwynavere stand before the wall and contemplate their next moves.

"Don't listen to our strategy you old- timers! I don't want you stealing our ideas!" Barley yells over to us. Duncan and I share a look knowing we are going to complete this obstacle in just a few moments. I note that Felicia is missing a glove. She must have lost it somewhere along the way, which means she is only able to operate with one hand. We sit back and watch what the group decides to do. Eilith and Davion come up behind us with the other recruits in tow.

"We figured they should see the end," Davion smiles.

"Are you two out?" Eilith asks.

"No, just giving them a fighting chance." Duncan watches the group whisper to each other before forming a basket with their hands. Gwynavere is the first up the wall. They boost her to the first ledge where she crouches low as to not fall. She reaches down and grabs Barley's hand while Felicia boosts him from the ground, barely able to do so with just one hand. Barley then helps Gwynavere to the top ledge and reaches down for Felicia.

"Taleria," I call over to one of the recruits.

"Yes?" she says stepping up next to me.

"When Barley goes to use his powers to pull a crystal from the ground and lift Felicia up, I want you to smash it, okay?"

"Why? I'm not in the game anymore."

"I know, but as someone once pointed out to me, the enemy doesn't play by the rules."

Taleria shares the same ability as Barley and I have seen her obliterate his crystals with ease during training. As I suspected, a crystal comes out of the ground and pushes Felicia towards Barley. Felicia reaches towards him and his hand locks around her gloved one. I know Barley isn't strong enough to pull her up by himself, so he will have a decision to make. Reach for her other hand and take the pain, or drop her and win the game with Gwynavere.

"Now, Taleria." The rock shatters beneath Felica leaving her legs dangling beneath her. "Continue to make sure his crystals don't hold."

"Yes, ma'am."

"Bets on what he will decide?" I ask Duncan.

"He'll drop her. Felicia's magic has to be brutal if she insists on wearing those gloves all the time."

"I can't hold you! Reach up with your other hand!" Barley yells down to her.

"I guess I was wrong," Duncan smiles.

"No, Barley you can't take it. Just drop me!"

"I'm not letting you go, Felicia!"

"I don't have my other glove and this one is slipping as it is! Just drop me!"

The glove starts slipping from her hand as each crystal explodes beneath her. As she starts to fall, her hand slips out completely from the glove. Felicia starts to fall, prepared to join her peers on the ground and fail. A small hand drops from the ledge and grasps her now ungloved hand.

Pain contorts Gwynavere's face, but she refuses to let Felicia go. Barley's look of shock makes him pause, but a moment later, he reaches down and grabs Felicia's other hand. Gwynavere and Barley both wince in agony as they hoist Felicia's body up the wall and onto the ledge with them.

The moment they release her hand, they don't miss a beat before boosting her to the top ledge, finding the rope to slide to the ground. Gwynavere struggles to push Barley's body to the top of the wall, but she manages to succeed. He reaches down and she jumps up to grab his hand, barely making it. The three recruits all make it over the wall and make a bee line for the finish line.

"I think they deserve a win," I say.

"Agreed." Duncan and I forfeit the obstacle and fail. We make our way around the wall and watch as the three recruits jump over the fire, signifying the end of the course. Barley turns to Gwynavere and picks her up, spinning her in his arms. They hoot and holler as the rest of the recruits run over to celebrate with them. Praise rings out from the group, yelling about how they beat us because we couldn't figure out how to get over the wall. I can't bring it upon myself to ruin their happiness. It comes in such short supply these days. We stand back and watch as the group celebrates before hoisting the three winners up into the air to carry them over to where we stand.

"Alright, alright. Calm down." Duncan's voice carries above the cheers as they set their winners back on their feet.

"So, what went wrong?" I ask.

"What do you mean? We won!" Barley shouts. The group erupts in joy once more.

"True! True!" I yell over them. "But why did *you* win, where everyone else failed?"

"Because we are the best!" Barley cheers once more.

"Barley." Duncan's clipped tone stops the cheers in their tracks.

"Sorry, sir." Barley sucks in his lips as if to seal his mouth shut.

"We worked as a team." Felicia's small voice cuts through the silence.

"Exactly," I smile. "I watched everyone else sabotage each other along the way to try and get to the end, yet these three were the only one's that worked together to make it to the end."

"But you didn't say we could work as a team!" one shouts.

"Did I say you *couldn't* work as a team?" Silence.

"What is the lesson you all learned here today?"

"We are stronger together." Gwynavere steps forward from the crowd.

"Precisely," Duncan smiles.

"Even when things got tough, you didn't stop working as a team. You were faced with a choice Barley. Let Felicia drop and fail, or take on the pain you knew would be inflicted if you touched her skin. But much to my surprise, Gwynavere was the one to make the decision for you." A smile creeps up my face knowing that Duncan was wrong.

"Why didn't you let me fall?" Felicia asks. "I told you it was okay to let me fail. You didn't have to do that."

"It's what Rory would have done. He would have taken the pain if he knew it meant you could cross that finish line with us." Barley lays a hand on her covered shoulder and nods his head. Tears well up in my eyes because I know he is right. Rory would have done that for Felicia, or for anyone if it meant they would succeed. I clear my throat before continuing.

"This is the lesson we wanted you to learn today. The odds will not always be in your favor during battle, but when you work together, the numbers don't matter. You might not always win, but you'll have lost knowing you did so together."

"Have you ever lost in battle before?" one asks. I turn to Duncan searching his face for any response. His eyes meet mine as tears start to line my lashes. Something catches in my throat and I can't seem to find the words to tell the recruits that some battles you win, but you'll lose something very special in doing so.

Chapter 29

ENZO

Leaving Jade with Tyros may be one of the cruelest things I have ever done, but sacrifices need to be made for the ones we love. Jade has to understand by this point I will do whatever it takes to get Aliyah back, including destroying a village that houses the worst of the worst criminals.

Kastoff is just a dot on the map and surely no one will miss those who live here. I need to do this for Aliyah. I am out of options and if this is the price I must pay Tyros to do it, then so be it.

Using this much of my power might kill me. If not, I will be able to go back to Tyros and bring Aliyah back. Either way, I will be with her again, in life or in death.

I make my way to the center of the village. I take in the window- front shops filled with different trinkets, baked goods, and other colorful items. This place is not what I had imagined it to look like. I expected broken down doors, homes with missing shingles on the roof, and unhinged anarchy consuming the town. For a village filled with murderers and criminals, it seems almost...peaceful.

Instead I look upon small homes with lights in the windows to cast out shadows in the night and a sense of harmony that brings goosebumps to my skin. I breathe in deep and let my eyes slip shut. When I open them again, Aliyah stands before me.

"Enzo, don't do this. Bringing me back is not worth blackening your soul."

I walk up to her and cup her face. She leans into my palm and places her hand over mine. I stare into her ocean blue eyes that start to brim with tears.

"You shouldn't be so concerned with my soul when you took it with you into death."

"You were never a bad person before I came into your life. Don't lose yourself to the darkness in my death. You are a warrior Enzo. You have fought to protect the ones you love time and time again. Do not throw away your goodness for someone like me.

"I'm not your forever, Enzo. I was a moment in your life to bring happiness and joy. You opened your heart to me, showed me every dark corner, and I loved you for it, but doing this," she waves her arm towards the village, "doing this will only hurt you further. It isn't worth it."

I pull her into my arms and wait for the smell of vanilla to invade my senses, but it never comes. Her soft hair slips through my fingers as I grip the nape of her neck. I feel her little hands drawing soothing circles on my back, as I once drew them on her.

I don't want to let this moment go. I think of that little boy sitting next to his mother as she died in his arms. The feeling of being helpless and lost in that moment crept into that boy's heart and lingered. I never want to feel that way again.

"I'm so sorry, little dove. I need to do this. I can't be in a world without you in it. You may never forgive me, but in time I know you will love me again. I'm doing this for you...for *us.*"

"Please, don't do this." Aliyah pulls back from me and fresh tears slip from her eyes as she holds me.

"I'm sorry." I close my eyes once more and when I open them, the vision of her is gone. I feel the pull of my power rise up within me.

"For you, Aliyah. I'll see you soon, one way or another."

Agony crackles through my skin as I push out my power to engulf the village. Not a single scream rises from the mouths of the murderers here. Homes are obliterated before my eyes and the sound of cracking wood and broken stone fills the night air.

Dust flies up as each building falls while my power reaches the next one. With each passing moment, a smile creeps onto my lips at the thought of how close I am to getting my little dove back.

"More! You're holding back! You're weak!"

My skin feels like it is going to burst open with power my father wants me to so willingly unleash on the fae in front of me.

Dark eyes lined with tears stare back at me as I hold back my power like an untamed alicanto, thrashing and bucking to be set free. I feel tears of my own pooling behind my eyelids.

"I can't do it." My voice is barely above a whisper, knowing if I cannot deliver on my promise to harness my ability, my father will deliver on his promise of pain.

"You can and you will. You are worthless to me if you cannot even kill a criminal. He is nothing but the scum of the realm. You will kill him and you will do it now. Break his neck without so much as a thought!"

My mind flashes back to a time when my father lay with me in bed reading stories of magic and adventure. How could the death of someone he loved turn him into such a creature of hate. This man was not my father, not the one I knew. I know I will disappoint him again today.

I want to be out in the training yard playing with my friends. I want to hold Jade's hand as she pulls me along to hide from Gunnar during tag. I imagine myself in another place where she is there to make me smile.

We have protected each other every day since I found Leyon beating on her, but some things you can't be protected from. I just want to learn how to be a child, not how to be a monster. This isn't who I want to become.

I shake my head to clear the memories of my father. I push out more power, watching this small village be torn to shreds brick by brick. I feel each and every neck breaking as my ability rips souls from this world and thrusts them into the next. For Aliyah, I will become the monster once again.

"Yes, son. Better!"

My father's praise comes in waves these recent years. I'm becoming the weapon he will wield against our enemies with each passing day. I stand before twelve fae criminals, all begging for their life. It took years before I could even kill one fae without hesitation, but now...

I close my eyes and find my place away from this dungeon room. In my mind, I'm sitting at the breakfast table, laughing with Gunnar and Jade about our most recent prank on the leading officers. Gunnar throws food in Jade's direction and her smile only grows brighter as pomegranate seeds stick in her hair and cheeks. Her eyes light up when they find mine with a matching smile. My chest feels lighter in these moments, like my father isn't about to come around the corner and pull me into the darkness.

In my memory, Jade's words of comfort over the years fill my mind, telling me I am safe. In my mind they are right outside, waiting for me to return to them so we can stir up trouble and blot out the stain of my actions.

I barely feel the necks of the fae snapping through my power as each one drops forward onto the floor, their spines at an odd angle. My father's words of approval pour through my mind, robbing me of the joy I find within my memories.

"You will be the most feared man in all of Olyrium, my son. I could not be more proud of the weapon of destruction you have become. No one will dare stand against us."

My father is right. I am nothing more than a creature of anarchy. The once black spot on my heart has transformed to a beating vessel of malice. I have become the nightmare I once feared. I am no longer the small boy crying in bed for someone to save him from the monster in the wardrobe. I am the monster.

My chest rises and falls at rapid speed and my vision begins to waver in and out. I bend over, placing my hands on my knees and sucking in oxygen like the last drop of water in the mountain pass. The village before me is silent. I feel weak as I look out over the decimated homes. A smile spreads across my face.

"I'm coming for you, little dove."

As I make my way out of the village, something catches my eye and pulls me to a complete stop. Laying in the debris by one of the homes is a small doll with a pink dress and little silver slippers. Soot from the destroyed home clings to her dress and the side of the dolls face has been torn off.

My heart beats faster as I walk over the rubble. I sift through the carnage and see blonde hair spilling out from under a large slab of roof that had fallen through the home. I shove the pieces of wreckage off the body that lies underneath and horror strikes my heart when I see Aliyah laying before me.

"No, no, no! Not again!" I fall to my knees before her and pull her into my arms. Tears flood my vision and I wipe them away with the back of my hand. When they clear, I look down to my little dove, but it isn't her face I see anymore. Laying in my arms is a women with long blonde hair, but her face is caved in and missing half the skin, clearly torn off by the roof. Blood smears down the front of her dress and her neck lays at an odd angle.

I hold her in my arms as I scan the rest of the chaos I've created. In what would have been another room in the house, I spot a leg dangling out of a crushed wall with a little silver slipper still on and the corner of a pink dress peaks out from the top of her leg.

"What have I done? What have I done!?" I scream. "I'm so sorry. I didn't know. I didn't know. I didn't—" I sob over the woman in my arms and cradle her to my chest.

As my tears dry, anger builds in my chest. Tyros knew exactly where he was sending me. I never should have trusted him. He knew this village was filled with innocent people, but I didn't even question it. My family was right, and I didn't listen. He was not to be trusted. I listened to him and now I have to live with these deaths for the rest of my life. They died at my hand. Not Tyros'— mine. They aren't the criminals I rationalized killing as a child. Instead they were innocent lives I took in pursuit *of* life, yet that same cause only led to more death.

I stand and begin to sift through the rubble of each and every home, pulling body after body out that I had destroyed. I lay them in a line on the outskirts of the city and get to work. I find a shovel amongst the fallen homes and begin digging a grave for each and every person I slaughtered here today. This village wasn't filled with murderers and criminals. The only murderer here is me.

These thoughts run through my mind as the sky turns to the darkened hues of twilight and I have buried the final body. I couldn't give them the traditional funeral they deserved, but I couldn't leave them to be trapped in unrest for all eternity. They deserved better. As I finish burying the final body, I look out over the horizon and see a woman in a tattered dress, her long blonde hair blowing in the wind. But this is not a dream, and Maker, I wish it were. She looks at me and reaches out a hand as if beckoning me to her, but instead, I lay the shovel on the ground and turn my back on her. I can't face talking to

Aliyah right now. She warned me not to do this, and I didn't listen. Now I have to pay the price for my actions. But I won't be paying that price alone...

"Tyros!" I storm into the throne room of the Banished Kingdom and lift Tyros up by the throat. He doesn't choke, or gasp for air, he just smiles at me.

"Welcome back, Enzo. I trust your journey to Kastoff was...productive?" he smirks.

I squeeze tighter on his throat, but his smile never falters. My anger seethes at his lack of candor.

"You knew! You knew what was in that village and you lied to me!"

"You are correct. I did know what was in that village. I told you murder and crime were rampant there, and here you are. A murderer and a criminal. An outcast, who based on recent actions, should not be allowed in society. You have a tendency to kill anything in your way to get back to Aliyah."

"Enzo?"

My hold on Tyros drops when I hear Aliyah's voice from behind me.

"Little dove?"

She races into my arms and holds me tight. The smell of vanilla fills my senses and a bright light beams between us, the mate bond snapping back into place. I feel her there, right at the end of that tether connecting us. I stroke her hair and gaze upon every inch of her face as though I have not seen it in a thousand years.

"Are you real?" I ask, placing my hands over every inch of her body, convincing myself she is actually real.

I'm real, Enzo. I'm here now. She lifts onto her toes and places a soft kiss to my lips. Pure joy erupts in my heart. I did it. I got her back. Everything I did, it was all worth it. I will grieve Rory's death, and every death I have caused along the way for the rest of my life, but with her by my side, I know she will put me back together again.

"I thought I lost you forever," I say.

"I'm here, Enzo. Today and every day to come." Her smile is just as I remember. A throat clears behind us and I remember Tyros.

"Stay here. I just need a moment to collect Jade and then we can be on our way." I turn and walk towards the Banished King.

"I don't know how you did it, or what sort of magic this is, but...thank you. Consider her life as recompense for the atrocities you have committed. While I was hell bent on killing you, I have what I want now. We are even. Where is Jade? It is far past time that we return home."

Muffled screams come from Jade as a few of The Kalari walk her out of a tunnel next to the throne room. Her eyes are wide as she finds me standing before Tyros. Her arms are tied behind her back and her mouth is gagged with a cloth tied around her head.

"Release her! I did what you asked. Now release her." I try to pull on my power to destroy The Kalari holding her, but I feel nothing. The well of my magic is too low to wield after what I did in the village. I curse under my breath at how stupid I am to come here unarmed with magic when I know Tyros is far superior at wielding spells alongside his own power. I don't even have my battle axes as The Kalari stripped me of my weapons upon arrival.

"You are correct. You have done what I had asked, however, what you asked of me cannot be done. There is no spell that can bring someone back from the dead," he smiles.

"What are you talking about? Aliyah is standing *right* there!"

"Is she?" he mocks.

I look to Jade whose eyes are flooded with tears as she looks behind me to Aliyah. I spin around so fast and watch blood pour through the front of Aliyah's tunic, right over her heart. She looks down to the source and then her eyes trail back up to meet mine. As she moves to speak, blood pours from her mouth and tears well in her eyes. I race over to her and catch her before her body can fall to the ground.

"Aliyah, it's okay. I'm here. Nothing is going to happen. I've got you now." I place my hands over her wound, but like that day on the battlefield, blood pumps over my fingers, unable to be stopped.

"Why didn't you save me Enzo?" she asks.

"What?" Confusion pulls at my mind as to why she would ask this, of all times. Anger laces her tone as she looks up at me, almost unaware of the blood pumping from her body.

"Why did you bring me to Olyrium? Why did you kidnap me that day? Everything that has happened to me is your fault. You did this to me. I wish I had never met you."

"Make it stop! Make it stop!" I yell.

"As you wish." Before me, Aliyah disappears from my arms like she was never there at all.

"Bring her back! You said you could bring her back! You swore on your soul you could do it!"

Jade is slumped on her knees as tears pour from her eyes. Sobs wrack her body as she goes limp in The Kalari's bony arms.

"If only I had a soul to swear on." The laugh that comes out of Tyros is maniacal and laced with venom.

I run at him intent on killing just one more person for the sake of Aliyah. Before I reach him, a familiar voice sounds to my left.

"Enzo." I snap my head in her direction and see Aliyah standing there. Then her voice calling my name again from the right. She stands there, tears streaming down her face with an ax buried in her chest. *Behind me.* Her back torn to shreds with fresh lashings. *Left.* Water spews from her mouth like the day at the Reflecting Pool. *Right again.* A sword through the heart and blood pouring down the front of her.

Every direction I turn there is a new version of Aliyah, ruined by my doing. She was right. I caused all of this. All I hear is the sound of Tyros laughing and Aliyah's voice ringing through my head. My vision blurs the faster I spin and the voices in my head grow louder, screaming at me all the horrible things I've thought to myself over the last few months. I slam my hands over my ears to try and make it stop, but it keeps growing louder and louder. Crazed laughter gnaws at my brain. I fall to my knees and put my forehead to the floor as every sound stabs at my ears like a sharp knife. I can't stop it. I can't drown it out. I can't take this anymore.

I scream as loud as I can and let out every ounce of denial, anger, sadness, *rage,* that has been pent up for so long. I scream and scream and scream until the only sound I hear is my own hoarse voice echoing back at me off the stone floor. My breaths are ragged and my throat feels like I am swallowing nails. Sweat drips down the back of my neck as the world around me falls silent. I can't get up. I'm too *scared* to look up. I can't see her face one more time.

Hands come around my shoulders and lift me up. Jade's muffled voice fills the space, but I can't make out what she is saying. I close my eyes as she lifts my head off the floor. I can't bear to look around for fear of what I might see. My body feels spent and my eyelids are like heavy curtains that refuse to move.

I feel nothing now. Truly and utterly, nothing as darkness welcomes me home.

Chapter 30

LILIANA

"Gunnar, seriously, stop tossing and turning! I haven't had any sleep the last two nights because of it!" I turn over to my other side, trying to get comfortable.

"I'm sorry! I can't seem to find a comfortable spot. Maybe if you weren't taking up so much room I'd be able to spread out more!" he huffs.

"Me?! I am shoved into the corner of this tent! *You* are taking up all the room! I don't know how Saraphena does this every night."

"Well Saraphena is not normally next to me. If you know what I mean," he says in a cocky tone.

"Ew! Gross, Gunnar! We are *not* talking about your sex life with my best friend. Nasty." I roll my eyes knowing he can't see me.

"Speaking of! How are you and Duncan?"

My cheeks flush at the mention of his name. I feel like a raw nerve being exposed to the world waiting for an answer from him. Asking to be Soul Bonded to someone is not something to be taken lightly. Your souls are literally tied together.

"I asked him to consider being Soul Bonded to me."

"You what?! Lil, that's a huge ask! What about your mate? What if you met them but were Soul Bonded to Duncan? Once the mate bond is in place, you could never be Soul Bonded to him again."

"I know. I've had a lot of time to think about it. I spent hours in the Citrine library looking for the spell, just to see if it would even be an option for us. When I found it, I knew what my answer would be right away. I love him, Gunnar. I don't care about finding my mate. I want to give Duncan the love he deserves."

"I mean, sure. You love him *now*, but Lil, if the mate bond snaps in place, you can't deny it."

"Why not? Why don't I get a choice? Just because some invisible tether snaps in place between me and someone else, doesn't mean they are who is *best* for me. Plus, look at mother and father. They aren't mates, and yet they are still married and faithful to each other. I want to decide who I am going to be with, not some fancy invisible leash."

"But what if you change your mind? What if you meet your mate and they won't let you reject the bond?"

"If they won't *let* me reject the bond, then they aren't the right person for me. I know you and Saraphena, and Enzo and Aliyah, got lucky in the mate department. You both love each other, but

I love Duncan. I feel the love he has for me. I may never be his mate, maybe you only get one in a lifetime, but I know he is my forever. I am his and he is mine."

"You never were one to follow the rules, were you?" Gunnar smiles.

"Rules were created by people who were too afraid to give in to their dark side," I smirk.

"Only you would come to that conclusion, sis." Gunnar laughs as he turns around again, trying to get comfortable.

"What do you think Kaleron wants to see us about?" I ask.

"He is king now. I am sure he just wants us to come see him flaunt his new title." Gunnar's tone is light, but his emotions are filled with trepidation. Our brother has always been unpredictable.

"I guess we will find out tomorrow."

"Brother! Sister! Welcome home!"

Kaleron sits on the throne before us as we walk into the throne room three days after arriving in SunSpark. Mother sits beside him with a soft smile on her face. The members of Kaleron's council sit to the right of the dais and scribble ferociously on parchment.

"Brother, good to see you. Shall we address you as brother or as king?" Gunnar asks.

"No need for formalities! We are siblings first, royals second." Kaleron rises and makes his way down the steps before embracing Gunnar and clapping him on the back. He turns and pulls me in for a hug that almost breaks my spine on contact. We have not seen Kaleron since our arrival because he has continually been pulled away for "important matters." *Thank the Maker I don't have to sit in those boring meetings.*

"Hey Kal. I've missed you."

"And I, you sister. We need to talk. Come, let's retire to the dining hall for some refreshments." He leads us out of the throne room and Gunnar and I follow behind him. I give Gunnar a side glance and he shifts his eyes to meet mine. I turn back to see my mother still sitting on the dais and I give her a soft wave. She smiles in return, but I sense the sadness coming off her.

As we make our way through the halls, I take a moment to look around my home. It feels strange being back here after being away for so long. The walls seem too bright, the floors too shiny, and the air too thick.

My mind wanders back to my shadow waiting for me back in Citrine. I never felt quite at home here growing up, maybe the darkness is where I have always belonged.

Court members stop Kaleron along our walk to ask him questions about important matters, sign documents, and give orders. He really was born to be king.

"Kal, why are we here?" Gunnar asks.

Kaleron stops walking and turns to face us. "How is your progress on finding a way to bring Aliyah back?"

The question catches me off guard. I hadn't realized he was so invested in us finding a way. I reach out my power to sense any ulterior motives, but all I am met with is genuine concern. I feel the nervousness through my ability and sense his unease. Why is he so concerned with Aliyah?

"No luck yet," Gunnar replies hesitantly. "Why do you ask?"

"Ah, I see." Kaleron's demeanor flickers with sadness for just a second before snapping back into his kingly facade.

"Kal, did you really drag us all the way here to ask us about Aliyah?" I ask.

"No, I just— I was curious is all. I'm sure Enzo is not taking it well. He always did have a wild temper."

Kaleron isn't wrong. Enzo isn't taking it well, especially after Rory's death. Going to see the Banished King was truly mad, but he's desperate at this point and desperation often leads to extreme measures. I just hope those measures don't get him killed.

"I called you here because I found something amongst father's things I think you would find quite interesting." Kaleron pushes the dining hall doors open and walks to the head of the table. It seems like just yesterday I sat in this same room with Duncan for the first time. That was certainly an interesting night. I laugh under my breath at the memory.

Kaleron sits at the head of the table and loads his plate with meats, cheeses, and fruits. His plate is piled high with food by the time he is finished and I can't help but laugh at the irony.

"Something to say, Lil?" he smiles.

"You are eating almost as much as father used to. Don't let yourself go now, *King* Kaleron," I smirk.

He lets out a boisterous laugh and tosses a grape at me before popping another one into his mouth. "The difference between father and me is that I at least train and exercise to have a *need* to eat this much food!"

"Can we please get back on topic, Kaleron? We have things happening back in Krystal that require our attention." Gunnar bounces his knee up and down, clearly impatient.

Kaleron stares at him for a moment and smiles. "I hear congratulations are in order, brother. Set to marry Saraphena now, are you? How wonderful! When the time comes, we would love to host your wedding here at the palace. It seems only fitting the prince of SunSpark be married in his own home."

"I'll speak to Saraphena, but we will get married wherever she feels most comfortable. I am going to give her the perfect day, minus one great detail. Because of that, everything else must be what *she* wishes for our big day."

Kaleron's mood shifts and feelings of guilt wash over him. "Kal, why are you feeling guilty?" I blurt out before I can stop myself.

"What? I don't feel— Don't read my emotions Liliana! You know I always hated that. Emotions are supposed to be private matters!"

"Sorry, I just— anytime someone brings up Aliyah your mood shifts to one of despair. Why? You literally tried to kill her best friend and you threatened her into attending the ball with you. Why would you suddenly care?"

"I don't care. I'm just feeling guilty I could not have done more that day during the battle in Twilight."

"We can't go back and fix our mistakes, but you can help now. Send troops to Citrine to train with the other recruits. Enzo is building an army to help fight against the Banished King. We could use all the help we can get," Gunnar adds.

"No. I will not be sending our troops to Citrine. We need them here." Kaleron's voice is firm.

"Need them here for what? There is no war here, Kal. Olyrium needs everyone to join this fight if we want to stand a chance." Gunnar shifts in his seat, clearly agitated.

"I am King of SunSpark. I will not be sending troops and I do not have to explain my reasons to you. They stay here until I otherwise say so."

"Kal! A war is coming, whether you like it or not! Send the troops!" Gunnar yells and shoots up from his seat, standing over Kaleron.

Kal pushes up from his seat and slams his fist on the table. "Enough! *I* am king! Not you! One day, Maker forbid, you become king, you can make a different decision, but until that fateful day arises, you *will* listen to me. Now, do you want to know why I called you here or not?"

"If I was king, I would not hide behind my crown while others gave their life for the safety of these lands," Gunnar seethes under his breath. Kaleron blows out a burst of air from his nose and glares at Gunnar. Sitting down, Kaleron reaches into his breast pocket and throws a stack of parchment onto the table, scattering the pages across the surface.

"I thought you might be interested in these," he says.

I pick up one of the pieces of parchment and note the jagged edges along one side. My mind flashes back to Twilight when we found the old king's journal detailing the fallen star. My eyes snap to Kaleron. "Where did you get this?"

"I found them amongst some of father's old belongings. It is quite an interesting read and I think you will find some of the information very...enlightening."

"Why would father take these? *How* could father have taken these?" Gunnar asks.

Confusion pulls at my eyebrows as I collect each page before me. "He didn't," I start. "but I know who could have."

Chapter 31

JADE

Sobs wrack my body as I watch Enzo face Tyros' hallucinations, knowing there is nothing I can do to help him. The Kalari grip my arms tighter as I fall to my knees. One of them try to pull me to my feet and I know his grasp on my arm will leave bruises for certain.

"Ow!" My muffled cry comes from behind the gag in my mouth. Tyros' head snaps in my direction and his eyebrows pull down into an angry furrow when he sees The Kalari hurting me.

He snaps his fingers and they burst into a cloud of bone sawdust. I slam forward onto the ground, unable to catch myself with my hands bound. I roll onto my back and look up as Tyros stands above me.

He leans down and unties the gag from my mouth and shifts my shoulder to untie my hands. The moment I am unbound, I scramble up and distance myself from Tyros.

"Don't say I never did anything for you, daughter."

"Do *not* call me that. I may share the same blood that flows through your poisonous veins, but I am *not* your daughter. You are no father to me." I look behind Tyros to see Enzo on the ground screaming with his head to the floor and his ears covered by his hands.

"Make it stop."

"On one condition," he starts.

"No. No conditions. Make it stop."

"Hear my terms and I will make it stop." When I don't utter a word, he continues. "When you're ready to accept your power, come find me here."

"Fine. Deal. It'll never happen, but if the time ever comes, I'll be sure to make this my first stop." I spit at his shoes and run over to Enzo. I wrap my hands around his shoulders and try to pull him up, but he won't budge. "Make it stop...please."

"Is it a deal?"

"Yes, yes. Deal."

"Shake on it." Tyros holds out his hand as a wicked smile pulls across his lips.

Disgust grips my heart as I reach my hand out and grasp his. Pain radiates up my arm like venomous snakes slithering through my veins. I watch as black lines race up my forearm and I feel sharp spikes radiate into my neck. I clench my teeth and rip my hand out of his.

Tyros stands there with that sinister grin still splitting his face. I have no time to decipher what he has done to me, so I turn and reach for Enzo's arms again.

Enzo falls silent as he slumps over onto the ground next to me. *Crap.* Enzo is huge. There is no way I am getting him out of here by myself. I look around for something to roll him onto to drag him out of here, but we have no way of getting to the pillar with him in this condition. I'll deal with that once I get him outside.

I pick up his wrists and start to drag him towards the entrance. *Maker he is heavy.* Sweat beads on my forehead as I make my way out and into the sunlight.

As I drag Enzo through the dirt, I pray to the Maker to send us help.

"Get up you big oaf! Come on, Enzo! Please wake up. I can't drag your big behind all the way back to Citrine."

I look up, and standing at the entrance to the palace is Tyros. He leans against the frame of the door and crosses his arms and one ankle over the other. Even if he had offered to help me get Enzo outside, I would never accept anything from him.

"I'll see you soon, daughter. Don't forget our deal."

"Go to hell, Tyros. I will *never* come back here."

"We shall see." Tyros stands there, watching me struggle to pull Enzo to safety. Anger boils in my chest.

The sound of beating wings fill the air around me and dust kicks up as over a dozen sphinx land around us. Some of the

SunSpark Flying Legion members stand guard as Gunnar yells directions at them.

"Jade! Enzo!" Liliana jumps off Molly and runs over to us. She throws her arms around my neck in a quick embrace.

"Maker am I happy to see you! How did you know—" I start.

"No time to explain! Let's get out of here." She points to the entrance of the palace and The Kalari begin emerging, weapons drawn. Clearly our presence here is no longer welcome.

"Gunnar, I need help. I can't lift him on my own." He comes to my side and loops an arm around Enzo, hoisting him up and taking most of his weight. I loop my arm around his back and help Gunnar guide him over to one of the sphinx.

Gunnar lays him across the back of one and I climb on behind him. We shoot into the sky as the others mount their sphinx and join us. I look down at the island below and something pulls at my heart.

The Kalari are nothing more than small dots now staring up at us as we make our way back to Olyrium. I hold onto Enzo to make sure he doesn't fall off as we soar through the sky.

I let my mind drift off to my conversations with Tyros during my stay. He said I could have real powers. If he is my father, I must have some ability, right? When we get back to Citrine I will have to do some more research on half-magic offspring.

If I do have powers, I certainly don't need him to help me access them. I will figure that out all on my own, just like I have everything else.

Enzo and the others, they are my family, and the only way I am ever going back to Tyros is on my death bed. He deserves nothing from me and I want nothing from him.

Blood isn't what makes you family, it's actions, and he has shown me no reason as to why he deserves to be in my life. If he wants me, he can come get me in *my* home.

I stroke Enzo's hair through my fingers as we fly over the ocean. I stare down at the pillar when we cross into Twilight and are shrouded in darkness. We need to bring that pillar down. We have been so focused on bringing back Aliyah and finding the heir we have lost sight of what really matters. *Protecting Olyrium.* Aramot may have repaired the pillar, but we destroyed it once and we can do it again.

It occurs to me that the pillar was above ground, but there wasn't a single fae in sight to hold it up. How did Aramot manage that? Another question on the never ending list.

I start making a plan in my head of all the things that need to be done. Our problems are piling up before us and we have not a single solution to any of them. It's high time we regroup and refocus. Liliana and Gunnar flank my position in the sky.

"How did you know to come to the Banished Kingdom?" I yell as the wind whips around us at brutal speed.

"We were visiting with Kaleron when a messenger came in with a report from the SunSpark Flying Legion saying on their recent round, there seemed to be a disturbance on the island. It seemed The Kalari were gathering near the pillar to bridge into

Twilight or so they suspect. We knew you were here, so we left right away, and thank the Maker we did," Liliana calls over the space between us.

"Did Tyros say anything about sending his troops over?" Gunnar asks.

"What? No. Why would he tell me anything? It isn't like he shares his plans with me!"

"Whoa. Defensive much? Calm down, Jade. I just meant, you were there. I figured maybe you overheard something or he pulls a classic villain move and monologued his whole plan to you about destroying Olyrium." Gunnar laughs, but I can see the hint of questioning in his eyes.

"I don't know anything about his plans. If I did, I would share them with you." I avert my gaze and shift to Enzo's back rising and falling in a steady pattern.

I feel Liliana watching me, but I don't have the heart to look at her. I know I'm not telling them the full version about my conversations with Tyros. Maybe I do owe them the truth about my parentage, but in the end, Tyros is not my father in the way that counts, so the less people who know the better.

I try to calm the pressure in my chest so Liliana does not pick up on my unease. When I finally risk a glance at her, her eyes are locked on me and her eyebrows pull together in question.

"What in the hell happened back there?" Gunnar yells over the wind. The fire in his hand illuminates a small circle around us casting out the darkness of Twilight's atmosphere. I swing my eyes away from Liliana, thankful for the reprieve of her glare.

"Tyros' magic creates your worst nightmare. He used it against Enzo. It's bad, Gunnar. Enzo agreed to destroy an entire village for the chance of bringing Aliyah back. Tyros led him to believe the village was filled with murderers and criminals, but it wasn't until after he returned that we learned the truth of who lived there. Innocent people died because of Enzo's relentless pursuit of bringing Aliyah back. I had no way of stopping him. Gunnar, this has to stop. We all want Aliyah back, but this is getting out of hand. We've already lost Rory, and now an entire village, all for the cause of something that has never been done in the history of the realms. Enzo needs to be stopped."

I look down at Enzo who is still passed out in front of me. I stroke my hand in soothing circles over his back and a tear slips from my eye at the thought of how much he is hurting. This is going to kill him, but we need to stop looking for a way to bring her back. Too many people have been hurt. She wouldn't want to be brought back if this is the price of doing it.

I turn to Liliana and she just shakes her head in agreement as tears well up in her eyes. Without another word, she banks right and breaks away from Gunnar and I. Gunnar sighs, but nods in agreement as well.

The search for a way to bring Aliyah back is over. It's time we move on.

I stare at my hand placed on Enzo's back and note the darkening of my nail beds. My mind flashes back to the moment Tyros shook my hand and those black tendrils closed around my veins. I feel a headache start to form behind my eyes and something thick and cool drips onto my hand.

I look up to the sky to see if clouds hang over us ready to unleash their raindrops, but the stars shine brightly and the moon is full and bright. I tip my hand to let the moon's light illuminate my skin.

Three black drops run down my hand and I feel a droplet on the tip of my nose. I touch my fingers to the liquid and find my fingernails are not the only thing turning black. Whatever Tyros put in me, it is taking hold fast. I just hope he isn't also the cure.

Chapter 32

LILIANA

"Duncan?!" I call, running through the front doors of the palace. "Duncan! Where are you?"

"Bring Enzo to his room and call for the healer in Korin who tended to Aliyah. He is the only one Enzo would trust to treat him," Gunnar says coming in behind me.

"You good if I—"

"Yes. Go. Find Duncan. And Lil," he starts.

"Yeah?" I smile back.

"Good luck. I hope he chooses you like you've so clearly chosen him." Gunnar gives me a soft smile before turning back to show the legion the direction of Enzo's room.

Joy erupts in my heart of being back here with Duncan. Hopefully he took time to consider what I wrote to him in my note. I'm crossing all of my fingers and toes, and saying every prayer to the Maker above, that he says yes. I run down the hallway to our room and push open the door. *Empty.*

I make my way to the training fields and find some of the recruits out practicing their sparing.

"Hey! Have you seen Duncan?" I ask them.

"No ma'am!" one of them calls back. *Hmm.* Where would he be?

I walk through the library doors and find him standing in front of the window, oblivious to the fact that someone has entered. I take this opportunity to try and sneak up on him. I push to my tip toes and be careful not to step on any creaky floorboards. As I approach him from behind, I leap at the last minute and wrap my legs around his waist and throw my arms around his neck, placing kisses to both his cheeks from behind.

"Hey shadow! Did you miss me?"

"Hey Liliana." His tone is somber and worry pulls at my senses. I try to reach out to his emotions, but find them muddled with confusion, sadness, and nervousness.

"What happened? Is everything okay?" I ask.

"Why don't you sit down?"

"Noooo, why don't you tell me what happened?"

"Lil—"

"Duncan. What's going on?" My tone is firm. I don't want to sit, I just want him to tell me what is going on.

"I've made a decision."

My heart beats a thousand times per minute waiting to see what he is going to say next.

"Twilight needs a king. You believe I would make a good king. I think it's time I started believing in myself. I'm going to take the throne."

"Duncan! That's wonderful! I'm sure it will be an adjustment for me going from constant sunshine to constant darkness, but hey, upside is that I won't have to wear sun lotion any longer! I guess there goes my plan for ever being tan! Maybe we can get some nice sunshine colored lamps to signal different parts of the day! Oh Duncan you are going to make such a good king! Truly I am so proud of you! I really think this is going to be good for us! I think—"

He holds his hand up to silence my ramblings. He pulls the note I wrote him before I left from his pocket.

"Sunshine. I can't ever let you be used as a weapon against me. I'm not strong enough to choose my kingdom if the choice ever came down to you, or them. I will become king, if you go back to SunSpark." His eyes meet mine and sadness washes off him, drowning me in his woe.

"But— but, I was just in SunSpark. There is nothing for me there. I want to be here. I want to be with you."

"If you truly wish me to be king, you will go back to SunSpark...permanently. You'll be safe there. Away from the fighting. Away from the war. Away from the Banished King."

"What are you saying? You want me to just...leave? But this is my home. This is my— This is my family."

"Your home is in SunSpark."

"No. You promised. You promised me I could always stay by your side! You promised!" Tears well up in my eyes.

"I can't do this Liliana. I can't be your Soul Bonded. I can't be— *We* can't be."

"Why?! Why are you doing this?! You said forever!"

"I'm doing this *for* you, Liliana. It wouldn't have worked out in the end anyways."

"No! You're doing this for you! You're taking the easy way out! You don't get to just decide what is best for me! You don't get to do that! You know I want you to become king! You know I would have you choose your people over me any day because that is what it means to be a ruler! This isn't a choice, Duncan!"

"I'm sorry, Lil."

"Bull! If you were sorry then you wouldn't be doing this!"

"I wish it could be different, but—"

"It can be different! You are making the choice for me, Duncan. It could be different if you let it be, but you are letting fear cloud your judgement! Look at everything that's happened! Enzo lost Aliyah. Gunnar lost Saraphena...twice! If anything, it should show you life is precious and we should take every moment to be happy that we can! Don't pretend like you are doing this for me, Duncan. You are doing this because you are scared!"

"Of course I'm scared!" Duncan's voice booms throughout the room. "I'm terrified, Lil! I can't lose you! I *won't* lose you! Everything you just said is the reason why I need to keep you safe!"

"How am I not safest with you?!"

"I am going to war, Lil! *War!*"

"I know! Let me go with you! Let me fight *with* you, not against you! If I am to die, I want to die with you by my side, knowing that we fought to save people! To save *your* people and my people! I have fought by your side before, why is this any different?"

"You will be safe in SunSpark. They have an army at the ready and the SunSpark Flying Legion to take you away somewhere safe if the situation calls for it. I can't provide that for you!"

"I'm not asking you to provide me an escape! I'm asking you to believe in us! To believe we can both make it out of this war together! Why don't you believe in us?"

"I believe in what I know and what I know is that SunSpark is the safest place for you to be."

"Fine. Let's say I go to SunSpark. I live through the war. You live through the war. Why can't we be together now and after the war?"

"I— Lil, I—"

"Exactly. *Fear.* You're letting fear influence your judgement. Fear has taken up so much room in your heart there isn't room for me anymore. Well guess what Duncan, you go be king. Be the greatest king that has ever ruled Twilight. Leave me behind. That's all *fine.* But do *not* expect me to stand back and watch everyone I care about go off to a war and risk their lives while I sit pretty in my palace. We may not be together, but this," I wave my arms around the room. "This is my home. *This* is my family. Like it or not, I am staying."

"Liliana, no you need to—"

"No Duncan. You listen here and you listen close, because I am only going to say this once. I love you. I will *always* love you, but you lost the right to tell me what I can and can't do with my life the moment you decided you no longer had room for me in your life. *I* rule my own life. Not you. Not Gunnar. Not General-freaking-Enzo. *ME.* I'm choosing to stay and to fight for my family. To fight for the place Aliyah called *home.* When you decide to get your head out of your backside, come find me. Until then, do not stand in my way."

As I make my way out of the library, all the anger dissipates from my body and is replaced with anguish. I walk down the hallway and stop in front of our room. I open the door and look at the bed we shared. Storming in, I grab my clothes out of the dresser and throw them into a bag. I make my way to a spare room, as far away from Duncan's as I can get, and throw open the door. The moment it shuts, the flood gates of my heart open and even my own ability cannot control what I am feeling. For the first time in a long time, I let myself feel every painstaking emotion that comes with it.

Chapter 33

SARAPHENA

E nzo's breath is steady as he inhales and exhales. He hasn't opened his eyes since he returned from the Banished Kingdom. After Jade filled us in on what happened with Tyros, the only conclusion I can come to is that Enzo's brain finally cracked.

"How long do you think he is going to be out for?" Duncan's voice is chipped as he addresses the healer. Thankfully the healer had arrived quickly, given the dire circumstances.

"I'm not exactly sure. It seems as though his physical body is not harmed, and he has no internal wounds. I cannot seem to find what would be causing this catatonic behavior." The healer's confused look does not bring me any comfort.

"He's depressed." Liliana's voice is somber as she enters Enzo's room. When I look back at her, I see her flick her eyes to Duncan before quickly averting them. He watches her as she walks into the room and kneels by Enzo's side. She lays her hand on his chest and her eyebrows pull together in concentration.

Fat, wet tears start to pour from Liliana's eyes and her chin quivers before she sucks in her bottom lip to bite it.

"Liliana, enough—" Duncan starts. He takes a step towards her and starts to reach out his arm.

Liliana's eyes flash open with a wave of anger as she looks at Duncan. "Don't you dare." Her eyes close again as she continues to use her power. Enzo's shirt soaks up Liliana's tears as she continues to sob, pulling off Enzo's turmoil.

His eyes open and he looks around the room. He doesn't utter a word to the rest of us, but instead turns and pulls Liliana's arm into his grasp.

"Thank you, but this is my pain that I must bear. Do not take my emotions on yourself ever again. Is that understood?" Enzo's voice is barely above a whisper.

Liliana nods her head and scoots off the bed. She exits the room without a glance at Duncan or anyone else.

Well that's definitely changed since her arrival. I push the thought down my bond with Gunnar.

Liliana asked Duncan to be her Soul Bonded since they will never be mated. Based on her chilly demeanor, I assume he did not wish to bond with her.

"Stop speaking into each other's minds as if I am not here," Duncan scolds. "Now is not the time and I can see the way your eyes shift back and forth between us."

I quickly glance at Gunnar before averting my gaze completely. Turning back to Enzo, he only lies there staring at the ceiling of his bedroom. A few loose tears drip from the corners of his eyes.

"Leave me." His voice is hoarse.

"Enzo, please let us help. What happened to you out there? We know what Jade has said, but we want to hear it from you." Gunnar sits on the edge of Enzo's bed, but makes no move to comfort his friend.

"Everything happened. I don't want to see anyone right now. Leave." Enzo can't even make eye contact with us. He rolls over onto his side, his back facing us. The healer pulls a few small vials from his bag and sets them on the bedside table.

"To help with whatever ails him. Call me if he needs anything. I will be back in Korin." The healer exits, leaving Duncan, Gunnar, Jade, and myself. I motion my head towards the door and the rest of them follow me out. I move to shut the door and take one last glance at Enzo. The vials go flying across the room and shatter on the wall opposite of the bed. I shake my head and click the door shut.

"What do we do?" Duncan asks.

"Not here." Jade leads us down the hall into the library and shuts the doors behind us. We all take a seat on the furniture in front of the fireplace. A heavy silence falls over us, no one daring to speak first.

"I think we should consider—"

"We need to let her go—"

Jade and I speak at the same time, knowing what needs to be said, but never wanting to say it out loud.

"Enzo won't allow it. You know he won't. He will never give up on the chance at finding a way to bring her back." Duncan sighs. "Liliana should be here for this. Aliyah was important to her and we may need to help managing Enzo's emotions when we break the news." Duncan disappears from his seat in an instant.

Each of us sit and stare into the fire, mesmerized by the flames. Gunnar leans over to me and whispers into my ear. "If I knew you were so bewitched by fire, I would have a flame lit by my palm at all times so your eyes would always be focused on me."

I know his tone is meant to lighten the somber mood hanging over us, but the weight of our situation is too heavy. I simply smile and rest my head on his shoulder as we wait for Duncan and Liliana to come back. I hear their arguing before they even make it into the room.

"Don't touch me. I'm walking! See! One foot in front of the other! I'm moving as fast as I can!" Liliana's voice is clipped.

"I'm not touching you!"

"Yes you are! Your hand is right there!"

"My hand is *hovering* behind you to make sure you keep up, but I am not touching you!"

"I can feel the heat radiating off your hand onto my back, which means you are touching me because it's your hand's heat I feel!"

"Liliana that is completely ridiculous! I could have just teleported us here, but instead I allowed you to walk."

"*Allowed me?* You seem to be *allowing* me to do a lot lately! I don't need your freaking permission to—"

Duncan and Liliana appear on the couch before us. The look of anger on Liliana's face is palpable as she turns and connects her fist with Duncan's nose. She flies on top of him and starts punching him in his chest and face. Duncan simply places his hands on her hips and takes each punch without fighting back.

Jade's face is in complete shock as she watches the situation unfold. Gunnar sits there and smiles before punching his own fist in the air with each hit Liliana lands. I'm not sure if I should do something, or let it play out. Clearly she is working through something with him because I don't think this is some sort of foreplay.

"You bastard! I said not to touch me! You promised me! You—" Liliana slows her punches when she notices that Duncan isn't fighting back.

"Lil, is everything okay?" I ask.

Liliana shifts off Duncan's lap and moves to the chair across the circle from him.

"Ask him." She nods at Duncan. "He apparently speaks for me now."

"Sunshine—" Duncan starts. She cuts him a glare. "Liliana. I'm doing what I think is best for you, for everyone."

Liliana only crosses her arms and turns her head away from his gaze. She points her nose up in the air and huffs.

"Liliana and I broke up. I've decided to take the throne in Twilight and I cannot have her by my side."

A blast of fire comes flying across the room and hits Duncan in the face. Duncan sits there completely impassive as the fire dissipates around him. "I deserved that."

"Yeah, you did," Gunnar and Liliana say in unison.

"Look this isn't getting us anywhere right now. Duncan, maybe just stop touching Liliana for a while and give her the space she needs. Lil, you need to keep your strength up right now. We might need you to help with Enzo and that is going to be a lot to take on. Feel what you need to feel with your emotions. Don't try to shove them down or use your power to snuff them out. We need you at full capacity. Jade, we need to know everything that happened in the Banished Kingdom. Gunnar, don't encourage."

How is it possible that I am the only one left with any sense around here? "Now, updates everyone. Any knowledge you have, spill it now."

"My mother had the torn out pages from the kings diary in Twilight." Liliana huffs out a breath as the information settles over the group.

"I'm sorry, what?" Duncan cuts her a look. Liliana doesn't even acknowledge him. "Lil, how did your mother have the pages?" he asks. He's met with silence. "Maker, are you seriously not going to speak to me?"

"Saraphena, can you please tell Duncan I don't know how my mother got the pages because she refused to tell me how she obtained them? Her exact explanation was *"royal business is royal business.""*

"Seriously, Lil!" Duncan huffs.

"I'm sorry, did you all hear something?" Lil looks around as if the Maker himself is speaking in the room with us.

"Real mature, Lil," Gunnar laughs. "Look our mother isn't one to share her secrets. She only said that Twilight was better off without the knowledge the diary held and that she kept them so they didn't fall into the wrong hands."

"Well, what did they say?" I ask.

"I would be happy to show them to you, however, *someone* brought me here against my will before I even had a chance to grab them."

"Oh for Maker's sake." Duncan rolls his eyes and stands before striding over to Liliana.

"Don't you dare! Duncan I swear to the Maker—"

Her voice is cut off as Duncan clasps her arm and they vanish into thin air. A few heartbeats pass before Duncan reappears in the room...without Liliana.

"Duncan, do you really think this is the best way to handle things with her?" Jade asks.

"I don't know *how* to handle anything with her apparently." Duncan runs his hands through his hair and lets out a long breath.

"Unbelievable, Duncan! You son of a—" Liliana comes crashing through the doors once more mumbling on about how Duncan disregards her wishes to not be touched and then teleported away, only to be left there followed by a string of words I swear I have never heard before.

"At least she is speaking to you again! I take that as progress," Gunnar winks. Duncan gives him a glare as he returns to his seat. Liliana slams the parchment down on the table and we each pick up a piece. The space quiets as we all read our entry of the diary.

Several beats pass before anyone dares to speak again.

"I don't know about anyone else's' page, but mine was rather bleak," Gunnar says. I take the page from his hand and quickly glance at the story detailed on the parchment.

"Are they all like this?" Jade asks.

"You mean are they all detailed stories about how you have to eat the heart of an innocent person in order to make a wish with the ring? I am going to assume yes by the blanched faces of everyone in the group."

"Gunnar this isn't a time for jokes. What these kings did—" I start.

"It's why the pages were torn out. Perhaps the ring was not lost, but hidden." Jade continues to shuffle through the pages, reading story after story as she speaks. "There are dozens of pages here, all detailing how the heart was harvested and which wishes were made from it. Some of these hearts were from...children."

"Why on earth would your mother have taken these?" Duncan asks.

"If I knew the answer to that question don't you think I would have told you by now!" Liliana's voice drips with distain speaking to him. Duncan's face is impassive as he locks eyes with Liliana in a stare down of the century.

"We can never show these to Enzo. After everything he has done to get Aliyah back, if we did find the ring, he would not hesitate to kill an innocent for her," Jade swallows.

"Agreed. In fact, these pages shouldn't even exist. If these fell into the wrong hands and the ring was ever found— Let's just say there are some who would not be deterred by the price of the wish." I pick up the pile of parchment and throw the entire stack into the fire.

"Imagine if my father had gotten his hands on the ring, or my brother, or worse...the Banished King. This knowledge dies with us. Are we clear?" Duncan says.

"Crystal. So the ring is out, the fallen star in general is out because the ring is made from the star. The Banished King has no ability to bring her back. We are completely out of options."

Gunnar sits back in his chair and runs a hand through his short hair, blowing a breath out of his nose.

"Who's going to be the one to tell Enzo it's time to move on?" I ask.

"Not it!" Gunnar blurts.

"Seriously, Gunnar? Dramatic much?" Liliana adds. "I'll do it. I can pull off his emotions as I tell him to hopefully lessen the fallout."

"Now isn't the time to tell him. He isn't in a place to handle this news and Liliana can't keep pulling him out of that pit. We have no idea how badly his mind is broken right now. There may not be a right time to tell him, but there is certainly a better time. For now, we should just support him and show him that there is a life after her death." I look around to the group to ensure we are all on the same page.

"Did anything else happen while you were in the Banished Kingdom?" Duncan looks to Jade for any more insight.

"Tyros caused Enzo to have hallucinations of Aliyah making him think she was back. It was horrible. This was right when he came back from murdering an entire village he thought was filled with criminals because Tyros tricked him. I think it was the final straw. I had no way of warning him it was a trap."

"You stayed with the Banished King while Enzo went to this village? Did Tyros share anything with you about his plans?" Duncan tips his head. Jade's eyes flash to Liliana and I note the slight hint of panic in her gaze.

"Yes. I stayed as collateral to make sure Enzo came back. Obviously it was all a trap. He didn't share anything with me while I was there. I mainly just stayed in my room."

"You had a room there? He didn't keep you in the dungeon or chained up with The Kalari?" Confusion pulls at my mind watching Jade's reaction to my question. She shifts uncomfortably in her seat and can't seem to settle.

"No. I think he just wanted some *living* company. Obviously his sad sack of a personality doesn't exactly bring in many friends." She tries to pass off a laugh, but I can hear the nervousness in her tone. Something else happened on that island, and I'm going to figure out what.

PART IV: DEPRESSION

Chapter 34

JADE

A chill racks my body as I wake. It's still night, but the cool air coming from my open window sends a shiver down my spine. I pull myself out of bed and close the window. A headache burns behind my eyes. I feel something drip from my nose onto my nightgown. Wiping it away, I stare at the black ooze that now coats my hand. I push my other hand under my nose and more goop drips to the floor. I head out of my room to try and find some bandages to stop the flow. Passing Enzo's room, I hear the screams that haunt these halls with each passing night. It's been over a week now since he came back from the Banished Kingdom more broken than when he left.

"Aliyah! Aliyah! Come back to me! Aliyah! Please don't leave me! Please!" Enzo screams. I hear the crashing of things in his room. At night his powers have been taking over when he dreams of her. We have tried to remove most of the furniture, but he always manages to find something to break. I wish he would just move on from her. I loved Aliyah and while we had our differences, we made it work. I know that Aliyah promised to never hurt Enzo, but I know she had no intention of dying that day either.

Something drips down the back of my throat and on a cough, black ooze shoots from my throat and into my hand. I wipe it on my nightgown and as I feel the thick membrane slide down my throat again, I swallow it down. It burns like acid in my throat and I try to hold off a gag. Enzo needs me right now. I don't have time to be sick.

Cracking open Enzo's door, a plate comes flying towards my head. Dodging out of the way, it crashes against the opposite wall in the hallway. I look around the room and every window is shattered and the washroom door is blown to pieces. Enzo's sheets are ripped into ribbons as his hands scramble to grasp something to hold onto. His eyes are still closed and pieces of wood float in the air before flying into the wall.

I walk over to the side of the bed, and repeat what I do every night I have heard his screams since first arriving in Citrine all those months ago.

"Shhh. Enzo, it's okay. I'm here. It's me, Aliyah. I've got you. I'm here."

The room calms around me and Enzo's rapid breathing slows to deep inhales. He never wakes up when I do this, and thank the Maker for it, because he needs rest.

"Aliyah, my dove. I thought I lost you forever."

He wraps his arms around my waist and lays his head in my lap. I stroke my fingers through his hair and hum a calming tune.

Before long, he is in a deep sleep. A tear slips off my cheek. I don't know how much longer I can keep doing this.

I shift out from under Enzo. As I head for the door, I look back and see him peacefully sleeping again. I make my way down the hallway, headed for the infirmary. With each step my muscles burn in my legs. I reach out my hand to steady myself on the wall. It's been harder and harder to breathe recently, but I thought it was just anxiety over Enzo's condition.

My stomach churns as I round the corner to the next hallway. My legs feel like the ooze now pouring from my nose; thick and slow. My slippers must be made of lead because each step is harder than the last. As I reach the infirmary door, I turn and vomit on the floor. Thick, black strings hang from my mouth that connect to the puddle of throw up on the floor.

I push open the door and stagger over to the shelves filled with vials and tonics hoping to find what I need. I try to read the labels, but my vision blurs and refocuses within seconds. I blink to clear away the haze, but it returns tenfold. I feel the thick ooze creeping up my throat once more.

"You're okay. You're okay. You got this. You're not going to get sick. You're not going to—" Chunks of black goop spurt out over the vials before me and slide to the floor with a *splat*. The sight of it makes me want to yack again, but I try to swallow it down.

"Jade?" Liliana comes up behind me and loops her arm around my waist as my knees give out.

"I don't know what's happening, Lil."

"*Shhhh.* You're okay. I'm here now. What were you looking for in here?" She begins sifting through the contents of the shelf while holding me close to her side.

"It's Tyros. He did this to me."

"What? What do you mean?"

"He— He made me shake on it. He held out his hand and when I touched it these black snakes slithered up through my veins."

"Crap. We need to get you to bed. I'll start researching right away for any cure. Don't worry. We will figure this out." Liliana shuffles me out the door and back to my room. She helps me change out of my now black stained nightgown and into something clean. A shiny metal bucket sits next to my bedside table. I feel so weak.

"Lil—"

"Yeah?"

"I don't want to close my eyes. What if they never open again? Enzo needs me. He needs me to hold onto what is left of his sanity."

"You just need to focus on getting better right now. We will take care of Enzo. I'm just going to grab some books from the library and I will come straight back here. I promise I won't let you die." She gives me a soft smile and it's the last thing I see before my eyes slip shut and the black ooze clouding my brain drowns me in its abyss.

Chapter 35

ENZO

*T*he field of wildflowers and wheat that used to grow bright and beautiful are now burned to ash. Embers of the burnt field flick up into the air and dark clouds loom overhead. I visit this place too many times, yet each night I can't help but return. There in the distance is the source of my torture. A long tattered dress blows with the gusts of ash that fly around her. She starts running towards me.

"Enzo! Oh my Maker, Enzo, please. You have to help me!" Even though she stands right in front of me, her voice sounds like a distant call that I have to strain to hear.

"Stop mocking me!" I scream back. "Leave! Just go! Whatever vile creature you are that plagues my dreams, enough with this torment! Aliyah is dead! I watched her die. I held her in my arms as she took her last breath! Screw you for showing me her face once more."

The thing before me bursts into tears and starts banging on the barrier between us. "Enzo please! Come back! I need you!"

I turn my back on her, but the scenery that appears in front of me is not the field of wildflowers. I snap my head back to see if the witch is still there, but she is no where in sight. Turning back to the vision before me, I know what part comes next. I walk forwards through the ashen field I stood on not too long ago.

I see Aliyah standing in the distance, but this is not the Aliyah in the tattered dress. No, this Aliyah stands in her leather pants and tunic, ripped and stained with her blood. She smiles at me and I hear her in my head "Enzo, I—". Just like that day on the battle field, I can do nothing to save her. I race forward right as the sword pierces through her chest.

"No!" I scream. I've almost reached her as she drops to her knees. Catching her in my arms, I hold my hands to her chest to stop the bleeding. It's too much. There is too much blood. I look down and it coats my hands. It pools beneath her and gushes out of her mouth. Five figures appear behind me.

"How could you?!" yells Saraphena.

"You failed her, Enzo!" shouts Duncan.

"Even now you could not save her," screams Liliana.

"You disgust me," spits Gunnar.

"You are what you always have been Enzo, a disappointment and a failure," Jade curses.

I look down to my little dove, so fragile in my arms. Her eyes are open and ridicule fills her voice.

"Why didn't you save me, Enzo? Why didn't you help me?"

I scream into the sky. Tears well in my eyes.

"I'm so sorry, Aliyah. I did fail you. I promised to protect you. Aliyah, come back to me! Please, come back to me!"

The vision fades and Aliyah disappears from my arms. The others vanish and the ashen field around me blooms into a beautiful forest.

"Shhh. Enzo, it's okay. I'm here. It's me, Aliyah. I've got you. I'm here." Aliyah lays down in the grass and I wrap my arms around her finally feeling at peace. She's safe. I knew she wasn't really dead. She's right here with me.

I open my eyes, and for a few brief moments, I feel at peace. I expect to turn and find Aliyah by my side, but reality comes crashing back in when I find the bed to be completely empty. My chest caves in at the reminder of my loss.

Pulling myself from the bed, I grab the half shattered bottle of amber sitting on my nightstand. I ignore the cuts on my mouth as I sip down the alcohol. Taking in the carnage that is my room, I can't seem to find a single crap to give about what I have destroyed.

Every day I wake up and repeat the same over and over. Wake. Drink. Sleep. Repeat. I can't even find the will to go through the basic motions of life. The recruits don't need me to train them. Gunnar and Jade don't need me to protect them like we did as children. Duncan has Liliana now, so the only other male who lost his love has been taken from me. Now, I truly am alone.

I move into the washroom and strip from my clothes. Walking into the stall, I let the water wash over me in hopes that it will also wash away my sorrow. I stare blankly at the wall. My mind is lost in time, floating in the alcohol induced haze. Even through the water pouring down on me, I feel the warm droplets of water escape my eyes. I want it to stop hurting. I want her back.

I fall to my knees with a crack on the stone. I lay my forehead on the stall floor and let the sobs come over me.

"ARGH!" I scream into the tile as I beat on the floor, shattering the tile beneath me. "Why? Why, Aliyah? Why did you have to come into my life? What was the point?! Maker, why did you let her come into my life just to take her away?"

My vision slacks and sounds of exploding tiles fill the air around me. Water shoots from the sides of the walls, bursting around the tiles I've shattered. I sit back against the wall amongst the carnage I've created. I pick up a shard of tile and grip it in my hand so hard that blood pools in my palm.

I lay my head back against the wall and close my eyes as I take the shard of tile and drag it up the center of my arm. Blood swirls with the water heading towards the drain. I feel nothing. Not the sting of the cut, the healing of my skin, nothing. *Again.* The sound of my father's voice rings through my head. Another slice up my arm, skin splitting, blood pooling at the base of the shower. *Again.*

I need to silence this suffering, yet my body refuses to allow such an end. I watch my skin knit back together as I push the shard deeper and deeper with each cut, praying this time my skin won't heal. Maybe with this new cut, my body will finally give up and let me join my dove in the afterlife. *Again. Again. Again.* My father's voice shreds through all other thoughts.

Enzo, you need to stay strong. Stay strong for me. Aliyah's voice cuts off the sound of my father's.

"How can I stay strong for you little dove? You ruined me."

"Enzo!" Gunnar comes running into the shower still in his clothes. Duncan slides into the washroom a moment later, almost slipping on the floor as water pours into the room.

"Enzo, stop." Duncan grabs the shard from my hand and sits down next to me. Gunnar pulls me into an embrace which I am too exhausted to return. I feel Duncan's hand rest on my shoulder as my brothers and I sit on the cold tile of the washroom together. I hang my head on Gunnar's shoulder and let the tears pour from my eyes.

"Enzo, no matter how bad things get, Aliyah wouldn't want this for you. She needs you to keep going."

"Then I will fail her once more."

"No Enzo, she would never think that you failed her. She knows you did everything you could. She loved you, Enzo."

"And I loved her. I loved her Gunnar. And I didn't say it. Why didn't I say it?"

"Aliyah knew you loved her. It isn't always about the words you say, but how you show love. You loved her more fiercely than anyone else in her life. That is what she will remember in the afterlife." Gunnar's words sting at the reminder she is no longer here. A broken sob slips from my lips as my heart shatters once more.

"Shhhh. We've got you, brother. We've got you, now." Duncan sits beside me, his soaked clothes cool to the touch, but he doesn't let me go. Neither of them do.

My brothers hold me for what feels like forever. The water around us has stopped pouring, and all that is left is the wreckage of my washroom and my broken heart.

Chapter 36

LILIANA

My feet rest on the end of Jade's bed with several large tomes scattered at my feet and over every surface available. It's been three days since Jade came clean about what Tyros did to her. How had I not noticed she was sick before? I glance up from my tome to see Jade's pale face contorted in pain and sweat droplets lining her forehead. Her fists clench the sheets around her and panicked moans come from her increasingly black lips. Setting the tome aside, I stand and grab the cloth and bowl filled with cool water.

"Hey now, you're alright," I coo. I dip the cloth into the bowl and lay it across her forehead. The fever set in yesterday and we haven't been able to find a way to keep her temperature down since. Jade barely opens her eyes anymore saying that the sunlight is too bright for her. That was the last thing she said before slipping into the coma. The room is shrouded in darkness from the thick heavy curtains over the windows, but even the candle light seems to be too harsh on her eyes. I look to her fingers as lay limp by her sides. Her nail beds have turned completely black and lightning shaped black lines continue to creep up her arm. I have found nothing in any of these books that could tell me what this might be. Tyros is a master of spells, along with his power, so I wouldn't be surprised if he concocted a special curse just for Jade.

"How is she?" Duncan's voice grates on my ears and my mood instantly sours.

"Getting worse."

"I'm assuming you haven't found anything on the spell?"

"If I had, I would have found a way to cure her already." Duncan puts up his hands in surrender. A small book is in his right hand as he makes his way to the edge of the bed. I watch him with disgust, but throw out my power to feel his emotions. Anguish claws at my mind and guilt that isn't mine sits heavy in my chest. Worry slams into me as Duncan takes in Jade's features.

"Do you mind if I sit with her for a while?" Duncan points to the bed, but doesn't sit as he waits for my permission.

"Fine. I think she might like the change in company anyway."

"No, please stay."

I find my way back to my chair and prop my feet up on the edge of the bed. I pick up a new tome and flip to the section on ancient spells. I try to read the lines on the page, but I can't seem to pull my focus together with Duncan in the room. I want to hate him. Every fiber of my being is screaming at me to fight for him with everything I have, but I know my worth. Duncan needs to choose me because he wants to, not because I force him too. I just pray to the Maker he doesn't wait too long.

"The recruits are really coming along. I have them running some drills in the yard together as we speak. Are we having a reading party?" Gunnar knocks on the door as he enters with Saraphena in tow.

"Just trying to spend some time with her," Duncan says. Gunnar and Saraphena sit down on the couch to the right of Jade's bed. Saraphena lays her head in Gunnar's lap and kicks her feet over the arm of the couch.

"Read to us, Duncan. I could use a good story." Gunnar runs his hands through Saraphena's hair and I overt my eyes, forcing myself to look at Duncan instead.

"What book is that?" I ask.

"It's silly, but this is one of the books my mother used to read to me when I was a child. When I would get sick she would sit with me on the bed and read me these absurd stories. I thought maybe hearing a childhood tale would be soothing to her."

Tears prick in my eyes as I feel love pouring off of Duncan. This is the only family he has left and if we can't find a cure for Jade, he will lose her too. Duncan opens the small book in his lap and brings one of the candles closer to illuminate the pages. He begins a story about a young girl who is poisoned by her evil twin sister.

"Maker Duncan! A little too close to home right now don't you think!" Duncan flashes a glare to Gunnar who interrupted his story.

"It's a children's book Gunnar, it always has a happy ending. If anything, this should give her hope!"

"Just keep reading, Duncan. I want to hear the end." Saraphena slaps her hand over Gunnar's mouth before he has a chance to protest.

"He always interrupted stories when we were children, too. He liked to pick apart the story line and point out all the things that didn't make sense." I laugh to myself at the memory of Kaleron, Gunnar, and I all piled in bed together listening to stories much like this one.

Duncan continues reading. "...she lay there in a pile of red rose petals with her lips cold as ice. Her true love loomed over her, confident that his love for her would be enough to bring her back from sudden death. He leaned down and placed a soft kiss to her lips and a bright golden light burst between them. The girls eyelashes flickered for a moment before opening. The prince knew his love for the girl could conquer any curse. They all lived happily ever after. The end."

"See this is exactly what I mean! *True love's kiss* my butt! That would never work in real life! It isn't a realistic ending!" Gunnar waves his hands around the room as if that will help prove his point.

"Gunnar *shut up!* It doesn't have to be realistic! It is just a fun story! If anything, I *wish* true love's kiss was the answer to cure Jade! That would make my job so much easier. I could stop reading these tomes and get back to more important things!" I roll my eyes at my brother.

"And here I thought I was your true love?" Saraphena winks at Gunnar.

"Oh baby, no you are! But the only magic in our kisses are the—"

Jade stirs in her sleep and her panicked moans return. Thankfully I don't have to hear whatever inappropriate joke my brother was about to make.

"Alright, everyone out. She needs rest, not your bickering." Saraphena rises, taking Gunnar's hand and leading him from the room. She glances back at me and tips her head in the direction of Duncan. I roll my eyes at her, but she says more with her eyes than she does with words. They say, *talk to him Liliana, you idiot. Get him to see reason, Liliana. Try again, Liliana.* On and on the list of things her eyes might be saying run through my mind. She closes the door behind her and leaves me with a man I wish to hate, but can't.

"Do you think it's possible?" Duncan's eyes are locked on Jade, but I know he is speaking to me.

"Do I think what is possible?"

"That love can conquer all."

Tingles spark in my nose and a sting slices behind my eyes. *Don't cry.* "I used to think so."

"What changed?"

"You did."

Duncan's gaze shifts down and I swear I see a tear drip onto the bed sheet beneath him. "I love you, sun— Liliana. I meant what I said in my vow to you. My heart is yours, forever."

My heart is breaking in two all over again. "Then choose me. Right here, right now. Choose *me*, shadow." His eyes finally meet mine and I see the unshed tears lining his eyes. I reach out my power and I feel his love crashing over me like waves in a raging sea. But I also feel his hesitation. The conflict he feels is why I know he won't choose me. He swallows hard and the tattooed wings around his throat bob and constrict with the motion.

His black hair falls in front of his face, shielding his eyes from me as he stands from the bed. My heart is beating so hard in my chest I swear I am going to crack a rib. He comes around the bed and stands toe-to–toe with me. I stare down at his black leather shoes and the small puddle forming on the ground from the cloth that drips in my hand. I fear if I move this spell between us will be broken and I will lose him all over again. *Please choose me. Just choose me.*

Duncan's large, calloused hand finds my chin as he pulls my eyes up to meet his. I feel it then. Devotion fills my lungs and it is a richer feeling than any amount oxygen could provide. I'm captivated by his eyes as if I look hard enough I could see straight into his soul. It feels as though an eon has passed between us when his mouth finally opens.

"I wish we never met that day in SunSpark."

My chest cracks open and every hope and dream spills onto the floor along with the pieces of my broken heart. Duncan moves his hand to the back of my neck and places a kiss to my forehead before turning and leaving. When I'm certain he is gone, I fall to my knees and clutch my chest. I thought there was hope. I thought he would come to his senses if I just gave him space and time. How could I have been so wrong? I kneel on the floor clutching my chest, but the tears never come. It is as if the well of sadness has gone dry. This build up of emotions in my lungs sits heavy on my chest. I feel it crushing me with each strained breath. My ribs won't expand enough to get air in.

Turn it off, Lil. Turn it all off. My emotions go up in flames in my mind. Every ounce of hate, every molecule of love, burned away and turned to ash. If the choice is between feeling everything and feeling nothing, I will choose the latter. To feel nothing means feeling safe. *Protected.* Emptiness is predictable. Nothing can hurt you when there is nothing left to harm. This is where I will exist now. In the spaces between my cracked heart; cold and lifeless. The stories I was told as a child were a lie. No one is coming to save me. There is no such thing as happily ever after. My brother was right.

True love doesn't exist.

Chapter 37

JADE

I feel the thrum of blood coursing through my veins as I creep down the hallway to where Enzo was always taken. I hear the screams reverberating off the walls the closer I get to the torture chambers. I lay my hand on the cool wooden door and contemplate my actions. If I do this, Enzo may never forgive me, but if I don't I could lose him forever to the darkness his father continues to thrust upon him. Enzo will thank me one day.

I push open the door to the chamber and my blood runs cold. The sight before me is not what I expected to find. Blood coats the floor in pools around Enzo's knees. Four fae criminals lay slumped over on the floor, their necks bent at an odd angle. Enzo is on his knees before his father, a look of shock on his face when he sees me standing in the doorway.

"Leave, Jade. Please." Enzo's voice breaks on his plea, but I've come to far to turn back now. Pulling a blade from my holster, I grip it painfully tight as my nerves light up all over my body.

"You don't want to do this child." The general grips the hair on Enzo's head with force and pulls a blade of his own, pointing the

tip at the bottom of Enzo's chin. Something clatters to the ground beside him and I note the bloody blade. Enzo could have used that to kill his father, yet he doesn't even attempt to get up.

"Enzo, come with me. Leave with me now." I keep my eyes trained on General Felix. Enzo makes no effort to get up. He bests his father in both size and strength. I don't understand why he can't end this for himself.

"He won't be going anywhere with you. You are a plague to him, little girl. You corrupt his mind with thoughts of love and compassion, yet the world will show him none of those things. He is built to be a warrior, not someone to be loved. Enzo has no room for love in his life for what he needs to become. You will only stand in his way."

My restraint snaps at the general's words and I sprint towards him, knife at the ready. He shoves Enzo away from him and turns to me, bracing for a fight. My feet lift from the ground beneath me as that invisible hand around my neck tightens. I claw at my throat trying to get air in, but it's no use.

My vision slacks and dark spots block out the room around me. My legs kick the air as panic ensues. At least I'll die knowing I tried to help the man I love.

"Father, stop!" Enzo stands beside his father, resting his hand on the general's forearm. "Let me. This is what you trained me to do. If she is to die, let it be by my hand. Let me eliminate her from my life once and for all. If you let me do this, I promise you

I will never fail you again. I can be the weapon you want me to be, I swear it."

I hear the icy tone in his voice, but when Enzo's eyes meet mine, all I see is regret. I collapse onto the floor and suck in oxygen as fast as I can. General Felix may be shorter than Enzo, but his rage towers over us all.

"You do this and I might just finally be proud of you. Fail me and I will line up a hundred fae for you to spend hours slaughtering until you get it through your mind that you are a monster. Understood?"

"I understand father. I won't let you down."

Enzo turns to me as I feel the tears well up in my eyes. "It's okay, Enzo. Do what you need to do. I will know that I died helping the man I love and that I died with honor for protecting my family. If this is what must be done to set you free, then so be it."

Enzo nods his head just once and takes a deep breath. I see the smirk on his father's face as he waits for his son to kill me. I close my eyes and prepare for the end. Memories of my time here with Enzo and Gunnar flash through my mind. I never thought I would find happiness here, but now I know what true family feels like. If I had more time, I would stay with them until the end of my days.

"Jade, run!" Enzo's voice snaps me out of my memories and into the present. I flash my eyes open to find Enzo holding his father in place with his powers, barely holding him back. "Run, Jade! Just go!"

Time seems to move in slow motion as I debate my next move. This might be my only chance to set Enzo free once and for all. I was willing to die for Enzo, but I am also willing to kill for him. I grab my knife and with all my strength I launch it into the air. I watch it turn over itself, flying towards my target. A spurt of blood shoots out as my knife embeds into the eye of my enemy.

Enzo's hold on his father drops. General Felix collapses to the floor in a heap of loose limbs. Blood pours from the wound as Enzo tries to pull the knife free. The small hooks carved into the blade prevent it from being pulled out, never allowing the wound to close before my victim can die.

"Father! No, no, no! Jade how could you do this?!" Enzo's screams fill the chamber and slam into my chest.

"Enzo you're free now. You can finally stop torturing people. He's dead now. I saved you."

"He was my father! He was the only blood family I had left! You had no right to take him from me!"

"Enzo, I— I'm sorry. I thought—"

"You thought wrong! He was my father! Despite what he has done and despite who he has become, he was my father! I know that he loved me somewhere deep down! He wasn't always this man! He loved me! I will never forgive you for this Jade. Never!"

I slowly back out of the chamber, tears dripping down my face at his words. I hear them echoing off the stone walls as I close the door behind me.

"I will never forgive you, Jade! You had no right! You had no—"

Enzo's voice is finally out of earshot as I ascend the steps from the chambers. My mind is blank when I finally reach my room. There were two things lost in that room tonight; Enzo lost his father, and I lost the man I love.

SARAPHENA

Jade's body thrashes on the bed before me. I leap from the chair I had been sleeping in and make my way to the side of her bed. I pick up the bowl of cool water and cloth Liliana left. I dab the sweat beads off her forehead and say soothing words to help calm her spirit.

With each swipe of the cloth, her nightmare dissipates. I inspect her arm and note the black lines creeping up her body, closer and closer to her heart. I fear what might happen when it reaches the organ.

"How is she?" Duncan's voice fills the space.

"Getting worse. I don't know what to do, Duncan. We can't lose her too. It will crush him."

"Let me deal with Enzo." Duncan teleports from the room and I pray to the Maker he can get through to Enzo.

Come to bed, my love. A smile creeps onto my face at the sound of my mate's voice filtering into my mind.

I'm taking care of Jade. I'll be there as soon as Duncan comes back to relieve me.

Don't take too long. You know I like to take up the whole bed when you aren't here. His soft laugh accompanies his light hearted joke.

And you know I will push you off to the floor if you do. Get some sleep. I'll be in soon.

"You're going to be alright, Jade. I promise. I'm not losing both of you."

Chapter 38

DUNCAN

"She's getting worse, Enzo."

"What do you think I could do that the others are not already doing?" Enzo's tone is clipped, but I know he is right.

"I don't know."

Silence passes over Enzo and me as I sit here staring out the window. Enzo lies in bed, like usual, and refuses to look at me.

"How bad is it? The infection."

"Her nails are completely black and those lines continue to creep up her arm. Her lips have started to take on a dark hue as well. I don't know what happens when that black ooze reaches her heart. Liliana can't find anything that is going to help Jade in any of the tomes and Gunnar and Saraphena have been so busy with the recruits they have barely had any time to look."

"And what have you been doing? Saraphena told me what happened between you and Liliana. Haven't we lost enough?"

"I'm doing this so I don't lose her forever."

"If that's what you need to tell yourself, brother."

"And you are one to speak, huh? All you do is lay here all day and all night! Jade needs you Enzo! She was there for you through it *all* and now she is in there fighting for her life and you are just in here wasting away over someone who is dead!"

The chair breaks into smithereens beneath me, but I quickly teleport before I hit the ground. I now stand beside Enzo's bed and he shifts so his back is to me.

"Break everything in this room, Enzo. I don't care. But you know I am right. I know you don't want to hear this, but Aliyah is *gone,* for good. I know you have been seeing her in your mind and hearing her voice, but it's time to block her out. It isn't real! She isn't real! You need to let her go."

"It's my fault!" Enzo shoots from the bed and stands before me, chest heaving and nostrils flaring in anger. "I'm the reason Aliyah is dead and I have to live with that for the rest of my life!"

"You think I don't understand that?" I yell. "Aliyah didn't die *because* of you Enzo! She died because that is the risk you take when you go into battle, which she would have happily done time and time again for you. For all of us! She didn't die by your hand, Enzo. You have got to stop punishing yourself for something you had no control over!"

Our chests are almost touching, neither one of us willing to back down from this fight.

"How would you know what this feels like?!"

"Because I killed my mate!"

Enzo staggers back, confusion pulling at his mind. "No. She died. Your father killed Zorellya."

"No, Enzo. I killed her. My father was going to kill Zorellya's brother if I didn't kill her. She loved her brother so much and my father used that love against her. I was the one to break her neck. I thought it would be the most quick and painless for her, but I can still feel the vibration of her neck snapping in my hands. *That* is what it means to be the reason for someone's death. Zorellya died because I brought her into my life and my father exploited her love for others. I refuse to let Liliana ever be used against me, because I will gladly give my life for her's any day. Yet that is not the role of a king. A king is supposed to choose his people over himself. I can't do that with Liliana in my life because despite what she thinks, I am choosing her, just not in the way she wishes.

"So stop shriveling away in here over someone's death that wasn't your fault. You have someone right in the other room who *loves* you, Enzo. She would follow you into the fiery pits of the below if you asked her to. Aliyah will always be a part of you, Jade knows that, but Aliyah would want you to be happy. I once told Aliyah to fight for you even if you couldn't fight for yourself. Jade is fighting for you, brother. She is clinging to dear life because of *you.* Before she fell into the coma, the only thing she asked about in the few moments she was awake was how you were doing. Go and fight for Jade."

"I— I don't know how."

"Just be there for her. Show her you would stand by her side as many time as she has yours."

Enzo's shoulders slump and he hangs his head. "She doesn't need me, Duncan. She has all of you. I will just be a reminder of how she became sick in the first place, by following me to the Banished Kingdom. Jade can fight this without me."

Enzo crawls back into bed and the door behind me opens at his command, my cue to exit. "You're a fool, Enzo. If Jade dies, maybe then you'll see how stupid you have been."

I slam the door behind me hoping something will get through to him.

Chapter 39

ENZO

I've never noticed the small pieces of chipping paint on my bedroom ceiling before. I suppose I never spent enough time looking at it to truly take in all its features. The silence around me amplifies the sounds of my body. I hear the whoosh of air that fills my nostrils and feel it slip down my throat and into my lungs. I feel my stiff muscles twitch in my body from lack of movement since arriving back in Citrine. I feel the burn behind my eyes from hours of crying over what I did to Aliyah. My tongue feels like sand in my mouth as I try to wet my pallet, but am unable to find any drop of moisture. I hear the beat of my broken heart in my chest. I feel the blood rush with each beat to the rest of my body, keeping it alive, but for what?

Why does my body continue to keep me alive when there is nothing here worth living for? I thought I could bring her back. I thought I could be whole again, but instead the world spins on when mine has been frozen in time since that day on the battlefield. When I held Aliyah's body in my arms, I felt her slipping away from me. I felt her slick blood sliding over my fingers as her life slipped from my grasp. I couldn't save her that day, so what is the point in saving myself now?

A knock comes at the door. I don't answer. Saraphena enters the room like she does each day and sets down a tray of food by my bedside. Two powdered doughnuts sit on the tray, but all I can do is stare at them. She asks me something, but I don't hear her. All I hear is Aliyah's voice in my head. The sound of her laugh, her cries, her *everything*. If I had known those moments would be the only ones I would get with her, I would have held on one moment longer in our hugs, kissed her once more each time, made her laugh just once more. I would have cherished every moment with her if I knew it would be my last.

Saraphena exits the room and closes the door behind her. I'm not sure how long I lay there staring up at the ceiling, but the next thing I know, she is coming in with another tray of food. My eyes float over to the window and see the black of night. The lights reflecting off the crystals used to be so beautiful to me, but now it is a stark reminder of what Aliyah looked like under those lights. The way the colors would bounce of her skin. How when the orange rays hit her normally gray eyes, I could see the blue flecks sparkle in her gaze.

I turn my back on Saraphena and gaze out my window until the golden rays of sun crest over the window sill, blinding me with their light. I feel the bed shift beneath me as someone sits down, but I don't have the energy to turn and look. Something warm flows over my chest and for the first time in what feels like forever, I don't want to die.

"Hi." Liliana's soft voice caresses my ears as she reaches over and grabs my hand. A few tears slip down her cheeks, tears that should belong to me.

"I thought I told you to stop doing that?"

"I know, but I can't let you sit in here day after day. I can't begin to imagine what you are feeling right now. I know you need time to heal. Time to...move on." Hesitation filters through her tone as she goes on. "The others don't know how to talk to you about this, but we need you Enzo. The recruits need training, but more importantly, Jade is getting worse. Whatever the Banished King inflicted upon her is taking hold. I feel it in her, Enzo. The darkness that lies below Tyros' own skin. I feel it in Jade. All of my research has failed me. Your family...they need you. They need a leader, Enzo."

"I am no leader."

"Aliyah thought you were. She believed in you Enzo." Liliana reaches out and places her hand over my chest. "You might be a little damaged, and probably a lot broken, but that doesn't make you worthless. Rory believed if enough people gave you a piece of their heart, you could be whole again. Everyone out there," she motions towards the door, "they all gave a piece of themselves to you the day they chose to stay in Citrine instead of returning to their homes. You, Enzo, are their home now."

"I'll never be whole again without Aliyah."

"Aliyah never left you. Not really anyways. A piece of her is always going to be with you. She brought out every good thing there was inside you. It's time to be that person now. Be the person she knew you were. Everything that's happened...everything you've done. She wouldn't want you to cost the lives of others for the sake of bringing her back. You'll see her again, Enzo. I know she is waiting in the above looking down on you right now. I felt how much she loved you Enzo. She'll be with you...always and forever. But in this lifetime, you need to let her go now. If not for you, do it for her. The Maker will keep her safe in the above. She won't feel pain. She won't be sad. Everything she went through she can finally be free of. It might hurt us down here, but Aliyah deserves a life where she doesn't have to suffer anymore. I think we owe it to her to be happy, too."

"You really think she isn't suffering up there? Do you think she has truly found happiness?" A small sob breaks free from my lips at the thought of letting her go.

"I think that when you join her one day in the above, she will be right there waiting for you to fall in love with her all over again. For now, you need to block her out. Free your mind from the guilt. You're hearing her and seeing her because she is the manifestation of the guilt you carry from her death. I know you love her, but it isn't real."

"I've done so many terrible things, Liliana. How can I mend everything I've done?"

"We all make mistakes, Enzo. Aliyah told me what you said that day to her about her scars. They made her who she is and the bad stuff that happened in her life doesn't define her. Don't let your mistakes define you. Actions speak volumes. Let the past go and start making better choices now. You aren't who you were yesterday or the day before that. Every day our cells die off and fall from our body, do you know what that means?"

"That one day I'll be nothing more than one of The Kalari?" I quip.

"No," she laughs. "It means in time, every cell of the person you once were won't be there anymore. You'll be brand new. Every day you are going to wake up and have a choice to make on who you want to be that day. The Enzo who lets his past dictate who he is going to be, or the Enzo who looks towards the future and chooses to grow, despite his past. So, today is a new day. Which Enzo are you going to be?"

Chapter 40

ENZO

Standing in the doorway to Jade's room feels too close for comfort, but I know Liliana was right. I have a choice in who I want to be and I don't want to feel this way forever. I look at Jade's skin filled with lightning cracks of black ooze slipping through her veins. Her eyes have hallowed out leaving only black rimmed lashes to match her inky lips.

The black lines lace her cheek bones making her look like a cracked porcelain doll. Her hands have gone completely black, and I don't want to imagine what the rest of her skin looks like. Jade's chest rises and falls in an uneven pattern.

"Go to her." Liliana stands beside me and clasps my hand in hers.

"I can't say goodbye to anyone else. This was a mistake. I am not as strong as everyone thinks."

"Enzo. This may be your only chance to say goodbye. You regret not telling Aliyah you love her, don't make the same mistake with Jade." Liliana tugs my hand forward and I follow her into the room. The heavy curtains hide away any light that might shine through. "Can we open the curtains?"

"The light hurts her eyes. We'd like to keep her as comfortable as possible."

"Oh." It is all I can manage to say. A strange sensation engulfs me as I stare into the black holes that were Jade's eyes. "I'd like a moment alone with her please."

"I'll be right outside. Call if you need anything." Liliana shuts the door behind her leaving me in silence. I reach out and take Jade's hand in mine. For someone so ferocious and strong, her hand feels small and dainty in mine.

"I'm so sorry Jade. I've done a lot of things in the last few months that I'm not proud of, but one of the worst is taking you for granted. I relied on the fact that you have always been by my side, even as children. You didn't deserve this, Jade."

"Enzo! Wait up!" Jade calls from behind me.

"Who's the slow poke now?! Looks like giving me that stupid nickname backfired on you!"

"Oh please! You're only slightly faster now, but you are still just as dumb!" Gunnar calls. Laughter fills the halls as we race each other around Citrine. I am still getting used to these long legs that seemed to grow out of nowhere. Jade's short brown hair swishes around her face as the wind from her speed races around her. Her

smile is bright and beautiful and her eyes glisten with tears from how hard she laughs. Gunnar pushes her shoulder and blows fire at her from his palm as if splashing water. She twists her head away and giggles before sticking her foot out and tripping him. Gunnar hits the ground with a thud as Jade keeps running.

"Hey Gunnar! You got a little something on your face there!" Jade runs her finger down the bridge of her nose, signaling Gunnar to wipe the dirt off his face.

"Oh why I oughta!" Jade grabs my hand and I look down to where our palms connect. Her hand is warm and firm in my grasp. Two small dimples form at the crease of her smile and her eyes crinkle with delight. Jade is so beautiful.

"Enzo! Enough of this nonsense! Time for your extra lessons." My father's voice sucks any joy present from the room.

"He doesn't want to go," Jade whispers.

"What did you say to me?"

"I said— I said he doesn't want to go. What you're doing to him— It's wrong." A crack across Jade's face has her blood splattering onto my cheek. Tears well in her eyes when they meet mine, but she doesn't back down.

"If hitting me keeps you from ruining his heart, then I can take it."

"Jade, stop. It's okay. I can do this. He won't ruin me. I promise." I pull her arm back and push her behind me. "I'll be right behind you father. Just one moment please."

"One moment. That is all you get and it is more than you deserve." My father's tone is clipped. I turn and wipe the blood from Jade's nose. She was going to take his abuse for me and I couldn't let that happen. She is too good. "I'm sorry, Jade. I promise he wasn't always like this. He just thinks he is doing what is best. I can take it, don't worry."

Jade pulls me in for a tight hug. "One day, you'll be free of him. Your heart is good, Enzo. Remember that. You are a good person. I'll be right here when you're done. I'm not going anywhere."

"You've always believed my heart was good. Even after the things my father made me do, you always believed I was good. I've been so lost, Jade. I used to think I was alone, but you were there the whole time. If we had more time, I'd show you I would stand by your side through anything. You're my best friend, my most trusted advisor, my first crush. I'm sorry for pushing you away all those years ago, but I am happy you didn't listen to me and stayed." I laugh at the memory of a time long before this.

Jade's breathing slows and I watch the black snakes in her veins slither their way closer to her heart. I lean down and bring my lips to hers in one final goodbye. I sit back in my chair and hold her hand as I wait for her final moments of life to pass. Our life together plays over in my mind. Every moment we shared together in the last 700 years. I smile as I think of the life my best friend and I have led together. In the end, it wasn't my heart that was good, but hers. I just wish I had more time to show her how wrong I have been.

A bright light blasts through the room and blinds me with its rays. I cover my eyes with my hands and as I stand, my chair tips over on its back. I stumble around the room, trying to find my way out. When the light fades, there, sitting up in bed, is Jade. The black vipers no longer present in her veins, the once dark eyes now shine brightly, and her lips are a light pink instead of black as coal. Jade's hand reaches up to her lips where my kiss still lingers.

"Oh my Maker. True love's kiss." Gunnar stands in the doorway, shock etched into his face. "It's real. That is the only logical explanation!"

"What's going on? Maker, Gunnar. I leave for one second and you blast through the door giving them no pri—" Liliana's voice is cut off as she sees Jade sitting up in bed, the image of perfect health. "Jade?"

"How can this be?" Jade looks to me as if my confused face will have the answer.

"I— I don't know. I— I was kissing you goodbye and then there was this light."

"Do you have the mate bond with Jade?" We both snap our heads in the direction of Gunnar who just shrugs like that would be the most obvious answer in the world.

"No. I don't feel that same tether between us as I did with Aliyah, but I don't understand how this could have happened. I don't know what I did."

"You kissed me. Maybe those stories Duncan read were true. Maybe there is such a thing as true love's kiss. Enzo, do you— Do you love me?" Jade's voice waivers at the word *love*.

"You heard Duncan's story?" Liliana asks. "We didn't realize you could hear us. We hoped of course, but we had no clue how sick you were, or what to do to help you get better."

Jade ignores her question and focuses her eyes completely on me. "Enzo. Do you love me?"

"I— Jade, I mean, of course I love you, but— I didn't think it was— like this."

"Aliyah may have been your mate, but that kiss. It can only mean that I am your *true* love."

"I—" I don't know what to say. True love doesn't exist. Mate bonds had to be the closest thing to true love, but Aliyah was my mate and I don't have the tether to Jade that I felt with Aliyah. Could they in fact be two separate things? I run the small ax around my chest back and forth over the chain, anxiously waiting for a better explanation.

"Holy crap! Jade! You're okay!" Duncan comes into the bedroom, but quickly senses the tension in the air.

"Liliana," I say. "Feel my emotions. Tell me what you feel between Jade and I. It is the only way to know."

"I feel— love."

Chapter 41

JADE

*E**nzo loves me.*

*E*nzo loves me.

I am Enzo's true love. All this time I thought true love was a thing of myths and legends. Yet here we stand. I rise from the bed and make my way over to Enzo. I stand before him and reach out to take his hands in mine.

"I love you, too. I always have."

"Jade, I don't— I don't know if I'm ready to love again right now." I hear the others back out of the room and close the door, clearly not wanting to be a part of this difficult conversation.

"I understand. I'll be here whenever you're ready. I always knew there was something between us. I thought we missed our chance, but maybe now we can have another shot." A smile pulls at my lips at the thought of all the possibilities ahead of us. Enzo and I can finally be together. He can perform the Soul Bond with me so that we have that mind connection for life. People are going to write books about our great love story one day. *The tale of real life true love.* We would tell our children this story, and our children's children. They would know the great story of true love running through their veins.

I look down to the small silver ax hanging around his neck. That pendant will always be a reminder of Aliyah. It will always be a reminder of the hurt. I reach around his neck and unhook the clasp.

"What are you doing?" he asks gripping my wrist.

"As long as you wear this, you'll never truly move on. You will always be hanging on to a part of her. How can you give us a fair shot if this reminder is always coming between us? You need a fresh start, Enzo. The past is forgotten. You and I are the future." I palm the small ax in my hand and place the other on his chest, his strong hand wrapping around mine.

"I think I just need some time." Enzo drops my hand and heads for the door. Shutting it behind him, I walk over to the windows and throw back the curtains. Light shines in from the bright sun warming my skin for the first time since I became ill. I didn't need Tyros to awaken any power in me. The power of true love was always inside me.

I spin around the room and the light filtering in through the window panes bounces off my skin in golden streams. I would paint every window golden in our home so when the light shines through, it will remind me of the golden light which surrounded Enzo and me in our love. I thought I had lost him to the memory of Aliyah forever, but this has to change things.

Enzo had been holed up in his room since we got back from the Banished Kingdom, but he got out of bed for *me.* When they told him I was dying he must have snapped out of his depression and come for me.

After all this time, Enzo and I finally have a future together. Aliyah needed to come along to open his heart to love, and while she will always be his first love, I am going to be his last.

"Thank you, Aliyah." I close my eyes and look to the above where I know she is happy and safe. "Thank you for showing him what love is, and what it can be. I promise I will take good care of him."

I smile and let myself sit in this moment with my thoughts. Every moment of every day I have been by his side. I have seen him at his best, and at his worst, and I know I love him despite everything he has done. That is the past, I am his future.

Opening up the window before me, I look out over the sprawling crystal mountains. My room overlooks the deep water surrounding the palace. I reach out my hand that holds the reminder of Enzo's pain. The silver chain sparkles in the sunlight.

"To our future." Opening my palm, I let the small ax plummet into the watery depths below, right alongside the last memory of her.

PART V: ACCEPTANCE

Chapter 42

ENZO

I stand in the library three days after I found out Jade is my true love. The bubble around the queen's sword ripples beneath my touch. I think back to the day in the library when Aliyah first found this and was able to reach inside. Some small part of me hoped she would be able to remove the sword, that maybe she was the heir to the Krystal throne all this time.

How wrong I had been. Jade is apparently my true love, which to my knowledge didn't even exist. How can it be that someone as unworthy as me could have not only a mate, but also a true love?

Am I worthy of love? The questions burn in my mind. Does love really and truly wipe out all the bad things we have done, or does it just place a rose-colored film over our past to hide the truly ugly parts of our pasts? Jade had seen me at my absolute worst, knows the things I have done, and yet still chooses to stay. But what if I was always meant to be this monster? What if my father didn't make me into a weapon, but instead, only brought out the monster already buried inside my very being?

Was I always destined to hurt others, and if so, was it fair of me to subconsciously punish Jade all these years for her past crimes? I knew I trusted her with battle strategy and to fight by my side, but I never trusted her with my heart. Not after what she did. But maybe, just maybe, I could let go of her past, and for her sake, let go of the monster inside me, as well.

Because maybe that's what true love is; seeing into the deepest, darkest parts of our lives and choosing to stay, despite the corrosion on our once innocent souls.

The kills were easy this time. Over the years I have learned the faster I can kill the fae my father puts before me, the faster I can leave this room. This isn't who I want to be, but it is who my father needs me to become. The most feared fae in all of Olyrium. That is what my father claims people will say about me. The life I dreamed for myself as a child of finding my mate, feeling unconditional love, being a father— It will never come to pass. In order to be who my father needs me to be, I need to become unworthy of those things. I need to break myself so no one can ever break me.

I almost gave into that dream today with Jade. After years of trying to deny my growing feelings for her, I thought maybe just once I could see what it might feel like to be loved. I know my father will punish me for my misguided thinking.

"Beautiful work as always, son. You have come so far over the years."

"Thank you, father. Am I free to go?" I know the answer, but I plead to the Maker I am wrong.

"You will never be free, Enzo. You know what you did today. You know the punishment."

I kneel before my father as he presents me with the small blade. I grip the cool metal in my palm and hold out my arm to begin my task. The first cut is always the worst. The sting shoots up my arm and it isn't until I have finished the final stroke that the first slice has healed.

"Again," my father commands.

I begin again. The first slice hurts less this time and I know by the end I will feel nothing at all. I watch the blood pool around my knees as I continue to carve into my arm. I focus on the skin knitting itself back together instead of the splitting of flesh. I dare not cry or my father will punish me with several more rounds.

"What you did today was criminal, boy. You are unworthy of love you stupid child. Love is what gets you killed on the battlefield. Love is what distracts you and ends your life. Love is pain. You do not feel pain, Enzo. You inflict pain. That is your purpose. You will never seek love for it will blind you to what your true purpose is in this life. Again."

I reset the blade at the crease of my elbow and make my first slash. I will never scar from these cuts on the outside, but if you were to peel back my skin and gaze into my soul, you would see the scars laid there from years of this torture. Etched into my being you would find the bleeding wounds of this life, never to be fully healed.

I stare down at my arm, at the soft pink lines before they have fully finished healing. UNWORTHY.

"Again."

I begin the soft curve of the letters with my blade.

"What are you, Enzo?"

"I am unworthy of love."

"Say it again until you believe it as you have so clearly shown me you do not grasp that concept by today's actions."

"I am unworthy of love. I am unworthy of love. I am—"

The door behind me swings open and I turn my head ever so slightly. Panic washes over me as I see Jade standing there. She can't be here. She can't see this.

"Leave, Jade. Please." I plead with her through my eyes. I watch her pull a blade from her holster. I know my father won't kill her outright with his powers, he is too arrogant for that. He will make her suffer first for even attempting to kill him. I cannot let that happen. I don't hear her response. My father pulls his blade and points the tip of it to my chin. Maybe this time he will really do it. Maybe this is how I will be truly free. My hopes are snuffed out as my body flies across the floor. Jade's gasps fill the chamber as my father strangles her with his power.

NO! I can't let him do this. I can't lose her. I will never survive my father's abuse knowing she isn't waiting for me on the other side of that chamber door. I need her.

"Father, stop!" I rush to his side and place my hand on his outstretched arm. "Let me. This is what you trained me to do. If she is to die, let it be by my hand. Let me eliminate her from my life once and for all. If you let me do this, I promise you I will never fail you again. I can be the weapon you want me to be, I swear it." My father releases Jade and temporary relief floods my system. I still need to get Jade out of here before he can hurt her again.

"You do this and I might just finally be proud of you. Fail me and I will line up a hundred fae for you to spend hours slaughtering until you get it through your mind that you are a monster. Understood?"

"I understand father. I won't let you down." I look into Jade's eyes and I can't help the regret that sits heavy in my gaze. I know what I must do. Tears well up in Jade's eyes staring back at me.

"It's okay, Enzo. Do what you need to do. I will know that I died helping the man I love and that I died with honor for protecting my family. If this is what must be done to set you free, then so be it." I nod my head slightly. Jade's life will not end today. I turn and throw my power out towards my father. I don't want to hurt him, but I can't let him hurt Jade either.

"Run, Jade! Run!" I yell. I keep my gaze fixed on my father, willing myself to not break in his presence as I have so many times before. "Run, Jade! Just go!" Time seems to slow as I watch my

father collapse onto the ground before me. My hold on him breaks and I watch as blood pours from his eye socket. Jade's knife is embedded into his skull. My father lays before me, motionless.

"Father! No, no, no! Jade how could you do this?!"

"Enzo you're free now. You can finally stop torturing people. He's dead now. I saved you."

"He was my father! He was the only blood family I had left! You had no right to take him from me!"

"Enzo, I— I'm sorry. I thought—"

"You thought wrong! He was my father! Despite what he has done and despite who he has become, he was my father! I know that he loved me somewhere deep down! He wasn't always this man! He loved me! I will never forgive you for this Jade. Never!"

I don't hear her leave the chamber as I sob over the loss of my father. My mind flashes over my early memories with him. Playing with me in the crystal fields, teaching me to ride an alicanto for the first time, the love he so clearly had for my mother. Once I made him proud he could have returned to that same man. I thought in time I could change him. Remind him of the man he once was. Now I will never get that chance. I will never forgive Jade for taking that opportunity away from me. Never.

A hand rests on my shoulder as Jade comes into view. She plants a kiss on my cheek and snaps me from my memories.

"Are you ready to go home?" Jade's smile is genuine. She is happy and healthy, but my mind and heart are still so torn. I wasn't ready to let Aliyah go yet, so Jade wants to take me back to Korin to find closure, whatever that means.

"Yes." My body may be with Jade, but my heart still seems to pull me across the ocean to Luar. I'm not sure I will ever fully let Aliyah go, but I owe it to Jade to give it my best shot. The Maker must want us together if He allowed me to find a true love. Maybe your mate isn't always your true love?

"The recruits are all set to continue their training with the others while we are gone. Saraphena and Liliana have dedicated themselves to researching for a way to bring down the pillar to the Banished Kingdom. They don't need you right now. We can take as much time away as we need." Jade's hand slips into mine as she pulls me towards the library doors. I look over my shoulder at the sword and take one more moment to think about how wrong I had been about Aliyah being the heir.

She has been quiet in my mind ever since I found out I apparently love Jade. I'm not sure if I am thankful for the quiet, or if I am just thankful I wasn't actually going mad at the possibility that she could still be alive. It's time to lay Aliyah to rest not only in the ground, but in my heart as well. The best place to do that is to go back to where my love for her started and start making new memories.

Chapter 43

SARAPHENA

The morning sun creeps through the curtains covering our windows. Gunnar's chest rises and falls with easy breaths and I note the small smile curving up his lips. I pull a tie from my nightstand drawer and push my long curls into a knot at the top of my head. I run my hands down my face and huff out a breath before shifting to get out of bed. It's been three months since Aliyah died. Three *long* months.

I walk out onto the balcony attached to our room and look out over the expanse of Krystal. Glittering mountains shine with the first rays of sunlight, the alicanto graze in one of the close crystal fields, and for a moment, everything is silent. I've enjoyed these moments knowing the stillness won't last forever. It is in these moments that I still feel her. I haven't talked to her since that day on the bridge, but she is never far from my thoughts.

I spot Mirage in one of the crystal clusters, her feathers looking healthier by the day. Daisy stands next to her, occasionally nudging Mirage's wing. I smile and watch the two best friends for a while. When I think about Aliyah these days my heart no longer sinks, but instead I can see something happy and find her within the moment. My heart aches a little less and my tears fall less often. I don't think I will ever truly be done grieving my best friend, but I've come to accept that choosing to be happy doesn't mean I'm not choosing to miss her. I can enjoy life's moments, the life she wanted me to have, and know that she would be happy for me, despite the fact she cannot be here to enjoy it with me.

I glance down at the sun tattooed on my forearm. *'Til the end.*

"Good morning, love." Gunnar's strong arms wrap around me and I lay my head back on his shoulder.

"Good morning," I sigh.

We stand there in silence for a few moments before I turn in his arms and interlace my fingers behind his neck.

"Let's get married."

"When?" His smile glows brighter than the rising sun behind me.

"As soon as Jade and Enzo get back from Korin."

"That soon?!"

"Having second thoughts?" I wink.

"No!" He kisses me lightly on the lips. "Never, but I just thought you would want to take some time to plan it all first?"

"I don't want anything big. I just want you."

"And so you shall." His kiss is more passionate this time, frenzied and needy. "But first, you need to put this back on."

He holds out my engagement ring before me and my heart squeezes.

"Gunnar...I...I can't. Look what happened the last time with Enzo. I can't put him through that again. I know he has Jade now, but I can't take that risk."

"Screw Enzo. I love you Saraphena and I would let Enzo destroy a thousand rooms if it meant you got to wear this symbol of my love for you. I am going to marry you, that fact has not changed. Enzo will have to learn to live with it eventually. I am done tip-toeing around in my love for you. You asked me never to hide from you, but I'm done hiding from the world too."

He slips the ring over my finger and tears spring in my eyes once more, a sob catching in my throat.

"Dang it all. Now I'm back to zero days without crying! I was doing so well," I laugh.

His thumb wipes off the tears from my cheeks as he wraps both his hands around my jaw. His eyes sparkle in the morning light as he looks at me.

"They always say the most beautiful eyes have cried the most tears." A soft smile tugs at his lips and I lean into his palm, closing my eyes for just a moment.

"I love you, too, Gunnar."

A knock comes at the door and the silence which once hung in the morning air is gone.

"They're leaving. Figured you'd want to know." Liliana's voice is muffled by the closed door.

"Let's go say goodbye one last time. After that, we will all be together again."

As we make our way out to the front of Citrine, something uncomfortable pulls in my chest. This feeling that something is off, but I can't quite put my finger on what. I shake off the feeling and focus on saying goodbye to my friends.

Duncan has Enzo pulled into a tight hug and Liliana stands off to the side talking with Jade.

"Be safe, brother. We will be right here waiting when you get back." Duncan's deep voice echos slightly in the entryway.

"Thank you." Enzo turns to Gunnar and me. "Try and help these two find some sense," he says in a lowered voice.

My eyes flick to Duncan who has moved to the opposite side of the room away from us and Liliana stares off to the other side. Jade joins us and the four of us shift uncomfortably.

I pull Jade to the side where Liliana is standing. Liliana's normally cheery attitude is painfully absent this morning, but I'm hoping to change that right now.

"Don't stay away too long," I say taking Jade's hand. "Gunnar and I are going to be married as soon as you return."

"What?! Saraphena that's so soon! We absolutely will hurry back as soon as we can! I don't think it will take Enzo very long to say goodbye now that he knows we are true loves," Jade smiles.

Lil remains motionless, simply looking at me with a small smile on her face, but you can tell there is no emotion in her eyes. "Congratulations, Saraphena. I'm so happy for you." Her voice doesn't have that same sparkle to it and I know there is no conviction behind her tone.

"Lil, are you alright?" I ask.

"What?" She blinks and it is as if her mind snapped back into reality. "Oh yes! So sorry, just tired is all. I truly am happy for you. I can't wait to help you plan the wedding."

I give her a questioning look, wondering where this sudden shift in mood is coming from. I can tell it is fake, like she is saying what she thinks I want to hear, but not what she actually feels.

"Lil—" I start.

"I am actually going to head back to my room and try and get some more sleep. I'll see you later today and we can talk more about this wedding." She starts walking up the right staircase leading to our rooms. Duncan dissipates into thin air the moment she is gone.

Jade gives my hand a squeeze and pulls me back over with the others. "Enzo guess what!" Jade bounces with excitement.

"What?"

"Saraphena and Gunnar are going to—"

"Miss you so much!" I cut her off. I ignore the look Jade gives me. "It won't be the same here without you and you have to promise to send for us if you plan to go to Adryanna's! I don't want to miss out on another night out," I laugh, a hint of nervousness spilling through.

"Absolutely, we will. Keep the recruits training while we are gone. I don't want them slacking," Enzo arches a brow at Gunnar.

"Boot camp a la Gunnar is now open for business! Sir yes, sir!" Gunnar mock salutes Enzo and we all fall into a relaxed laugh.

Another wave of unease washes through me, but I push it aside once more. *Nothing is wrong.* I watch as Jade slips her hand into Enzo's and I don't miss the slight tension in his shoulders as she does. The doors to Citrine close behind them and this time when the feeling of despair pushes into my mind, I don't shove it away. *Maybe something is wrong, I just don't know what.*

Chapter 44

LILIANA

I stomp up the stairs to my bedroom, needing to be alone after that encounter with Saraphena and Jade. Saraphena is getting married, and Jade has found her one true love. *Something that as of a few days ago didn't even exist.* I roll my eyes at the notion. I reach for the handle to my bedroom door. Why do they get to be happy and I get stuck with the non-committal, brooding, grumpy, irritating, selfish—

"Liliana."

Sitting in the arm chair before the fireplace in my room is Duncan.

"Out."

"Please talk to me. You've changed. I never wanted to make you unhappy."

"UGH! Seriously?! Did you ever consider that being *with* you makes me happy?!"

"I don't want to fight." He moves to stand, making his way over to me.

"No." I put my hand up as a barrier between us.

"Lil. I'm— I'm sorry."

"You're sorry? Really? Say it then. Say the words you know I want to hear."

"I— I can't."

"Then we have nothing left to say to each other, Duncan. You can't keep pushing and pulling me around like this. One moment you wished we never met and the next you're apologizing for making me unhappy. I'm not some toy you get to pick up and play with whenever you want and then cast aside when you decide it no longer suits you."

"I know you aren't a toy. I just—" He huffs out a breath. "What if you find your mate?"

"What?" That question stops me in my tracks.

"Let's say we Soul Bond. You won't be able to find your mate, or you would find them and our Soul Bond would be broken. On one hand, you would never be able to find the true person you are destined to be with, and on the other you would have to choose between your mate or me. I would *never* ask you to choose me in that situation."

"There wouldn't be a choice, Duncan. Mate or not, you are my forever. At least...I thought you were."

His face grimaces at my words and for a brief moment, that dry well of emotions in my chest springs a leak.

"Duncan, listen to me." I take a step closer to him, risking breaking the foundation of the wall I have build up to keep him out. "If I were to be on the side of the bond that could never find my mate, I would always be blissfully unaware even if I did meet them. I would be happy knowing I got to spend the rest of my life with you. If I was on the side of the bond where I could find them, I would chose you every...single...time. Just because some magical, mystical tether exists, against my choice might I add, and you know how I feel about my choices, doesn't mean you suddenly become nothing to me. I know what I feel for you."

"Liliana, you have never felt the love of a mate before. The pull is...undeniable."

"You're standing in *my* room after clearly having told me you wish we had never met, pushing me away back to SunSpark, and yet here you are." I step further into him, his smell of spiced rum filling my senses and I fight the urge to reach out to him.

"Here I am..." His hand reaches up to cup my cheek, my eyes closing at the feeling. "Sunshine," he whispers.

"Shadow," I whisper back. His lips find mine and the hurt between us evaporates for a moment. My arms wrap around his neck, pulling him closer to me. His kiss is pained...desperate and filled with need and all the unspoken words I wish he would say.

He pulls away and places his forehead on mine, hands gripping painfully at my waist. My eyes remain closed because if I open them this moment will end.

"Choose me," I say. The world seems to stop spinning as I wait for his answer. *Please just say the words and let this torment be over.*

"I can't." His hands withdraw from my body. It isn't until I hear the soft click of my door and the silence settles in once again that I realize he will never choose me. Our love isn't enough to conquer his fears and I can't wait around for the day he decides he wants me again. I mentally patch the leak in my heart and once again I am left in the comforting feeling of emptiness where nothing can hurt me again.

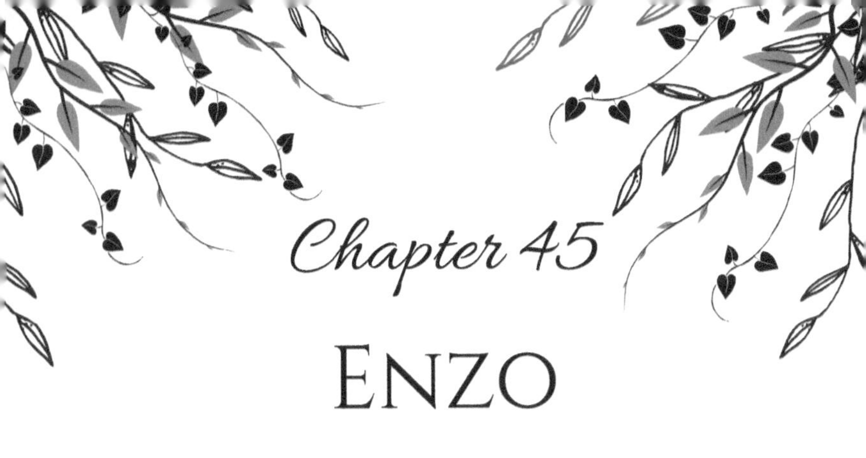

Chapter 45

ENZO

I look around our dusty home in Korin. Every surface is coated with a thick layer of dust. For three months this home has sat empty. Painful memories come flooding in of my time here with Aliyah. The look on her face the first time she saw the village. The night that we danced at the tavern.

The guilt sits heavy in my chest of everything I have done in her name trying to bring her back. She would be ashamed of me. Maybe it is a good thing I wasn't able to bring her back. There is no way she could ever forgive me for the things I have done. Destroying that village filled with women and children at the chance Tyros would bring her back. Pushing Rory too far causing him to burn out. Almost losing Jade to that black poison because I left her alone with Tyros. Aliyah would never forgive me. I turn to look at Jade who brought me here.

"I don't want to be here, Jade."

"You need to be here Enzo. It's time to move on. We have tried everything to bring her back. The star, the bargaining, pushing

Rory and the others, it needs to stop. You've hurt too many people in her name. You know she wouldn't have wanted that."

"I know. What am I supposed to do now? I held onto the thought of bringing her back so tightly that I'm not sure what to do with my mind now."

"You need to let her go. Move on, Enzo. You need to face the reality that she isn't coming back. Look at everything it has cost you." Jade makes her way over to me and wraps her arms around my waist. I think back to that first morning in Korin when I almost strangled her for even mentioning the thought of Aliyah not coming back, but now, maybe she is right. I wrap my arms around Jade and let my head fall on top of hers. Tears slip from my eyes as I let her words soak in. I need to move on, even if it kills me.

"Jade. Thank you for being here. Thank you for being here with me every step of the way." I pull her back away from me so that I can see her face. Her bright eyes look up at mine and a smile crosses her face.

"No matter what, I will always stand by your side, Enzo."

"I don't know what I would do without you. I've been so lost these few months. The things I have done—"

"Shhhh. There is no need to remember that now. Let it all go, Enzo. Let everything go."

Her hand moves up to cup my cheek and her thumb brushes away the tear that drips from my eye. Her smile is warm and inviting.

"I don't want to feel sad anymore, Jade."

Enzo! I'm coming for you! Aliyah's voice drifts through my head clearer now, but I need to move on. I need to stop imagining her coming back for me or me coming back for her.

I need to let you go now. Goodbye forever, little dove. I'm sorry. I block her out of my mind and focus my gaze back on Jade.

"Enzo," she says under her breath. She lifts up onto her tip toes and places a hesitant kiss to my lips. It feels strange having her lips on mine. "I have loved you since I was a child. Since that day you saved me from those other mean boys at the academy, I have loved you. I thought I had missed my chance with you, but maybe now— Maybe now the Maker has given us a second chance."

"Jade—"

"No. Don't say no, Enzo. If you can look me in my eyes and tell me you feel nothing for me, then I will never bring it up again. But if there is a chance for us, I want to try and take it. True love's kiss had to mean something deep in your heart or I wouldn't be standing here today."

I hesitate, not knowing what to say. She has been here for me all these months. I promised her on her death bed that if I had more time, I would show her that I took her for granted. Maybe I could learn to be happy again.

"I want to be happy again, Jade. You help make me happy. I don't know if this is really true love, but I think I'd like to see what it might become." Her smile broadens and her lips meet mine again. The kiss is more passionate this time and her touch feels like fire on my skin. I pick her up and her legs wrap around my waist as I walk her back to the nearest wall. My hands find her hair and I run my fingers through her soft tresses.

"I'm yours, Enzo. Forever and always," Jade says between kisses. I deepen the kiss and a soft sigh escapes her lips. I move to pull the tunic over her head. A heavy knock at the door reverberates through the small home. I pull back from her breathless. Her chest rises and falls with the heat of what almost happened.

"Ignore it. They will go away," Jade says. I place her back on the floor and walk over to the door. My hand reaches for the handle and pulling it open, Kaleron stands before me.

"Kaleron? What are you—" A familiar voice sounds behind him, the faint smell of vanilla assaults my nose, and wisps of blonde hair blow in the wind behind him. Kaleron steps out of the way and my heart stops.

"Enzo?"

Before me stands Aliyah, but not the same one we buried in that iron grave. No, this Aliyah is new— Transformed. Huge feathered wings sprout from her back, stuffed full with black, orange, red, and yellow feathers. The tips lightly dust the ground behind her, and the tops curve up into sharp points, black horns accenting the crest of her wings. My dove can fly.

EPILOGUE
THE BANISHED KING

I watch my daughter fly away with her little friends, that idiot Enzo slumped over and broken on the back of the sphinx.

"Enjoy him while you can, my child. Fate's clock ticks on." A wicked grin scrolls across my face as I turn and enter my dilapidated palace.

The halls of my prison suddenly feel empty without her presence. Her anger filled these stone walls with such warmth during her stay and I itch to have her back here, training to become the daughter of chaos I know she is. I saw so much of her mother in her, the fire in her snark, the cutting sting of her quips; it has been some time since I felt love, but it is only fitting I feel it for my daughter once more.

As I stride into the throne room, I remember the day her mother told me she was pregnant. It killed me to send her away, back to her husband in SunSpark, but I knew my daughter would one day return to me. What an unfortunate change of events it has become that I now may never get that chance to forge her into her true form. Let's hope Enzo takes the bait.

I settle into my stone throne and look out over my gathering skeleton army, a thing of nightmares. Two of The Kalari stand on either side of my throne, one wearing the skin of a recent victim. I don't know where they decided to pick up such a filthy habit. The Kalari scratches at his face and several pieces of skin slough off onto the ground, revealing his skeleton jaw. Bile rises in my throat at the sight.

"Long have I waited for the day when my enemy is at their weakest. Queen Dione played her hand too early and left her kingdom vulnerable. The seed of darkness has been planted in my daughter and soon she will rise to take her place by my side and slaughter those who banished us to this island. My final foe has fallen. Queen Dione's daughter was slain by King Aramot at my command and as long as she remains in her grave, my fate will not come to pass. I had hoped she would remain in Luar, clueless to her birthright, but that buffoon Enzo had to go poking around.

"If Queen Dione's daughter possesses the same ability as her mother, as I suspect she does, the girl must remain dead. Well, at least they need to *think* she is dead. If left in her iron coffin, I can annihilate Olyrium's forces and make them pay for what they have done. Enzo has fallen into madness, and my daughter will be the one to pull him out. The curse I thrust upon her will take hold soon and Enzo will be tricked into believing that *true love's kiss* is real. Aliyah will be forgotten, and my reign will begin."

I look to my minions who stare blankly back at me. A splattering sound comes from beside me as more skin falls to the stone with each scratch from The Kalari's bony fingers.

"I really need to get out more. The lack of *competent, conversational,* people around here is going to be the death of me." I roll my eyes and stand, walking to the end of the dais. "Creatures of destruction! Take up your spears, notch your arrows, and sharpen your blades! War is upon us and soon my child of darkness will return to bring Olyrium to its knees by my side! Destiny is calling, my friends, and who am I to deny it my answer!"

Acknowledgments

I can't believe book two is officially a wrap! It has been such an emotional journey going through the stages of grief with my characters. While I have been writing the character's development, I can genuinely say, I often surprise myself with the direction they decide to take themselves. Often times I have an idea in my head about what I want to happen, but the character decides their own path.

A huge thank you as per usual to my best friend, Jacque, for helping me write this book. Our constant FaceTimes and texting over plot points is the best part about my day! Once again, you have created the most beautiful cover for our book and I can't wait to see what you come up with for the rest of the series. None of this would be possible without you and there aren't enough words in the English language to express how grateful I am to you for everything you have done to help make this series possible.

To my father, thank you for reading the roughest of rough drafts and helping me work out ideas! I always think I have a great book until you get your hands on it and make a thousand corrections. I consider myself an ideas person and you the grammar person. Your continued support throughout this process means the world to me. To know you are proud of the things I have accomplished is a dream come true. It feels like just yesterday we were sitting in my bed reading books together and filling my head with visions of fantastical beasts and worlds far cooler than the one we live in! I still remember the day I came to you with a question about one of my characters and you called me back an hour later saying, "So I've been thinking about that character..." It made my day knowing that you are just as invested as I am.

To my family who have supported me and cheered me on this entire time! You all pushed me to keep going, even when I wasn't sure I could. My husband is always a constant support throughout this process and without him there would be no book. You have pushed me to keep writing, even through all the Lyme Disease issues and you never stopped believing in me. Here's to book three!

These are the authors behind Jane Rose Publishing, LLC.
Two best friends who spend their time talking about books,
FaceTiming over plot points for their next novel, and who share
a love for all things fictional.
Jacque (right) is responsible for the beautiful cover designs,
while Julia (left) brings their ideas to life through the written
word. Being long-distance best friends doesn't stop them from
coming together over the things they love.
Find them here on:
Tiktok: @janerose_thebookbesties
Instagram: @janerose_thebookbesties
Email: janerosepublishing@gmail.com
www.janerosepublishing.com